·The Demand

M I Hattersley

Dark Corridor Books

Read my books for free...

To show my appreciation to you for buying this book I'd like to invite you to join my exclusive Reader's Group where you'll get the chance to read all my upcoming books for free, and before anyone else.

To join the group please click below:

www.subscribepage.com/mihattersleybooks

1

Freya Lomax saw the car the second she stepped out of the school gates. Parked a little way down the street, it was one of those expensive types of cars with overly polished surfaces and blacked-out windows. In fact, it had black everything. Windows, paintwork, tyres. Freya had little interest in cars, so she had no idea of the make or model, only that the vehicle exuded a certain amount of gravitas sitting there on the side of the leafy south London street.

Gravitas.

She liked that word. She'd only learnt it recently but now endeavoured (another good word) to use it whenever she got a chance. But it was also very apt for this particular car. It was the sort of car you might see important people being driven around in. Pop stars, politicians, actors.

She looked around, wondering if it belonged to one of her classmate's parents. But she didn't think so. It seemed too big, too imposing. Most of the parents who sent their girls to St Bernadette's High were of the upper-middle-class variety. They wouldn't have blacked-out windows. Because Freya also knew that, along with VIPs, this was also the sort of car drug dealers might drive. Or gangsters.

"Come on, Mum. Where are you?"

She held a hand over her eyes, squinting through the late afternoon sun at the car, still sitting stationary and silent like a sleeping beast. Those dark windows were so impenetrable, especially from this distance, that there could have been twenty acting agents sat in the back and she wouldn't have known.

The thought tickled Freya's imagination. Acting agents. Whatever she was doing, whoever she was with, wherever she was, her thoughts always seemed to come back to the same thing. And then the disappointment was felt all over again.

Stupid mum.

Freya didn't have an acting agent. But she certainly wanted one. Especially since Denise, her drama coach, had said she had what it takes to be a star (not her exact words, but that's how Freya interpreted them) and would benefit from representation. Yet, playing to type, as usual, her mum had put her foot down and said no. Over a series of long, tearful and angry rows, she'd spelled out to Freya in no uncertain terms that she had to wait until she'd finished her exams before approaching any agents. To get 'proper qualifications' under her belt before pursuing her acting dream.

She continued to watch the car, raising her head slightly and giving it her best side. There could just as easily be a casting agent sitting in the back. Or some famous director. Actors got discovered in all sorts of situations and Freya knew the importance of creating opportunities for oneself whenever the chance arose. The car did look kind of threatening though.

She glanced back towards the school, wondering if she should wait for her mum inside. But she decided against it. It wasn't unusual for her mum to be running late. Instead, she pulled her phone out of her blazer pocket and switched it on. If she didn't arrive soon, she'd call her.

Probably forgotten all about me.

Freya had argued her case, of course, regarding her getting an acting agent. She might have been one of the quieter and more reserved members of her friendship group (because being a talented actor wasn't about being gregarious or a show-off. Look at Jessica Chastain, Keira Knightley, Nicole Kidman, who all professed to be shy) but when it came to her mum all that reservation disappeared. They'd fought often these last six months, and the theme was always the same: Freya's creative dream versus her academic journey. And of course, her mum's response was always the same too. Whilst under her roof... yadda, yadda, yadda.

So, Freya would have to wait a few more years before she got herself an agent. Of course she would. Wasn't that always the way? All she ever did was wait. Waiting for her life to begin.

She was still waiting.

She wondered if she should go over to the car and knock on the window, introduce herself. She'd read that casting agents liked bold statements like that. It showed confidence and drive and individuality. She pictured the back door opening and a tanned woman with big hair inviting her inside to join her on the plush leather seats.

Tell me more. Tell me more. Freya Lomax, you say? What an amazing name, and such good bone structure, too. You'll go far, my dear. Very far.

Freya's phone vibrated in her hand as it powered up, knocking her out of her daydream. She chuckled to herself, getting carried away. It was this very habit - getting so caught up in her imagination at the expense of other things - that seemed to annoy her mother so much of late. She was constantly yelling at Freya to pay attention. To *focus*. To be a good little girl, even if that meant rejecting her dreams.

But screw her.

As far as Freya was concerned, she was a typical fourteen-year-old girl, with the same ideals, likes and attention span as most girls her age. The only difference was she had a clear idea of what she wanted to do with her life. She had a goal. And wasn't that half the battle? Having a clear goal, something to set your sights on. And so what if it wasn't the same goal her parents had for her? That wasn't Freya's fault. Plus, she was an excellent student and didn't have to try too hard to get the grades, which meant she could put extra emphasis on her acting without her schoolwork suffering.

She had wanted to audition for the Brit School last year, but with the divorce and everything, the timing was bad. She'd accepted that but now her mum was saying she had to wait until she was sixteen.

More waiting.

And what did her mum know about anything? She was old and stressed and focused on her own stupid problems. Bitter too, since dad left. She didn't want Freya to have her own life. Didn't want her to be happy. But she'd be sorry. When Freya won her first award, she planned on thanking everyone but her mum. Because why should she thank her? She'd not helped. If anything, she'd blocked her.

So, being a fourteen-year-old girl from South London, with the same self-obsession as most fourteen-year-old girls, Freya's sliver of concern over the strange car with the blacked-out windows lasted only a few more seconds before her attention was firmly back on herself. The world around her faded to flashing lights and glitter as she ran her future acceptance speech in her head.

"Hey, Frey."

A voice snapped her back to reality, and she turned to see her friend, Mia, walking towards her.

"Want a lift?" She gestured over to a car parked across the street. But this one was bright red and Jan, Mia's mum was smiling and waving behind the wheel.

Freya waved back before glancing down at the phone clasped in her hand.

"No, it's okay," she said. "My mum's finishing early today so she's going to pick me up."

Mia pulled a face. She knew what Freya's relationship with her mum was like. "No worries. See you tomorrow."

Freya waved her off and turned her attention back to the phone. Opening up iMessenger, she reread the last text from her mum.

**Hey Frey. Will pick you up tonight.
Love u. X**

Love u.

The text elicited a sneer from Freya. Who the hell used 'u' for 'you' since the advent of auto-complete? Lame people, that's who. And words were cheap. Texts cheaper.

"Love you," she muttered, in a sneery voice, before letting out a dramatic sigh.

Although it had been a regular occurrence for the last year, she didn't enjoy clashing with her mum. But at least now she only saw her for about an hour each day and they didn't have time to get into any major fights.

Freya's thumbs hovered over the screen, about to tap in a reply - *Where are you?* - when the thought bubble with three dots appeared to show her mum was typing something. Freya paused, already knowing what it was going to say. It took another minute of waiting before the message appeared.

Sorry, Frey. Stuck at work. Have to see you at home. Get a lift with Mia if you can. Love u xx

Freya glanced up as Mia's mum's car disappeared around the corner at the end of the street. Great. It looked like she was walking home on her own. Again.

"Thanks a lot, Mum."

She pulled her headphones from out of her blazer pocket, annoyed more than was appropriate at the mess of white spaghetti that had formed since she stuffed them there this morning. Hoisting her backpack onto both shoulders, she set off, unravelling the wires as she walked before stuffing the earbuds in her ears and hitting play on the music app. As Billie Eilish filled her ears, she took a right down Wimbledon Park Road, heading for home.

And that's when she saw the car again.

It was parked ten metres in front of her. Close up, the enormous vehicle appeared even more imposing than it was outside the school gates. She froze, her breath caught in her throat as her overactive imagination fired up once more. What if it really was drug dealers? Or gangsters? Or worse, human traffickers. She pictured grotesque, sweaty men with black shark eyes and lusty sneers, prowling for young girls to sell as sex slaves. She glanced around, scanning the area for a way out. Was this really happening? Surely not. Things like this didn't happen to normal people.

She was ready to run when from around the corner, came salvation in the form of a man and woman. They were holding hands and smiled at Freya as they approached. In turn, she gripped the straps of her backpack and followed them as they passed by. Her palms were sweating but she stuck close to the couple, matching them step by step. A second later the car trundled past and took a left at the end of the street.

Freya let out a sigh. Deep down she knew it was a coincidence. That the car wasn't really following her. Because things like this *didn't* happen to normal people. There were no bad men out to get her. No gangsters prowling the streets. It was just another case of her mind playing tricks, her creativity working against her. But this didn't stop Freya from turning her music off and running as fast as she could along Morris Gardens, up Merton Road, and into the cover of King George's Park.

Here too, she didn't slow her movements, walking briskly along the wide concrete pathway that intersected the grass. Because of the hot day, unusual for early April, the park was full of people. Mothers with young children frolicked on the grass, old couples sat quietly chatting on benches. The notion crossed Freya's mind that she should approach someone, tell them her fears, that she was, possibly, be being followed. But even as she articulated the words in her head, it sounded absurd. So, instead, she pressed on.

Freya loved the park normally, especially in the summer, but today she barely noticed the sweet-smelling shrubs and scampering squirrels as she headed for the exit on the other side. Once there, she slowed her step and came to a stop, breathless now with the exertion as she inspected the street both ways.

"Stupid girl."

She laughed at herself, the vocal release on doing so threatening to conjure up deeper, untapped emotions. Usually, when this happened Freya allowed it, knowing if she was to make it as an actor, she had to utilise every feeling at her disposal, good and bad, difficult and joyous. It was this idea alone that had kept her going the last few years. The knowledge that, despite her parents going through a messy divorce, she could one day use her pain and anguish in her craft. It was a small mercy, but mercy all the same. She leant against the concrete gate post and let out another laugh. The heavy ball of fear that had formed in her chest these last few minutes was now dissolving as her mind cleared.

Being followed? How silly.

She'd convinced herself of this so much that as she walked along Mapleton Road and turned onto Garret Lane, her attention was already running through the monologue she had to learn for the next week. Marina's speech from *Voices in the Trees*. It was a good scene, filled with emotion. Maybe she could use some of her experience just now to drive the scene, give it real gravitas.

The thought provided a welcome boost of energy, but as she crossed the street, that energy quickly morphed into dread and fell like a lead weight into her stomach. The car was at the end of the street. Freya froze as it revved its engine. It was facing her. Then it was driving towards her. Fast now, with none of the stealth or ambiguity of earlier. It was coming for her. And it was almost on her. Freya looked desperately up and down the street. Fifty metres down, on her left was an old hotel, but it was boarded up, with a *To Let* sign nailed to the front. Up to her right stood the Griffin Tavern, but it too looked inhabited, devoid of life. Freya let out a gasp.

"Oh, god!"

The voice didn't sound like hers. It was too high pitched. The vocal cords tightened with panic. The car was screeching to a halt in front of her. A few seconds more and the doors would open, and the demonic forces inside would emerge, reaching for her, grabbing at her, pulling her into the hellish cavity of the vehicle before transporting her to a dark place where they would.... Where she would...

Her eyes fell on a passageway down the side of the Griffin Tavern. It looked wide enough for two people to pass but far too narrow for a car. Especially one so wide and imposing as the one in front of her. As the doors of the car opened, she ran for it, doubling back on herself around the side of the building where she sprinted down a winding passage that led to the back of the pub. A low wall blocked her path, but she vaulted over it with little effort, running alongside a row of modern terraced houses. In the next street, she paused, bouncing on her toes as she assessed her next move. Before she had a chance to think, the car appeared at the top of the street, like a mechanical Death Eater, hunting her down. Letting out a thunderous roar, it tore down the street towards her. Head down and with every muscle in her body aching, Freya leapt into the road and over to the other side, where she raced down a side street.

What was going on?

Who were these people?

What did they want with her?

The sun was setting, casting long shadows over the pavement. As she got to the end of the next street, she realised she'd reached St Anne's Hill. Her house was a block away from here. Five minutes on foot. Two if she was running. But what if they saw where she lived? Or did they know already?

Full of adrenaline and with panic clouding all but her basic motor skills, she carried on, running up the street towards where St Anne's Hill became St Anne's Crescent and then Aspley Road. She'd almost reached home when she looked up, and there it was.

No.

Please no.

The car was driving towards her, but she had to keep going. The end was in sight. She craned her neck, casting a desperate gaze down the empty streets. There was no one else in sight, but Freya had one last move. Veering left, she ran into the grounds of St Anne's church and up the stone steps, launching herself at the large wooden doors. They swung open, and she staggered through into the large vestibule beyond, steadying herself against a stone column as an old woman sitting on the back pew turned to glare at her.

"Sorry," Freya mouthed, before gasping back a breath.

The air inside the church was heady with spice. It reminded Freya of the scented candles her mum would burn at Christmas. Back when Christmas was a joyful time. When it was still the three of them in the house.

She glanced over her shoulder. The church doors were still hanging open, but the street outside was empty. They wouldn't come into a church after her, would they? With her heart still playing a high-energy dance beat in her chest, she walked over to the doorway and peered outside, looking left and right. The car was gone.

Thank you.

Thank you, God.

They weren't a religious family, but Freya felt safe here. Straightening her hunched frame, she waited a few more seconds, but no car appeared from around the corner, and she could hear no revving engines. She puffed out her cheeks. Had she imagined it? Was this another one of her flights of fancy?

Feeling confused and scared, as the adrenaline response dissipated, she shuffled back inside the church. Her mind, now back online and in full effect, spun with crazy ideas and mixed-up notions. She hadn't been inside St Anne's for so long, not since she attended Sunday school here when she was nine, but she remembered there was a side exit out to the car park that was accessible via the annexe on the far side. Careful not to disturb the old woman for a second time, she tiptoed over and slipped through the door into her old classroom. Here the spice smell was even more pungent, the walls adorned with rudimentary finger paintings of flowers, but Freya hardly noticed, focused as she was on the red fire door in front of her. As she got up to it, she peered through the frosted glass, half-expecting to see a sinister black outline on the other side. But it was clear. She pushed down on the release bar and swung the door open when she heard a noise behind her and a voice.

"Wait!"

Freya jumped, the pent-up anxiety in her body manifesting itself in a warbled squeal. She spun around, expecting to see a shadowy figure advancing on her, evil-eyed and with grasping sinewy fingers. But it instead she was greeted by a small man with a kind face. Admittedly, he was dressed in black, but the white square of his dog collar told her he was no threat.

"Can I help you?" he asked. He sounded foreign. Polish, maybe.

"Oh, no. Sorry," Freya gasped. "I was just... I used to come here... When I was younger. I need to go. Sorry."

She hurried out the fire door, leaving the vicar muttering in her wake. The warm breeze enveloped her like a benign blanket as she hurried down the steps into the car park, letting the door swing shut behind her. She glanced furtively around the area, like a meerkat on high alert, searching for predators. But there was no big black car. No danger. She could even see her house from here. Thirty seconds and she'd be at her front door. One minute more and she'd be in her bedroom. She'd be safe. Raising her head, she hoisted up the straps of her backpack and sprinted the short distance home.

2

The train for Teddington was already waiting at platform twelve as Beth hastened up the final few steps of the escalator and ran the final fifty metres, all but diving through the train doors as they slid shut.

Once safely on board, she steadied herself against the side of the carriage and pulled a piece of hair out of her mouth as nonchalantly as she could. She was sweating profusely, and her tights had slipped down - the material creating a gossamer hammock that hung a few inches below her crotch - but she'd made it. She was also more out of breath than she'd have liked, but that was expected. Her daily ten-kilometre run had recently slipped down to five kilometres and was now less of a daily run and more a when-she-could-be-bothered run or a when-she-had-the-time run. Which was, increasingly, never.

But sweat and ruffled hair be damned. She was on the train home. A whistle blew, a buzzer sounded, and they set off. Beth tightened the belt on her Max Mara trench coat, an attempt to rebuild an air of calm and decorum. Then, with head raised, she shuffled between the two businessmen, deep in conversation outside the toilet cubicle, and entered the carriage. Most of the seats were occupied, but Beth was eagle-eyed enough to spot a vacant one halfway down, alongside a grey-haired woman with a face like death.

With her eyes fixed on the empty seat and muttering the obligatory pleasantries as she squeezed past a rotund man standing in the aisle (and making a big deal of placing his brief-case in the overhead compartment), Beth made her way along the carriage. The woman next to the window gave her a nasty look as she wilted into the seat beside her, but Beth didn't care. She had a seat. She was going home.

As the train left Waterloo Station, she sat back, happy that for once she'd be home for dinner. All right, late dinner (all right, it would technically be supper by the time she got home) but it meant she and Freya could eat together. They could spend some time together. Beth couldn't remember when she last had a proper chat with her daughter and the thought she might now get the chance warmed her. This despite knowing all too well the meal would likely be eaten in awkward silence, or with her asking Freya a series of questions to which she received only grunts or sighs in response. But that was fourteen-year-old girls for you. Fourteen going on twenty-four.

Beth pulled her phone out of her jacket pocket and puffed out her cheeks. The glimmer of happiness that had been arising inside of her was already fading to guilt and self-hatred, but that wasn't unusual. In fact, these days it seemed her default state. She knew she was as much to blame for her and Freya's fractious relationship, but that only made things worse. She was stuck in the mother of all vicious circles. Couldn't do right for doing wrong. When Adam had left, she'd vowed to herself that she'd ask him for nothing and do whatever it took, so Freya's life would remain exactly as it had been. Adam still paid his way, of course, but even with his extensive monthly maintenance payments, it was a struggle to keep her only child in the manner to which she'd grown accustomed. Beth's recent promotion helped, but it also meant she'd taken on more responsibilities, was working longer hours, some weekends. She worked her arse off to provide for Freya and give her a good life, but in doing so she had no life of her own and no time to spend with Freya. But wasn't that the same for every single parent? Once this year was over and her position was more secure, she'd stand up for herself a little more at work, explain to her colleagues she had to be home at a reasonable hour. And then maybe, finances permitting, they could book that holiday to New York they'd talked about.

She switched her phone on and tapped through to the messages, hoping for, but not expecting, a reply from her daughter. There was the message from her, telling Freya she couldn't pick her up and then another hour later, asking if she was home safe. That was the last one in the thread. It had been read but not replied to. Beth imagined that was deliberate. Freya's way of punishing her. But maybe she deserved it.

Beth closed her eyes, trying her best to shut out the hum of people and the clatter of the train tracks. This time, she succeeded in putting the troubles of the day behind her and drifted into a semi-trance. She focused her attention on her breath, attempting to clear her mind of strategy meetings and the impending budget review. By the time the train pulled up at Wandsworth Town station, she was feeling almost herself again. Better, at least. Beth Lomax had no idea what feeling 'herself' felt like anymore. She hadn't felt like herself in a very long time. And even if she had done, she suspected she would no longer recognise that person.

"Freya," she called out as she opened the front door. "I'm home."

There was no answer.

She went into the hallway and bolted the door behind her. The heating was on, but it was controlled by a pre-programmed app so that meant nothing.

"Freya?" she tried again. "Are you in your room?"

When no reply came, she went through into their large kitchen-diner - the part of the house where they congregated most frequently - and placed her bag down on the kitchen table. She'd always liked this table. They'd found it in a vintage furniture shop in Finchley when Adam and she were still newlyweds. Beth had dreamed of it being the centrepiece of their family home. And it had been, for a time. These days all meals were eaten at the island, or in front of the TV. The table once reserved for family mealtimes, was now where she sat alone, hunched over her laptop with a glass of wine close to hand.

Speaking of which, she slipped the bottle of Chablis from out of her bag and moved over to the fridge, laying the bottle down between an unopened box of artisan cheeses she'd bought for Christmas and a stack of Waitrose microwave meals. She'd bought these for when she got home too late to even think about cooking, but she saw now the top two were already past their use-by-date. She stared into the fridge for a moment longer before taking the wine back out and pouring a large serving into the solitary glass she found on the draining board. Having had only seconds to chill, the wine was lukewarm, but it was necessary, and she drank two-thirds of the glass in one go. Along with Chardonnay, Chablis was one of Beth's favourite types of wine, but Adam had always scoffed at her choices when they were together. Every time she had a glass of it now it felt like a tiny victory.

She put the glass down. "Freya, if you are home, will you please answer me?" She waited. "I'm making pasta, okay? Ready in twenty minutes."

She listened, no response. No sound of any movement whatsoever. She grabbed up her phone to check the time. 8:22 p.m. Where the hell was she?

She placed the wine glass down next to her bag and went through to the hallway, clutching her phone to her chest.

"Freya, if you're ignoring me..."She hauled her tired limbs up the stairs. "Look, I'm sorry I couldn't pick you up. But I'm here now. We can have dinner together."

She walked along the landing towards Freya's room. The door was closed, but it always was. It had been that way since she was twelve years old. Beth knocked once, pushed the door open, and stepped inside, bracing herself for a blasting. But the room was empty.

"Freya?"

The first frisson of panic bubbled in her guts. Typically, if she wasn't downstairs, she was in her bedroom. Always.

"Freya!" she called louder, employing her serious tone. "Where are you? Answer me!"

She gave her daughter's room a final once over and moved along the corridor towards her own room. There was no reason Freya would be in there, of course, but something felt wrong. Beth's sense of reason was shaken. As she opened the door she saw here too the lights were off. With no sign of her daughter.

Despite a growing concern tightening the skin around her eyes, she told herself to stay calm. Asking, what was the most innocent explanation here?

Well, that was easy. Freya would have gotten a lift with Mia like Beth had suggested, and her parents would have invited her to have dinner with them. Yes. That would be it. They were probably all sitting around the family dinner table right now, eating a delicious home-cooked meal. An idyllic scene, with a full complement of parents and probably dessert too. Beth raised her phone and was swiping through her recent call list when she saw a sliver of light under the door at the far end of the corridor.

She padded softly over to the door and listened. No sound came from inside, but why was the light on? It was never on. This room had been Adam's study, his 'sanctuary' as he called it (pretentious twat that he was) and she hadn't stepped inside since he left. Initially, he'd set it up as a rudimentary office for when he was working from home, but for the last few years of their marriage, she'd suspected it was the place he came to hide from her. Probably where he came to text Izzie. So maybe Beth should have been thankful. Even Adam would know, taking photos of his penis to send to his much younger PA was disrespectful, done from their shared bathroom.

Beth eased open the door and poked her head around the side, feeling a strange fluttering sensation in her stomach as she did. She wasn't entirely sure what her body was trying to tell her by this. It could have been trepidation, unease, at stepping into Adam's domain after so long, but as she opened the door wider, it felt much more like relief.

"There you are."

Freya was sitting at Adam's large leather-topped desk with headphones over her ears. Her eyes were closed, and she was listening to whatever music was coming out of the record player sitting on the shelf to her right. Adam had promised, on more than one occasion, that he'd come and clear out the rest of his stuff, but his record collection and costly state-of-the-art music system were still here. No room for it in his new swanky Lambeth apartment, perhaps. Or he didn't want to put Izzie off with his collection of hoary old vinyl.

With her eyes shut and engrossed in the music, Freya didn't notice Beth until she was standing beside her. She put her hand on her shoulder. "Freya?"

"What the fuck!?"

Freya jumped up, her eyes snapping open. She stared at Beth like she was a ghost before dragging the headphones off, her dark hair trailing over her face as she did.

"Don't you ever knock?"

Beth stepped back, any relief she'd felt at finding her daughter safe and well morphing quickly to anger.

"Excuse me. I did knock. You didn't hear me with those stupid things on your head." She gestured at Adam's headphones, castigating the inanimate object with more wrath than they deserved. "And please don't swear. I've brought you up better than that."

Freya slumped back down on the leather chair and chucked the headphones onto the desk with a dramatic huff.

"Why didn't you text me back? Let me know you were okay?" Beth asked. "I was worried."

"Were you?"

"Yes. I was."

Freya snorted dramatically. "Surprised you even had time to text me to say you weren't coming. Seeing as you're *soooo* busy and important these days."

"Oh, grow up," Beth told her. But a part of her was softening. A part of her knew her daughter had a point. "What are you doing in here?"

"Don't know," Freya said, not making eye contact. "Fancied listening to some music, that's all."

Beth nodded, taking in the room for the first time since she'd entered. Nothing had changed since the last time she was in here. Since the day Adam left for good. She turned her attention back to her daughter. She looked tired, but there was something else too. Something Beth couldn't quite put her finger on.

"Are you okay, Frey?" she asked, her tone gentle now.

"Yes. Why?"

"You look... I don't know... Like you've got the weight of the world on your shoulders." She knew how she felt.

But Freya just scoffed and got to her feet. "I'm fine."

"Hey." Beth put her hand on her daughter's arm as she tried to shuffle past her out of the room. They were almost the same height. How the hell had that happened? "Is there anything you want to tell me?"

Freya rolled her eyes.

"What is it?" Beth asked.

Freya opened her mouth, but before she could speak, Beth's phone vibrated in her hand, chiming its intrusive melody into the room. Like it always seemed to do at crucial moments.

Beth looked at the screen, then at Freya. "It's fine, I can leave it," she lied. It was Louise, head of operations at the Royal Farringdon Hospital and Beth's senior manager. So, she couldn't just leave it. But this was important, too.

Beth grimaced, waving the phone around as if doing so would make it stop ringing.

"Oh, God! Just answer it," Freya spat the words out as she pushed past her.

"One minute, I swear," Beth yelled after her, swiping the phone open and holding it to her ear, adding. "Then we'll talk. And I'll make dinner."

"Beth? Is that you?"

"Sorry, Louise. I was talking to Freya. Is everything okay?"

The line was silent for a moment. "Yes, everything is hunky-dory," Louise said in her usual breezy manner. "I was just calling to make sure you were around first thing. Damien is coming into the office."

Damien Broadhurst. Head of the Farringdon Trust. He was a nice enough guy, but one of those men who seemed to have got where he was purely on charm, familial links and the fact he went to Eton. But wasn't that true of most men in positions of power in this country?

"That's not like him," she replied.

"Yes, I know. But he wants to be more hands-on apparently. Plus, some new trustee is being appointed. I think he wants you to help with the paperwork or something."

Beth cringed inwardly. It was the last thing she needed.

"Lou, I'm swamped at the moment. I've got five new starters needing full work permit audits, and then there's the budget review..."

Louise chuckled at Beth's outburst. "I know. It's not what you need. But it's what Damien wants. So... First thing tomorrow. That good?"

"No problem. See you then."

They said their goodbyes and Beth pocketed the phone before striding down the corridor to Freya's room, which was now very clearly occupied if the music blaring through the door was any indication.

Beth knocked and waited. Best way rather than barging in. When nothing happened, she knocked again. "Freya?"

The music was promptly turned down, and the door swung open.

"What?" Freya asked, holding onto the door with an outstretched arm and a look of disdain crumpling her pretty face.

"I thought we were going to talk?"

"You thought wrong."

"But..."

"I've nothing to say to you, Mum. Go do your work or whatever it is. I'm fine."

Beth swallowed. "Come on, Frey, I was only—"

"I said, I'm fine. Leave me alone." She went to shut the door, but Beth blocked her. "What the hell?"

"Hey. What about dinner?"

"I'm not hungry." She went to shut the door again. "Stop it."

"Come on Frey. Let's talk. Over a nice bowl of pasta."

"I said, I'm not hungry! Now leave me alone. Jesus!" Beth stepped back, allowing her only child to slam the door in her face.

"Well, fine then," Beth shouted through the door. "Go hungry."

"Fine! Piss off!"

"Oh, you ungrateful brat!"

Beth clenched her fist before letting out a guttural groan. Why did it always end up like this? At what point had her dear little Frey-Frey become such a horrible, surly teen?

She turned from the door and was about to go downstairs when she realised Adam's study light was still on. As she walked across the wide, L-shaped landing, she also noticed the stereo was still on and as she got nearer, heard the music coming from the headphones on the desk. She picked them up and placed them over her head. Bowie's dulcet tones filled her ears. The song was *Heroes,* one of Adam's favourite songs. They'd listened to it often when they first got together. Then, when Freya was a toddler, Adam would sit the small girl on his knee and they'd listen to it together, both singing along at the tops of their voices. It became their song, but Beth didn't mind that. She still didn't. But the fact Freya was listening to it tonight...

Oh, my baby girl.

Something *was* wrong. Beth removed the headphones before switching off the stereo and then the light. But as she closed the door behind her and headed across the landing to Freya's room, she stopped. She had so many questions, but she doubted Freya was in the right mood to answer them tonight, and she couldn't face another fight. Instead, she went downstairs and back into the kitchen, where she made a beeline for the

21

fridge. The Chablis would be chilled by now, and there was a large glass with her name on it. After the day she'd had, she deserved it.

3

Freya was expecting to find her mum in the kitchen when she got downstairs the next morning. She even wondered whether she'd get an apology. She deserved one, after all. But all she found was a note on the kitchen island with a five-pound note paper-clipped to the back. In her mum's impatient scrawl, she'd written that she was sorry for shouting but that she couldn't give Freya a lift to school as she had a 'BUSY DAY' (the words all in capitals and underlined three times for emphasis).

"Well, that's just great, mum. Thanks a lot," Freya muttered to herself.

She grabbed a pop tart from out of the cupboard and stuck it in her mouth as she pulled on her blazer and hoisted her rucksack over her shoulders. So, she was walking to school. Again. And if that big scary car was out there waiting for her, then so be it. If she got kidnapped now, it would be her mum's fault. She almost wished for it to happen. That would teach her.

But that was a silly thing to wish for and she took it back immediately, saying sorry to the cosmos for being rash. The

Lomax's weren't a religious family, but Freya had been getting more spiritual lately. And she shouldn't tempt fate.

She also wasn't sure why she hadn't told her mum about the car the previous evening. She'd meant to, had even rehearsed what she'd say in her head, practising how best to explain it so as not to panic her already stressed-out mum. But then they'd argued. And even before then, she'd felt nervous about telling her. As though, if she vocalised what had happened, it would make it more real. Once she was safely inside her warm suburban house, she'd even wondered if all the drama involving the black car was just that – drama. Her imagination running off into flights of fancy. So, she'd kept her mouth shut. Told herself it wasn't important. And maybe it wasn't?

She grabbed her keys from out of the bowl and headed out the door. It was a bright morning, warm for April, and as she set off for school, the idea that a car of shadowy villains were trying to snatch her seemed fantastical. It was good she hadn't mentioned it. The last thing she needed was her mum going all weird and stressed about that as well. She'd probably tell her she *didn't need this right now*. Like she had done when Anne-Marie Miller got the part of Tallulah in Bugsy Malone and Freya had been distraught for days. So why tell her anything? She didn't care. All she cared about was her work and that stupid hospital.

At the end of the street, she stopped to place her earbuds in and turn on her music. Billie Eilish picking up where she left off yesterday.

Stupid Mum.

She kicked an empty Coke can that was lying in the gutter and immediately felt bad about it. She'd been brought up to respect her environment. To never drop litter. But it was her mum's fault. She made her so angry.

Why did she have to be so stressed all the time?

As she got up to the Coke can, she picked it up and carried

it to the bin on the corner before crossing the road and entering the park.

Stupid flipping mum.

But her anger was already fading. She knew deep down her mum was only working so hard because she wanted to do right by her. Especially after Dad left. The divorce had been hard on them all. For the first few months, her mum had just sat and stared out the window for hours on end. Later Freya would listen at the bathroom door, her mum's sobbing scarcely masked by the running shower. Despite Freya having a good relationship with her dad (and Izzie too, who was pretty cool, once you got to know her) she knew he'd put her mum through a lot of pain. And whilst she could be a total pain in Freya's neck, she deserved to be happy.

But that was what made her so angry if she thought about it. Her mum was working long hours, tiring herself out so Freya could have a good life. Yet all she wanted was a mum who was happy and less stressed, who was fun to be around and at home more than she wasn't. It certainly was a conundrum. And one that Freya didn't have the answer to this warm April morning. Maybe tonight they could sit down and have a chat and Freya could tell her mum how she felt. If she was struggling and unwilling to ask Dad for help, maybe *she* could ask him? Or she could get a Saturday job? Would that work? She'd never had one. How much did people earn in part-time jobs these days?

Freya was so up in her head - thinking about what she'd say to her mum - that she was walking along on autopilot, tracing the path she walked every day when her mum wasn't able to drive her to school. As she left the park behind, she took a left down Merton Road. She was outside Party Chicken Shack when she looked up.

No way.

A yelp caught in her throat. Her skin went cold. There it

was, like an insidious shadow loitering by the curb a few metres in front of her. The same car from yesterday. The sight hurtled her back to the present moment. Then time slowed to a stop. She glanced up and down the street, but except for an old man walking his dog near the corner; the area was deserted.

"Help!" she cried after him, but he didn't turn around. "Help me!" she tried again, hoping someone, anyone, might hear.

Then the car doors were opening. On both sides. Two people were getting out. Men. Large men. Tall. Wide. That was all Freya saw before she turned on her heels and ran. With her head down, she raced down the street as fast as her legs would carry her, veering across the road and down the next one. On a normal day, she'd have made her way through a series of back-streets, which would eventually bring her out on Sutherland Grove, where her school was situated. But at this time in the morning, that way was quiet and more secluded. Right now, she needed people. A person. Anyone.

She ran fast. Ran until her calf muscles burned, and she had a stitch in her side. The road was long, and Freya wasn't the most athletic of girls. She was slim, slight framed, but had put all her energy into her acting these last few years at the expense of sports or any pursuit that would have made her stronger and fitter. And better able to deal with being pursued by two evil giants. Because they were still coming for her. Gaining on her fast. At the corner of the street, she risked a glance back at them. They didn't look like paedophiles, or sex traffickers, or whatever the hell they were. But then, what did people who did those things look like?

She carried on down the street, clenching her fists as she ran. Long before she'd even decided on being an actor, Freya would lose herself in extensive role-play, creating new and fantastical personas for herself. In any one day, she might be a magical princess, a mermaid queen, a fierce warrior woman. Anyone but the scared young girl from South London whose parents wouldn't stop shouting at each other. Now she channelled that fierce warrior woman once more. She was Mulan and Moana and Merida from Brave all rolled into one. An unstoppable being whom the forces of evil could never capture. She was courageous, strong, the fastest runner in the world. She could do this. She could make it. She could...

No!

They were still coming. Advancing fast. Now she could see the end of the road where it opened out onto the much busier and more populated Wimbledon Park Road. Cars were going past; parents walked their young children to school. Another thirty seconds and she'd be safe. But another fifteen and they'd be on her. Without looking back, she veered around the side of an Indian takeaway and down a side street. She was searching for a newsagent, an off-licence, any shop that might be open where she could hide out, ask the owners to ring the police.

The police!

Why didn't she think of that sooner? Scrabbling about in her blazer pocket, she pulled out her phone and swiped it open. Not easy when running at speed, but keeping one eye on the road ahead, she found the phone keypad and was tapping in 999 when, up ahead, she saw salvation. A man, about her dad's age, walking towards her. He had a kind face and a newspaper under his arm.

As she ran up to him, he stopped, and his face creased into a concerned expression.

"Helmeeepleease!" Freya gasped, as she ran towards him. "Some men...Some men are..."

"Whoa, whoa, hold up there darlin' what is it?" He stepped back, holding his arms out wide to stop her. He frowned. "Is everything okay?"

Freya swallowed back a mouthful of fear. Trying to get her words out, to explain what was going on. "I'm.... being... chased," she managed. "Some men. In a car. They're after me. Please help me."

"Jesus, okay. Let's calm down," the man said, patting the air with his outstretched hands as he looked around. "You're safe now."

But there was something in his eyes and the way he spoke that sent a chill running down Freya's back.

You're safe now.

Like he was mocking her. No. No, this wasn't happening. What would the warrior woman do? Freya stepped back to move around him, but he blocked her path. "What's going on darlin'?"

She shifted to the other foot, but he matched her movements once more. She lurched around the other side of him, but he grabbed for her, his hand closing tight around her wrist. It felt cold and rough, like an animal's paw. Freya went to scream, but he yanked her toward him and then his other hand was around her mouth, thick leathery fingers gagging her. She struggled hard, tried to scream, but only managed a muffled whimper.

"Don't be stupid," he growled in her ear. "It's going to be so much easier if you don't fight it."

But Freya fought it with everything she had, conjuring her inner beast and clawing desperately at the man's hands, trying to scream through the calloused palm covering her mouth. It was useless. This smelly ogre was twice the size of her and was not playing games. She thrashed about, tried to wriggle free, but the more she did, the tighter he squeezed. Then she saw the car.

No. Please no.

Her body went limp. She had no control over it. Fear had taken over, quickly turning to despair. She went dizzy. Her arms and legs weren't her own. As the car drove towards them, the man walked her over to it like she was a rag doll. Then the car stopped, and the doors opened. A man got out. One of the ones who'd been chasing her. Up close now she saw he had short brown hair and eyes so dark they were almost black. He was holding something in both hands and Freya's eyes widened as he opened it out. It was a black bag, more of a sack really, made of thick material. She let out a wail as they shoved her forward and shoved the sack over her head. Now she could scream, but it was too late. As the world went black, she felt herself being bundled into the back of the car. She heard the doors slam shut, then a crackle of electric static and a man's voice.

"It is done," he said. "We have her."

4

Beth squinted at the clock hanging over the doorway. It was only a few minutes after ten, but she felt like she'd already done a full day's work. It didn't help that Damien Broadhurst was still standing at the front of the room, still blathering on about funding and the advancement of the trust. Although to be fair to the man, he could have moved on to talking about his favourite film or what he was having for dinner by this point. She'd stopped listening.

Louise caught Beth's eye and widened her own, expertly articulating to Beth she should sit up in her seat and pay attention, which she did. She might have found this entire experience rather tiresome, but she was a professional. She switched her attention to Damien as he finished his speech.

"I know you all do exceptional work here in the HR department. It's not just the amazing surgeons and medical research teams that make Farringdon a world-class hospital. You are all such vital members of the team. So, thank you again and as I said, I'll try and come into the hospital much more, going forward. It's good for me to see things on the factory floor, as it were. Does anyone have any questions?"

Beth stayed quiet, willing everyone to do the same. She was dismayed and a little surprised when Carla raised her hand.

"This new heart drug everyone's talking about. Will we be getting it too?"

Beth glanced over and raised her eyebrows.

"What?" Carla said. "I watch the news. Apparently, some big American company is developing it and everyone's fighting over the rights. Something like that, anyway. And isn't the government trying to sign a big deal with the yanks at the moment? Worth billions I heard."

"Damien's wide smile did little to hide his disdain. "I heard the deal hasn't been finalised just yet. But when it has been, it'll be a good thing for the entire country, I'm sure. Braxxon Kleiner are world-leaders in heart medicine research."

"Why are we giving money to the US?" Carla continued. "I mean, I know we're a private hospital, so it's a bit different, but the NHS doesn't need the likes of them interfering. A lot of nonsense if you ask me."

She sniffed and crossed her arms and Beth met Louise's eye once more. This time they shared a stifled grin. Carla Johnson. God love her. From Leeds originally and despite living in London for the best part of fifty years she'd never lost her northern brogue or blunt way of speaking.

Ignoring Carla's mutterings, Damien turned to Beth. "Now Beth, I need to ask you a favour. We've got a prospective new trustee ready to come on board and I wouldn't mind a little help with their proposal. I've to present a paper to the existing trustees in relation to the appointment and it would be wonderful if you could help out."

Help out. As in she writes it and he takes all the credit.

She raised her chin. "I'm sorry, Damien. I can't."

The words were out of her mouth before she could stop herself, and she instantly regretted them. She never would normally speak out in such a way, not to a senior figure like Damien Broadhurst. But she was stressed and exhausted and not thinking straight. And drinking an entire bottle of Chablis with only half a pipe of Pringles to soak up the alcohol last night didn't help.

"Oh?" He frowned, appearing all at once like a confused elderly king. Someone who'd never been told 'no' in his life. He looked at Louise. "I don't understand."

Louise opened her mouth and shut it again before glancing at Beth. "What she means is she has a lot on at present, don't you Beth? We're working them hard here. But you can help Damien, can't you Beth?"

Her eyes were like laser beams trained on Beth. She bit her lip, having a fast word with herself.

"Yes. Sorry, Damien," she said. "I didn't mean to sound negative. It's just, I've got so much on at the moment. How would it be if you draft the proposal and I'll have a look at it for you?"

Damien looked at Louise with a fatigued expression, then back to Beth. "Yes. Fine," he said, before turning his attention to the entire office. "Now we may have something exciting happening over the next week or so. I can't say too much at this stage but all that I will say is it will be very good for the hospital. So, watch this space." He clapped his hands together and smiled, which seemed to indicate the end of the meeting.

Phew.

She'd swerved that one. Now all she had to do was complete all the tasks on her 'To-Do' list, start getting home at a reasonable hour and carve off more time to spend with her daughter. Maybe then Freya wouldn't look at her like she despised her. As the meeting adjourned Beth sat back in her seat and let out a deep sigh. If only they could invent a day with at least four more hours in it.

It did bother Beth that she and Freya hadn't spoken since their fight. It bothered her a great deal. She never let a fight fester if she could help it. She'd even considered waking Freya to apologise before she left for work, but it was so early it could have made things ten times worse, so she'd decided against it. But now she had an overriding urge to contact her only child. Just to make sure she was okay. That she didn't hate her mother quite as much as she professed.

It was a selfish act, Beth knew that. It could even be construed as her playing the victim like Adam always said she did. But that didn't mean it didn't hurt. A text would be enough. A few words of reassurance. An 'x' or two.

She'd turned her iPhone off for the meeting, but now she slipped the phone out of her trouser pocket. Holding it on her lap under the table, she pressed the 'on' button, thankful she'd left it on silent. She waited whilst a flurry of notifications vibrated through her thigh before lifting it to the lip of the table and peeking a look at the screen. The text was small, and her eyesight was not as good as it once was (the remnants of the hangover didn't help) but she could see most of the notifications were forgettable. An email from a cosmetics company she didn't remember subscribing to, a calendar update telling her she had a meeting with Damien Broadhurst an hour ago, a text from DPD informing her she'd missed their call, plus six messages from the WhatsApp group she shared with her friends from uni, which were all just silly memes. She cleared them one by one and was about to put her phone back in her pocket when it vibrated again, and a text message flashed on the screen.

It was from St Bernadette's High School. Freya's school. Beth narrowed her eyes at the screen, assuming the message would be one of those usual round-robin type missives, informing her of an upcoming charity drive or parents' evening. But no. The message addressed her by name, Mrs Lomax, and as she read it, she forgot all about her hangover and writing Damien's proposal. The muscles in her abdomen and pelvic floor contracted as she read the message again, making sure she hadn't misunderstood anything. She felt her palms moisten. She sucked back a breath, but it became wedged in her throat.

The message told her there was an issue with Freya.

It told her to ring the school as soon as possible.

5

Beth got to her feet, mumbling something about an urgent phone call as she shuffled around the back of Jazmine's chair and, once clear, ran for the door. She was already scrolling through her contacts list for the school as she reached the corridor, calling the number as she strode through to the landing by the elevators. She paced up and down in front of the steel doors as the dialling tone chirped and whirred on the line.

"Come on, come on..."

The line clicked, as though being answered. "Hello," Beth said. "This is Freya Lomax's mu—"

"Thank you for calling St Bernadette's High School, Wandsworth. All our lines are currently busy, but please hold and someone will take your call as soon as they are available."

"For fuck's sake," Beth hissed into the receiver.

She didn't need this. Not on top of everything else. She walked over to the window and looked out over the city in an attempt to calm herself. Yeah, right! She hadn't taken a proper breath since she got the text. She closed her eyes, inhaling slowly and deliberately through her nose, but it did little good. Her heart was racing and her mind running wild with ideas and notions and possibilities.

None of them were good. Out the window, she could see the green expanse of Charterhouse Square and, over to the right, Smithfield Market. Down below people went about their business, unaware she was watching them whilst having a bloody heart attack.

"Calm down, Elizabeth," she told herself. "Everything will be fine." And she did know that - hoped that - deep down. If Freya had been hurt, the school would have called her, wouldn't they? They wouldn't send a text. Even though logically this made sense, it didn't help. Nor did the fact Beth knew a big part of why she was acting so fretful was her state of mind prior to the text. Because when you're worried about your child, nothing makes sense. Nothing is logical. She looked to the sky, pleading with whoever was up there. She needed this to be just her mind messing with her. The usual toxic mix of work pressure, fatigue, guilt and hormones causing her to assume the worst.

"Hello, can I help you?" A woman's voice came on the line.

"Yes. Hi. My name's Beth Lomax. I'm Freya Lomax's mother. I've just received a message from you." The woman didn't respond. Not as quickly as Beth needed her to. "I was told to call," she continued. "You said it was about Freya. You texted me. Five minutes ago. Less than that. What's going on?"

The woman huffed gently on the line; it didn't sound like a huff of impatience, but Beth was close to interpreting it that way. "It wasn't myself who messaged you, Ms Lomax, but if you hold the line a moment, I'll find out what's going on."

"Yes, please do," Beth said to the hold music. An instrumental Coldplay song. She was back to pacing across the landing. But with head down now, staring at the black and beige carpet tiles laid out like a chessboard, making sure not to step on any of the cracks.

Anything bad is only in your head.
Anything bad is only in your head.

"Ms Lomax?"

"Mrs."

Mrs? Why the fucking hell did she say that? Why did it matter?

"Is Freya all right?" she asked.

"Erm, yes. Well... we don't know. You see, she never arrived at school this morning. Is she at home? You know you really are obliged to ring us if..."

The woman continued talking, but Beth had lowered the phone. She checked her notifications but there were no texts from Freya, no WhatsApp messages. She lifted the phone back to her ear.

"She should be at school," she said. "that's where I thought she was."

The woman went quiet. "Oh."

"We had a big row last night," Beth said. "I don't think she's talking to me."

"I see, well maybe that's it? We all know what teenage girls are like. Ms Hargreaves, her form teacher, is off work today as well. This is why we've only just logged this issue. But I'm sure there's a perfectly innocent explanation."

"Yes. Me too."

"We will need to know what's going on though, so when you do hear from her, can you ring us? And make sure she attends tomorrow if she's well enough."

Beth's grip on the phone tightened. "Yes. I will. She will," she replied, speaking through gritted teeth. "I'm sorry, I have to go. I need to ring around, see where she's got to. As you say, she's probably sulking somewhere. Thank you. Goodbye." She hung up and screamed silently into the ceiling.

Freya. Where the bloody hell are you?

With her phone still out, she scrolled to her favourites list and called Freya's mobile. It rang for half a beat and then a robotic voice came over the line.

"The mobile phone you are calling has been switched off. Please try again later."

Freya didn't have her voicemail set up (none of the kids did, apparently) but she never switched her phone off. Ever. Beth hung up and tried again. Same story. Opening iMessenger, she tapped out a brief text.

Call me darling. Please it's important. Love u. xx

She tapped the send arrow and stared at the message as it appeared in the thread, waiting for it to be marked 'delivered'. She waited a minute. Two minutes. But the notification never came. Freya's phone was switched off.

Beth paused and peered out the window again, this time not really seeing anything. What now? She went back to her phone and found Adam's number, calling him before she could talk herself out of it.

"Is Freya with you?" she asked before he had a chance to say anything. "She's not at school."

"Excuse me?" He said it in that same way he always spoke to her since the divorce. Patronising, like he already suspected she was being ridiculous.

She bit her lip and waited a beat before speaking. "I've just had a call from Freya's school," she told him. "She's not turned up to any of her classes today. I've been trying to call her, but her phone is off. It's never off, Adam."

This time the words must have sunk in because her ex-husband was silent. When he spoke next, his voice had lost all its supercilious timbre. "When was the last time you saw her?"

"Last night. We had a row, and she stayed in her room. I had to leave early this morning, so I didn't get a chance."

Adam sighed heavily down the line, overplaying the subtext like always. Still, he said it anyway. "What was it this time?"

Beth bit her lip harder. "It wasn't a big fight. Something and nothing. It's fine."

"Is it? What about her friends? Have you tried ringing them?"

"That was my next move. But they'll all be at school, won't they? Unless they've all bunked off together, but surely the school would have mentioned that. They would have, wouldn't they? Because that's a very different thing than—"

"Beth! Beth, calm down. This isn't helping."

She glared through the window, her perspective shifting from the world outside to her reflection in the glass. Illuminated by the harsh fluorescent light above, she looked haggard. The skin under her eyes sagged with the weight of absolutely everything. She shook her head. "I am calm. Thank you, Adam. But I'm a little concerned about our daughter. Aren't you?"

"I'm sure there's a perfectly reasonable explanation to all this." He already sounding impatient. "Are you at the house now?"

"No. I'm at work."

"Oh?" he barked as if this was preposterous to him. "Well, she's probably at home then. Bloody hell, Beth, you're calling me up, getting me all worried and you haven't even checked if she's at the house?"

"I'm at work, Adam."

"Yes. So am I. And I'm busy."

"And I'm not?"

Another sigh. "Well, when you do get home. Why don't you call me then? And in the meantime, I'll text her. Tell her to get in touch. If you've upset her, she might just be fielding your calls."

"Her phone is off. I told you that."

"Yes, and I told you, she's probably at home. Wait a second." The line went muffled, as though he'd placed his hand over the microphone. Then it crackled, and he was back. "Look, Beth. I'm at work and I'm needed. Go home and I'll call you when I hear from her."

He hung up, leaving Beth staring at her phone, fighting every impulse she had to throw the bastard thing through the window. But the call had silenced some of the voices in her head, at least.

Despite being a prize shit of the highest order, Adam loved his daughter and the fact he wasn't panicking offered some relief. But only some. Because she knew Freya. This was not like her. Not at all. She and Beth were very similar. Both were only children, both accustomed to getting their own way. They clashed often, especially these last few years, but it was never serious, and it never lasted long. They could be having a massive stand-up row one minute and all would be forgotten the next. This idea that Freya was holding a grudge, that she'd turned her phone off and was hiding out to spite her mother, it didn't seem likely.

Beth pocketed her phone and walked over to the elevator, pressing the down button and jabbing at it with her finger a couple more times when the doors didn't immediately ping open. It was too early for lunch, but she needed fresh air and to clear her head. Once she'd calmed down, she'd ring around Freya's friends and their parents too, ask them if they knew where Freya was. Hopefully without sounding like the hysterical fool Adam assumed her to be.

She bounced from foot to foot, not taking her eyes off the lights above the elevator as they moved from floor three to four to five to six. The elevator pinged.

Finally.

Beth readied herself to jump inside, but when the doors slid open, her heart sank. Standing in the middle of the elevator, holding a paper folder of medical notes to his chest, was Dr Raul.

"Hello there, Beth," he said with a smile. "Fancy seeing you here."

6

"How are you?" Dr Raul asked. "You look well."

Beth nodded and stepped into the lift, immediately facing out and standing shoulder to shoulder with the doctor. "Do I?" she said. "It must be the wonderful lighting in here."

Dr Raul chuckled as he leaned forward and stabbed at the already illuminated button for the ground floor. "Where are you heading?"

Out! Just out! She wanted to scream. Her head was banging, and her heart felt like it was going to burst out of her chest. She nodded at the illuminated panel. "Ground floor is fine," she told him.

"Are you okay, Beth?" Dr Raul asked. Frowning now, concerned. "Sorry, I shouldn't pry."

But the question, coupled with the gentle way he'd asked, set something off inside of her. She turned to the wall, widening her eyes as they filled with tears, less one escape.

"Oh shit! What is it?"

Dr Raul was a nice man, and she wouldn't normally have

been so dismissive of him. But she didn't want to talk to anyone from work right now. Only Freya. There was also a certain amount of awkwardness between her and Dr Raul, which had existed ever since he'd started at Farringdon. Beth had been slap bang in the middle of the divorce but had stupidly mentioned to Carla she thought the new anaesthesiologist was rather handsome. Carla, being Carla, had then mentioned this to one of Dr Raul's colleagues. No one had ever said anything directly, but Beth suspected he knew what she'd said, and that was bad enough.

"Beth?"

She gritted her teeth and pouted. Her upper body was shaking as she put all her effort into not crying. But it was useless. A shiver of emotion shot through her, and she burst into tears.

"I'm so sorry," she wailed, waving her hand in front of her face in a vain attempt to stem the waterworks. "I'm being stupid. I know I am. I'm just frazzled. It's nothing."

"Come on now," Dr Raul said, taking a step toward her but maintaining a gentlemanly distance. "If you want to talk about it, I'm happy to listen. You never know, it might help."

Beth shuddered and shook her head. "It's my daughter," she heard herself say. "We had a row last night and now I don't know where she is. She's not at school, not answering her phone. I'm trying to stay rational about it but... I don't know... I'm probably making a mountain out of a molehill."

Dr Raul sucked back a sharp breath. He hadn't signed up for this. Poor guy. "I'm sure she's fine," he said, resting his hand on her arm. "She's a teenager, right?"

Beth nodded and snivelled a reply. "Fourteen."

"There you go," he said, as the elevator came to a stop. "I know when I was fourteen, I had a lot going on and would often go off on my own without telling anyone. I'm sure she's fine. Just exerting her independence. But why don't we put your mind at ease, regardless?" He let go of her arm as the doors slid open and gestured for her to follow him over to the reception desk.

Agnieszka looked up from her computer, smiling at the two of them as they approached. "Good day, Dr Raul. Mrs Lomax."

"Aga, I don't suppose you could do us a massive favour, could you?" Dr Raul asked, leaning an arm on the front desk and looking at Beth as he continued. "Can you ring around every A&E department in..." He narrowed his eyes at Beth as if trying to remember. "Clapham?"

She smiled. "Wandsworth."

"That's it. Call every A&E department within a twenty-mile radius of Wandsworth and ask if they've admitted a Freya Lomax. Fourteen years old. Say you're following up for Dr Raul at The Royal Farringdon if you think it will help?"

"Oh?" Agnieszka's darted a look at Beth, the concern in her eyes making her want to scream once more. "Yes. Of course. I will do that."

"Just to put our minds at rest," added Dr Raul. He leaned closer to Beth and lowered his voice. "Why don't you take yourself home in the meantime? I'll wait with Aga and call you the second we're done. I'm sure she'll come up with nothing. In fact, I bet you'll be calling me first to tell me she's at home."

"I can't go home," Beth whispered, the two of them moving away from the front desk as Agnieszka picked up the phone. "I've got so much on and—"

"—And you're no use to anyone stressed out and upset."

She sniffed. "I'm sorry. I know I'm being bloody daft. She'll be fine. I know she will. I'm so angry at her for doing this. As you say, bloody teenagers... Shit!"

She shut her mouth as she sensed more tears rising inside of her.

"Get yourself home," Dr Raul said, guiding her towards the security gate in front of the main entrance. "Do you need anything?"

"My bag," Beth cried. "It's in my office. My house keys are inside." She wiped at her cheeks with the heel of her thumb, ready to head for the elevator.

But Dr Raul held up his hands. "You stay here," he told her. "No point having to explain yourself to everyone. I'll get your bag. I'll also tell them you've got a migraine and I've recommended you take the afternoon off."

"Thank you."

He smiled, and she almost lost it. "Give me five minutes."

Beth watched as he strode over to the elevator and pressed the button, but on seeing the lights were up on the eighth floor, headed instead for the stairwell. He turned in the doorway and held his hand up, fingers spread. *Five minutes.*

Beth walked over to the side of the entrance where the hospital's glass frontage looked out onto the street. The sun was shining, clashing with the storm going on in her head.

"Come on, Freya," she muttered to herself. "Be at home."

She walked back to the front desk just as Agnieszka put the phone down. "That's St Helier and Royal Marsden so far," she said. "Neither of them has her."

Beth forced a smile. "Thank you for doing this," she said. "It's my daughter. She's not turned up for school."

"It's no problem."

"It's probably a colossal waste of your time," Beth added. "She'll be at home when I get there, annoyed I've made such a fuss."

"I bet," Agnieszka replied, smiling as she picked up the receiver. "But it is good to check."

She raised her eyebrows at something across the room and Beth turned to see Dr Raul jogging towards her.

"Blimey, that was fast," she said, accepting the bag from him as he got closer.

He grinned. "Yeah, my gym membership is paying off finally." He was out of breath, but his overall appearance was as neat and unflustered as always. Beth was glad she'd bumped into him.

"Thank you," she said. "And you'll call me?"

"As soon as Aga has finished ringing around. Unless you want to stay?"

Beth glanced at the receptionist and then at the exit. "I'll get back and see if she's there," she said. "I'll take a cab, so I'll have reception the entire way home. Shit. You need my number."

"Oh, yes." He pulled his phone from his pocket and opened it up before handing it to her. "Easier if you do it."

Beth swiped open the address book and quickly keyed in her number and name ('Beth Work', keep it professional) then she handed it back. "Speak to you soon then. Thank you. Both of you." She looked to Agnieszka who was finishing up the call. She made eye contact with Beth and shook her head with a smile. Three down. All clear.

"Now, go." Dr Raul said.

Beth didn't need telling. She hoisted her bag over her shoulder and, with her phone gripped to her chest, she swiped herself through the security gate. Once outside, she headed for the taxi rank opposite - where a cab was already waiting. At this time of day, it would take her around forty-five minutes to get back home. Forty-five minutes of torment, but then all would be well. Dr Raul and Adam weren't just saying things to placate her, they were right. Freya was more than likely at home. Maybe she'd slept in and decided it wasn't worth going to school. Maybe she was feeling down and needed some time alone. It happened. God, there were many days recently when Beth wished more than anything she could spend it in bed.

Yes. Freya was safe and well. She was at home. Beth had to believe that.

Because if she wasn't, where the hell was she?

7

Beth slammed the front door behind her and ran up the stairs, calling out as she went. "Freya? Are you there?"

She took the last few steps in one stride, using the bannister to haul herself around the corner and onto the upper level.

"Freya. It's me. Come out, will you?"

Beth hurried along the landing towards her daughter's bedroom. Harry Styles looked down at her from the poster hanging on the door as she grabbed the handle and pushed it open without breaking her stride.

She stopped.

The room was empty.

Moving over to Freya's desk, Beth laid her hand on the MacBook that lay closed on top. It was cold. She strode over to the bed. It hadn't been made, but that wasn't unusual. Freya never bothered with such things, and Beth had long ago given up on that particular battle. She felt at the recess in the pillow before picking it up and hugging it to her. It was cold but smelled of her daughter's shampoo. Now, from her position in the room, she could see into the wardrobe and the space at the left-hand side where Freya's school uniform would normally be hanging. Only it wasn't there.

Dr Raul had already phoned whilst Beth was in the taxi, reporting there'd been no admission of anyone fitting Freya's description at any of the nearby hospitals. Now the relief she'd experienced at that news was wiped away. In its place, a new kind of dread. She padded over to the wardrobe and rifled through the vast selection of dresses and cardigans and sweaters. But she found no blazer, no grey V-necked jumper with burgundy trim detail, no starched white shirt.

A thought came to her, and she returned to the laptop and prised it open. The login screen flashed into life as Beth sat down on the stool and said a brief prayer that Freya had the same password she'd always had.

They'd agreed some time ago that Beth would be privy to all her daughter's logins and passwords but on the proviso, she wouldn't check up on her unnecessarily. Despite her growing surliness, Freya was a good kid, and sensible, too. This was the first time Beth had ever needed to exorcise her right to view any of her daughter's social media accounts. But today it was necessary. It was very fucking necessary.

Leaning over the keyboard, she bashed in the password and hit enter. The box with the row of dots in the middle of the screen quivered, informing her she'd got the password wrong.

"No. Don't do this."

Beth tried again, tapping out the word using one finger, taking her time. As she hit enter, the screen opened up and her stomach muscles unclenched a little. The beauty of modern browsers meant once she was inside Freya's account, most of the other logins were auto-filled and she could get onto her Facebook and Instagram accounts with just two clicks. She went straight to direct messages and narrowed her eyes at the screen, unblinking as she scanned the rows of messages. What she was looking for exactly she didn't know, but it all appeared innocent enough. Mainly, it was a bunch of messages between Freya and her two best friends, Mia and Lauren. The messages were many but brief, predominantly threads where the three of them were discussing other girls in their class and things they'd posted online, complete with screenshots and an absolute plethora of laughing-face emojis. Freya sounded rather bitchy and unkind in places, but it was nothing you wouldn't expect from a four-teen-year-old girl trying to fit in.

Satisfied her daughter hadn't been involved in any question-able communication with shadowy men off of the internet, Beth closed the laptop and pulled her phone from her pocket. She knew Mia's parents, Jan and Mike, well. Indeed, there had been a time when she and Adam had considered the Sackler's good friends. There'd been dinner parties, nights out, even talk of a holiday at one stage. But since the divorce, she'd not seen them. It was hard. She understood that. People didn't like to take sides.

She dialled Jan's number, but it went straight to voicemail. She was a solicitor at one of the big firms in the city. "Hi, Jan, it's Beth, Freya's mum," she started. "Sorry to bother you, but Freya didn't turn up to school today. I just wondered if you or Mia had seen her. Can you call me as soon as you get this, please? Thank you." She hung up and slammed the phone down on the desk. Her voice had wobbled at the end there. On the words *thank you.*

"Come on, Beth, pull yourself together," she whispered. "This isn't helping."

She took a deep breath and picked up her phone, ready to ring Lauren's mum next when the screen lit up and a new call came through. There was no name, just a number, but as she hadn't yet saved Dr Raul's details into her phone, she assumed it to be him again, seeing if Freya was at home.

She ran her tongue over her dry lips, rolled back her shoulders, and then answered the call as confidently as she could.

"Hey there, Beth speaking."

The line was silent for a moment. Then she heard a click and whir and a voice said. "Is this Beth Lomax?"

It wasn't Dr Raul. She wasn't even certain it was a real person. The voice on the line sounded odd. The vocal pitch was deep and robotic. Like on documentaries when they distort a person's voice to keep their identity a secret.

Her stomach flipped over.

"Who is this?" she asked.

The line went silent. Then the whirring and clicking again. Then the sinister voice. "I asked you a question. Is this Beth Lomax?"

Beth swallowed hard. "Yes. This is Beth Lomax," she said, her heart trembling in time with her top lip. "What do you want?"

"What we want will soon be clear," the voice told her. "But first, what you need to know, Beth Lomax, is that we have your daughter. And if you want to see her alive ever again, you need to listen very carefully."

8

Beth had always thought it strange how one coped with moments of heightened stress or emotion. If you'd have asked Beth five years earlier what her reaction would be on discovering her beloved husband, the father of her child, was one day going to tell her he'd been screwing his pretty young PA and that he was leaving her, Beth's response would have been that she'd want to die. That she'd crumble. Go to pieces. Yet the reality when she found out was that an overwhelming calm descended over her. Maybe because the weeks and months leading up to his bombshell were so vile, so full of unanswered questions and second guessing herself, that the actual news came as a relief. It meant she wasn't mental after all and it meant that at least now she could do something with that news. She had some control again. She'd listened to Adam's demands and ultimatums (about who should have what, when he'd see Freya) with a grace and decorum that surprised even her. At the time, at least. After he'd packed his suitcase and she'd finished off a bottle of wine, there was a little less grace in evidence. But still.

Similarly, if you'd told her this morning that she'd be soon speaking to someone with a digitally altered voice who was - by their own admission at least - holding her darling daughter captive, she'd have told you once again that she'd want to die. At the very least, her assumption would have been that she'd experience a rush of blind panic. She'd be terrified, angry, distraught, unsure what to say. Yet, as the caller's words echoed through her head, a stillness and focus descended on her. It could just be that she was scared stiff. Desperate to stay calm less she miss one word of what was being said.

"You have my daughter?" she whispered, leaning over the desk.

"Correct."

"What's her name?" She wasn't sure where that question came from, but she was glad she'd asked. Because she needed to know this was real. As the words left her lips, Beth felt empowered, proud of herself that she was taking control of the situation. A mother bear's instinct. Maybe that's what it was.

The phone went silent. Then the voice crackled on the line. "Freya. Freya Louise Lomax."

Beth gasped for air, her heart exploding as she asked, "What do you want? Who are you? Why are you doing this?"

The person on the line coughed, causing static distortion to blare down the line. Beth took the phone away from her head for a second and checked the time on the screen. It didn't register at all.

"Calm down, Beth," the voice told her as she lifted the phone to her ear. "Like I already told you, we will explain the situation to you in due course. But for now, you need to listen to me very carefully. Are you listening?"

Beth swallowed. "Yes."

"Good. So let me be very clear to you about what's going to happen. If you phone the police, Freya dies. If you tell anyone about this phone call, Freya dies. If you panic, try and find us,

Freya dies. If you do anything but what we ask of you, Freya dies. Do you understand?"

Beth nodded, lips trembling, trying to form words.

"Do you understand, Beth?"

"Yes."

"Good. We have taken Freya for one reason and one reason only. Because we need you to do something for us."

"What? What is it? Money? My husband, my ex-husband, Freya's dad, he's rich. We can—"

"It is not money we want."

"Then what?" It felt like her heart was going to burst.

"Our plans are still being finalised. We shall explain fully when everything is in place. Not before. All you need to know is that your daughter is somewhere you will never find her and she is safe. For now."

"Please don't hurt her," she gasped. "She's all I have."

"Beth, we need you – and Freya needs you – to stay calm. Don't change your routine at all. Go to work. Do your job. Tell no one about this call. Alert no one. If you do, Freya will die. For now, she is being looked after, but if you do anything that we are not happy with, if you deviate in any way from our instructions, that will not remain the case."

"Whatever you want, whatever your demands are, I'll sort it out," Beth told them as adrenaline took over. "But don't you dare hurt my baby."

"We have one demand," the voice said. "That is all. We will convey this to you soon. But for now, go about your life as best you can and await our instruction."

"Wait," Beth cried. "How do I know you have her? How do I know she's safe?"

The voice sighed, or snorted, or did something to elicit more static distortion. Then the line went dead. Beth waited, clutched the phone tightly to her ear. Then a new voice came on the line. One she recognised.

"Mum?"

"Freya. Oh god, Freya. Are you okay? Have they hurt you?"

"No. Not really." Her daughter let out a whimper. "What's going on? I'm scared."

"I know, baby. I know you are. Me too. That's normal. But I'm going to sort this out. And soon. I'm going to get you back. Just hang tight, sweet pea. Try not to worry."

Try not to worry? Jesus. Even as the words fell out of her mouth, she wished she could claw them back. Talk about lame platitudes. Talk about unhelpful bullshit.

"Are they treating you okay?" she asked. "Have you eaten?"

Freya sniffed. "Mm. I guess so. I had a McDonald's before."

"Oh well, that's something, then?" Beth replied, trying to stay upbeat but failing miserably as a sound halfway between a laugh and a wail bubbled up inside her. "I'm going to get you back, Frey," she said, more resolute. "I'm going to bring you home safely, I promise. You just hang tight, yeah? I love you."

"That's enough."

"Freya?"

But she was gone, the voice back. "We are ending the call now," it said. "Do you understand what you have to do, Beth Lomax?"

"Please don't hurt her."

"Do you understand?"

"Yes."

"Good. We will contact you shortly."

The phone went dead and Beth let out a loud wail. Not even a hint of laughter behind it now. She went again, a desperate guttural wail she hoped might remove some of the pent-up emotion currently crushing her lungs. "Oh, Freya," she cried out. "Oh, baby."

She stared at the phone gripped in her claw until the screen faded to black and then for a long time after. Tears were running down her face, but she made no move to wipe them away. They were her penance. She deserved them.

"Shit."

Why hadn't she just told Louise she was coming into the office a little later this morning? Why hadn't she been more bloody forthright? Hell, the contents of that 'important meeting' could have been summed up in a half-page email. Her presence there wasn't that imperative. Why hadn't she stood her ground? Louise wasn't an ogre. She'd have understood. Then she and Freya could have had breakfast together, cleared the air after last night's row. Beth could have driven her to school, said goodbye properly, told Freya she was proud of her, that she loved her. She might have even said it back. And none of this nightmare would be happening. Freya would be safe. She wouldn't be... With those horrible people... She'd be here with Beth. She'd be...

Beth sat upright and sniffed back. No. This wasn't helping. This wasn't getting Freya back. She stood and went downstairs. In the kitchen she filled the kettle for tea, attempting to inject normality into her situation. Because what else could she do? This was a waiting game. As the kettle boiled, she leaned her back on the island and went over the phone call in her mind, the sinister inhuman voice still reverberating in her consciousness.

Beth already knew she was going to follow their instructions to the letter. She had to. She had no power. One demand, they'd said. But if it wasn't money then what the hell was it. Drugs maybe? Access to medical records? Was that why they'd chosen her daughter? Was it planned that way? Or was she just the first girl they found?

Beth sighed. There were too many questions and no answers. All she knew at this moment was Freya needed her and she was the only person who could help. She had no reason to believe these people weren't serious about what they'd do if she told anyone.

...Freya dies.

The remembrance of this, of the way they'd spoken those chilling words, had Beth running to the large Belfast sink and dry heaving into the porcelain bowl. Once done, she turned on the tap and lapped at the stream of water. Her throat was so dry, and the cool liquid offered some nourishment. Cupping her hand under the water, she splashed some on her face, cleaning away the salty tears and mascara tracks. She straightened up and reached for a tea-towel. She could do this, she told herself as she dried her face. For Freya, for her darling daughter. For her only child. Beth would do whatever was needed to do to get her back. Whatever these people's demand was, she'd do it. If they wanted money and she had to rob a bank to get it, so be it. Her daughter's life was on the line, and it was down to her alone to save her.

9

Freya strained at the ties around her wrists. They were made of hard plastic, like the ones that came wrapped around new toys, making it impossible to remove the doll - or whatever it was - from the packaging without her parents' help. She stopped struggling as the sharp edge rubbed painfully at her skin.

What was the point?

Even if she broke free, where was she going to go? After that horrible man had thrown the black sack over her head and bundled her into the back of the car, she'd lost all sense of space and time. An all-encompassing panic response had flooded her system, her mind spinning at a million miles an hour as she tried to make sense of what had happened to her. She'd screamed until a hand gripped around her throat and a gruff voice with a foreign accent told her to, "Shut it or you're dead," kicked and elbowed until her hands were pulled behind her back and the plastic ties applied. They could have been driving for over an hour, she couldn't tell, but from the sounds, she heard whilst being dragged from the car, her guess was they were still in London. Possibly by the river. Even though her entire body had been trembling, and she was gasping for air in short, fitful breaths, Freya had picked up the sound of overhead machinery (cranes, possibly) and a distant horn reminiscent of a Thames River barge.

Once out of the car, one of the men had dragged her across dusty uneven ground and then across the tarmac before a second man grabbed up her legs and they carried her the rest of the way. It was a few minutes before she sensed they'd entered a building, the warmth and close air enveloping her sensibilities. Here her captors stood her up, the same voice as before snarling in her ear, ordering her to "Keep your mouth shut. Don't do anything stupid."

A minute later and they were in an elevator, the men whispering and muttering over her head. Now, she counted three voices. She'd tried to listen to what they were saying, but she was shaking so much, and her imagination was swirling with every probable scenario that she couldn't concentrate. They had then dragged her from the lift and carried her down a long corridor, the bright fluorescent lights above filtering through the thick material covering her face. None of the men spoke as they came to a stop and Freya heard the beep and click of an electronic lock opening.

"Put her down there," one of the men had instructed. "I'll call them. Inform them the mark is now in situ."

That was a few hours ago, and she was still 'in situ'. More specifically she was sitting on a thin air mattress with her hands tied around her back and a bag over her head. Through the thick material, she could just make out a row of windows over on the far side. Her guess was she was in some kind of office or even a classroom, but that was all she knew. As the panic she'd felt on being snatched subsided a little, she began to feel cold and regretted opting for her socks rather than tights this morning. But at least the panic that had tightened her throat and made her think she was dying had indeed lessened. She no longer felt like her heart was about to stop or that her lungs would collapse. Her limbs felt like her own. And whilst her thoughts remained in dark, sinister places, she could now focus on her situation.

She'd been kidnapped. That was certain. But why? Was it money that people were usually after when kids got taken? She tensed, fists tight with hope, trying not to focus on the desperate dark thoughts on the cusp of her awareness. It may have been money these people were after, but a part of her suspected that was wishful thinking. The innocent, childish elements of her personality trying desperately to win the battle in her psyche. Because whilst Freya was only fourteen and inexperienced in many ways, she knew enough about the world to know what some men did to young girls.

She sat upright and rolled her shoulders back. What would the warrior woman do in this position? What would a world class spy do? Despite already being blindfolded, Freya closed her eyes, doing all she could to side-step the bad thoughts and imagine herself into the role of someone stronger, braver, more experienced. The sort of person who might work out a way of escaping these evil men's clutches. The notion made her feel sick and dizzy, but she breathed deeply through the course material and attempted to steady herself. As well as having an overzealous imagination, Freya was also intelligent, one of the cleverest in her class, and good at problem-solving. She might be small and lacking in athletic ability, but she had this to her advantage. And she had to try, didn't she?

A new thought popped into her head. Something she'd seen in a Netflix documentary a while back, another of her true crime ones. Her mum didn't like her watching them, saying they'd give her nightmares (the usual lame parent stuff) but as she was rarely at home to stop her, Freya watched them regardless. Plus, as Freya had told her, they were educational, good for her acting career, providing as they did a chance for her to study people from different places and demographics which she could use in her character work. The documentary that came to mind was about people who had been abducted. She recalled someone saying that if you're snatched and taken to a single location, it means your captors are probably waiting for a ransom. But if they take you to a second location after that, it means you're most likely going to be killed.

"Oh, god." Freya let out a whimper.

What was best? Try to stay present and realistic, in case an opportunity arose to escape - or try to distract herself from the terrifying reality of her situation lest she lost all hope?

Maybe she didn't get to make that decision.

Freya opened her eyes at the sound of shouting outside the room. It was muffled, but she could pick out the odd word. The man sounded angry. As his muffled shouts grew louder and clearer, the door beeped and clicked, and he stepped into the room.

"Yeah, well, I don't care," he bellowed before pausing.

Freya froze as the door clicked shut and whoever this was paced across the room. She heard the floor creak as he walked past the mattress.

"Yes, I know that," he said. He was on the phone. She heard the tinny sound of a response, but nothing fully audible.

The man stopped a few feet away.

"Well, they should have told us, shouldn't they? I might not have taken the fuckin' job if I'd known. Yeah, well, it's done now, isn't it? Speak to you in a bit."

She sensed him walking up alongside her and the sound of a chair scraping against a hard floor. She turned the way of the noise and through the rough material, she made out the fuzzy outline of the man silhouetted against the row of windows.

"What's your name?"

Freya gasped. She wasn't expecting a direct question. "Sorry?"

The man sighed as though easing himself onto the chair. "What's your name?" he said again, but his tone was gentler. Freya paused, unsure what to tell him. Would it help to give her real name? Or not? If they'd taken her because they wanted money, then surely, they'd know who she was. Wouldn't they? How could they ask for a ransom if they didn't know who to ask?

But if they didn't want a ransom, then what did they want?

"Calm yourself down," the man told her, huffing out a joyless laugh. "It's Freya, right? I was only asking. To open up lines of communication, as they say."

"Okay," Freya said, wishing her voice didn't sound so weak and wobbly. "Yes. It's Freya."

The man growled. "Well, we might as well get ourselves comfy, Freya. We're going to be here for a while, by the looks of it." He sounded angry at that fact.

Freya struggled once more with the ties binding her hand. The plastic ripped at the thin skin around her wrists, but she found the pain focused her. Turning slowly, she peered around the room, but except for the windows over to her right, she could make out no more features in the space. It could have been a black cube for all she knew.

"Why are you doing this?" she asked the man.

"Not for me to say," came the sharp reply.

"Please. I just want to go home," she cried. "Please, sir. I've done nothing wrong. I'm just a young girl. I'm no one and I won't tell anyone. I swear it. Not a single person."

"Stop this."

"Please. Just let me go home... My dad has money. He's rich. He'll pay you what you want. Please, I just want to—"

"Hey! I said stop this," the man snapped. She sensed him

getting to his feet, and then his head was next to hers. He spoke quietly, gruff voice crackling against the phlegm in his throat. "Listen, Freya. We can do this the hard way, or the easy way. And I suggest you opt for easy. Which means you sit tight, keep quiet and don't cause me any bother. If your mum does everything asked of her, you might get to go home in a day or two."

An icy chill spiked Freya between the shoulder blades. She sat back as the man stood and his footsteps moved toward the door. "I'll be back later," he said. "Don't you go anywhere. Will ya?"

He let out another chuckle, and the door clicked open. Freya held her breath, waiting for the sound of it closing and the lock clicking before letting out a loud wail. "Please!" she yelled. "Please, someone help me!"

But she knew it was useless. As her torso shuddered with emotion and tears poured down her face, she attempted to make sense of what she'd just been told.

If her mum does everything asked of her, the man had said.

What did that mean?

Yet it wasn't this that had Freya rocking back and forth on the mattress and praying to a god she didn't believe in that this was all a terrible dream.

Might, the man had said.

She *might* get to go home in a few days. Meaning she *might not* just as much.

10

Beth's initial rush of courageous resolve disappeared faster than the large glass of wine she poured herself once certain she wouldn't throw up. The alcohol was no crutch at all. She was still shaking. She poured herself another and took a large gulp. Downing strong Malbec was probably not the cleverest thing she could do right now. But she was unsure what she should do in the circumstances.

They'd told her to stay calm. To go about her usual routine. To wait for instructions. But all that was much easier said than done. She was full up to the eyeballs with brittle pent up energy and there was nowhere for any of it to go. She could have turned her rage and frustration inwards, of course, but that was inevitable and there'd be plenty of time for that later. Right now, all she cared about was staying sane long enough to make sense of what she'd just been told. And really, what sane person wouldn't be drinking after finding out their beautiful, fragile, fourteen-year-old daughter had been abducted?

She tapped her fingernails on the marble top of the kitchen island, rolling from pinkie to pointer, rapping out a staccato beat as she chewed her lip. What the hell was she going to do? She normally had a certain amount of nervous energy to deal with, but this was now amplified to the point she felt like she'd taken something. She slid off her stool and stretched. The house felt too quiet, the air too still. It was like being at a museum. Or a hospital.

Or a morgue.

Shaking the thought away, she paced the length of the kitchen and peered through the large patio doors into the garden beyond. Despite it being an unusually hot day for the time of year, it was barely spring, and the sun had already set over South London. She narrowed her eyes into the gloom, eyeing with suspicion the inky trees looming over the house, the shadowy shrubs and dark corners.

"Go to hell," she spat, before grabbing the curtains with both hands and yanking them closed.

Freya had sounded positive on the phone, Beth reasoned. As positive as any young girl might sound who'd been snatched off the street on her way to school. And she was a plucky girl. Clever too. She'd stay strong. She'd....

Beth huffed out a deep sigh of emotion. Who was she kidding? The poor girl would be terrified. She'd been abducted, kidnapped. Her poor baby.

She strode back over to the island and picked up the glass of wine, swallowing the whole measure down without tasting it. She went to pour herself another before but paused, clenching the bottle in her hand. It was one of Adam's special bottles. A vintage.

"Bastard."

An intense fury rose within her and as she lifted the bottle, a voice in her head told her to chuck it, to smash it against the wall. Her arm quivered, knuckles whitening as she gripped the neck. But then a wave of despair washed over her, and it felt as if all her strength had ebbed away. She placed the bottle down and burst into heavy sobs. Hot salty tears gushed down her face as she wailed into the ceiling. Slamming her fist on the table, she cried out again, louder now, a primal scream coming from deep within her soul. She sounded like a wild animal. But it helped. A little.

She sank back onto the stool and reached for her phone. Instinctively, she opened iMessenger. The thread between her and Freya was still open. She couldn't bring herself to read of any of it.

"I'm so sorry, baby girl," she sniffed. "Please be okay. Please don't worry. Mummy is going to get you back."

She closed the app and opened her address book. And there he was at the top of the screen, Adam Lomax. At the top in both name and status. The bastard. She clicked on his profile, her finger hovering over his number. Should she call? The kidnapper had been quite specific that she was to tell no one. But he was Freya's dad. Not only that, he was the one with the money. If their demands involved sending them a large sum of money, then he'd have to be involved further down the line.

Spurred on by the wine in her system, she hit 'call' before she changed her mind. As the dial tone began, she put the phone on speaker, hoping the noise would break up the morbid calm that had descended over the house. It also meant she maintained a further distance between her and Adam when he answered. The phone rang out three times and then his deep voice echoed into the room.

"Hey there, this is Adam Lomax. I'm real sorry I can't take your call right now. But please leave a message and I'll..."

Beth hung up with a dramatic tut. "I'm *real* sorry," she sneered, doing his voice. "It's *really* sorry. You're not American, you pretentious prick."

She spun the phone away from her before getting to her feet and picking it up again. She checked the battery, checked the ring volume was on and turned up high and stuffed it into her trouser pocket.

What did she do now? Stay here until they ring back? When would that be? Tonight? Tomorrow? Next week? Why didn't they just tell her what they wanted when they'd called? It felt like they were toying with her, mocking her. She felt trapped and adrift all at once. It was horrible. But this whole situation was horrible. And it would only be worse for her poor little Freya.

Beth shuddered. She was going around in circles and would drive herself mad if she wasn't careful. Then she'd no use to Freya at all. She had to get out. She had to do something. Striding through into the hallway, she grabbed her coat off the end of the bannister where she'd flung it earlier. Her keys were still in the pocket and after slipping the coat on she moved over to the front door and unlocked it.

A cool breeze hit her in the face as she eased open the door, chilling the tracks of tears still wet on her face.

Bloody hell.

She stepped back inside and glanced at her reflection in the large Regency-style mirror on the wall. The woman looking back at her was an absolute wreck but, physically speaking, the perfect embodiment of how Beth felt inside. Her dark hair was still relatively neat – having been freshly washed and straightened this morning - but that was where any semblance of neatness or normality stopped. Her eyes were tired and bloodshot, ringed with dusky circles of eyeshadow. Tracks of black mascara ran down her cheeks, into her mouth and down under her chin.

"Jesus, Beth."

She leaned forward into the mirror, wondering how the hell this woman, bedraggled as she was, could still operate. Didn't she realise her baby girl was being held captive? How was she not crumpled in a foetal position on the floor? How could she even think straight? But then again, maybe she wasn't thinking straight. Maybe she'd flipped completely and wasn't even aware of that fact. She was about to leave the house looking like a goth clown after all. And where the hell did she think she was going to go?

Her phone buzzed in her pocket, and she pulled it out to see it was a text from Jazmine at work. It was brief and to the point, so she could read it on the notification screen without opening her phone.

Hey B. Might be in a bit late in tomorrow. Got to take my cat to the vet. Hope that's OK? xx

Beth liked Jaz, she was a nice person and had been through a lot herself over the last few years. But she stared at the text now without reaction or emotion. She felt empty, numb. With the phone in her hand, the thought came to her to call the police. It was what any sensible person should do when their daughter went missing. Yet those words still reverberated around in her soul.

"...Freya dies..."

But how would they know if she called the police? Surely they had special units for this sort of thing. If she told them what the voice on the phone had said, couldn't they send some covert officers to help her? She shoved the phone back into her pocket.

No.

Couldn't risk it.

Not yet.

She glared at her reflection and shook her head. She had to stay resolute. Had to try to, at least. Freya wasn't the only one in the family with a vivid imagination. Ever since she'd taken the call, Beth's mind had been spinning with increasingly dangerous thinking.

If you do anything but what we ask of you, Freya dies.
Freya dies.
Freya.
Dies.

She couldn't get the voice out of her head, and now images plagued her mind. Freya, alone and terrified. Calling for her mum. She'd read somewhere that when people feared they were about to die, they often called out for their mothers. Even as adults, they did it. Even when their mothers were long dead themselves. But it was human nature, instinct, a desperate desire to return to safety. Beth puffed out her cheeks.

Stop it. Stop it now.

She had to hold on to the facts. One of those being it was unlikely the kidnappers would have called at all if they planned to do something unthinkable to Freya. They had demands, they'd said. Meaning Freya was a leverage tool. Meaning they needed her alive.

Beth flung her coat back over the bannister and moved back into the kitchen, glancing around for inspiration, for something to occupy her attention and get her out of her head. She filled the kettle and switched it on. While it boiled, she opened the door of the fridge and stared into its depths, not really seeing anything but her daughter's face.

Not for the first time, Beth was overcome with a powerful sadness caused by the realisation she had no close friends anymore. How she longed for a cool, sassy girlfriend. Someone she could talk to without prejudice, who'd listen to her problems, make all the right sounds, but never push her to do anything she didn't want. The kidnapper had said to tell no one. But Beth may have risked a call to a close girlfriend - her rock - who would be around in an instant to hold her while she sobbed and tell her it would all be okay, that she was doing the right thing by following the kidnappers' instructions.

But she had no one like that. Not anymore. Her parents were both dead and over the years, she'd lost touch with every one of her close friends. At university, there'd been three of them. Beth, Andrea and Gillian. They were so close, the three of them. When they were all together, Beth had felt unstoppable. But then she'd met Adam and over the next few years, she grew further and further apart from her two besties. It wasn't that Adam had made her stop seeing them or anything toxic like that (regardless of what she now thought of him; he wasn't always a shit) but more so it was Beth herself who'd drifted away. In Adam, she thought she'd found her soulmate and wanted to spend every available moment with him. She'd long assumed Gillian, especially, was jealous of her and Adam's relationship. And why not? They were a golden couple. So in love and best friends too. It was the two of them against the world. Right up until it wasn't.

Beth ran her fingers through her hair, feeling more alone at that moment than she'd ever felt in her life. She considered calling Adam once more, but then a thought hit her. What if they'd tapped her phone? What if they knew she'd rung him? Would that anger them? Push them to hurt Freya? She wandered through into the lounge but didn't turn on the lights. Instead, she slid along the nearside wall and over to the large bay window. Concealing herself behind the gathered material of the curtain, she peered out into the night. Aspley Road was quiet this evening, with not a soul in sight. Not even Mr Andrews from twenty-nine, who walked his dog around this time. Down towards the end of the street, she noticed a car parked up with its headlights on. It was hard to tell the model, but the outline didn't look familiar.

Was that them watching her?

She backed away and ran upstairs to her bedroom, where she found her laptop lying on the bed. Sitting, she lifted it onto her lap, the screen lighting up the room as she eased open the lid. Then a thought hit her and she twisted around, her attention darting to the window in case whoever was watching saw she was on her computer. But that was okay, wasn't it? It meant nothing.

"Come on," she mumbled to herself. "Pull yourself together."

She was letting her fears and her imagination get the better of her, and it was not helping. And yes, she was probably more justified than she'd ever been in her life to be paranoid, but she had to keep a clear head if she was to get Freya back safely.

Still, this didn't stop her from opening up a new browser window and typing, *How to tell if your phone is bugged,* into the search field. She hit enter and scanned the results, clicking on the top one and opening a site called *On Guard.* Her eyes darted over the words, speed reading the post but seeing little that gave her cause to believe her phone was bugged – or 'tapped', as the site called it. Weird noises on the line? Not that she'd heard. Increased battery usage? Not really. New apps appearing or weird text messages? No, and no.

The knowledge of this didn't make her feel any less nervous or frantic, however. She clicked back to the search window and typed in, *What to do if your child has been kidnapped.* She felt ridiculous doing so, but she was desperate. As she scanned the results, she saw that once more they were of little help. Most of the linked pages were giving advice about family law, what to do if your spouse abducts your child, that sort of thing. Other articles talked about sex trafficking and what to do if you suspected a child is being trafficked. Nothing about her situation. Because why would there be? There was only one thing to do if your child went missing. Call the bloody police. Trust the professionals to deal with it. She clicked open a new window and was about to search for ways to contact the police with no one knowing when she heard a noise from downstairs.

She froze, all her focus shifting to her hearing. There it was again. A shuffling sound and then footsteps. Her mind shot to the blue car. Shit. It was them. They'd been watching her and now they were in the house. They'd come for her.

11

With her heart beating heavy in her chest and her entire body tense with fear, Beth placed the laptop down on the bed. Moving slowly and methodically, she slipped off the bed, placing her weight onto her feet before easing herself upright. As the floor creaked under her, she froze, her face fixed in a tight grimace as she listened for movement downstairs.

She may have been overwhelmed with anxious paranoia, but someone was down there. She could just sense another presence in the house. Moving to the bedroom door, she grabbed a metal vase from off the chest of drawers. It was long and slender with a heavy base and turning it around in her hand, it felt like a decent enough weapon. And it was all she had to hand. As she stepped onto the landing, she heard another noise. It sounded like the kidnappers were in the kitchen. And was that someone speaking? She raised her head. Yes. A voice. Deep and low. A man's voice. It was unclear what they were saying, but it dispelled all doubt. They were here. They were inside her house.

A torrent of adrenaline flooded Beth's system, but she held

her nerve as she padded along the landing, her makeshift club raised at her shoulder, ready to strike if needed. She wondered if she should call out, let them know she was up here. If they were here to get her, did that mean they were going to take her to where Freya was being held? Would that be a good thing? She'd be with her scared little girl. But who would come to rescue them, or carry out the kidnappers' demands? A million fractious thoughts invaded her mind, none of them helpful. She reached the top of the stairs and paused, not daring to move less she make a sound. Whoever was down there was still in the kitchen.

"Hey," she called out. But her voice got stuck in her throat and all that came out was a soft croak. Keeping the vase raised, she made her way downstairs, leaning into the bannister and letting it take her weight so the stairs wouldn't make so much noise. At the bottom of the steps, she stopped again, inching around the side of the staircase to see into the kitchen. Her stomach turned over.

There he was. Standing in front of the island with his back to her. He didn't cut a hugely commanding presence, being not much taller than Beth's five-seven frame. But he was broad and the large, hooded parka he was wearing made him appear doubly intimidating. That and the fact he'd broken into her home. The bastard.

Beth gripped the vase with two hands, holding it like a baseball bat as she tiptoed along the hallway towards him.

Don't turn around. Please don't turn around.

She hadn't taken a proper breath since she'd first heard the intruder, and a wave of dizziness washed over her. She screwed up her eyes and then opened them wide, fighting the fatigue and stress pulling at her resolve. Three more steps and she'd reach him. Her hands tightened around the vase. She was going to strike him down. Knock him out. Kill him if she had to. If this man had her daughter, then he deserved everything he got. He was scum. He was...

"Beth! Whoa!" He spun around, a look of shock on his face as he noticed her.

"Dr Raul!" Beth gasped. "What the fuck?"

His eyes moved to the vase, and he held up his hand. "I'm so sorry," he said, spitting out the words. "Your door was open. Like, actually hanging open. I called out for you, but there was no answer. I was worried, so I stepped inside. I'm sorry. I shouldn't have."

Beth lowered the vase. Her hands were shaking. The adrenaline pumping around her body, unsure where to go.

"I— I almost hit you," she stammered.

"I know and what an absolute idiot I am." He moved toward her, reaching for the vase and taking it from her as he guided her through into the kitchen. "I should have rung you, rather than come inside. But I left my phone in the car and when the door was open I just..."

"No, it's fine," Beth muttered.

Dr Raul led her over to the dining room table and pulled out a chair. "Here, sit down. You look to be in shock. Let me get you a drink. Tea?"

They both eyed the bottle of Malbec at the same time. Her with desire, him with a look of concern. Beth gave a resigned nod. "Yes, tea would be good."

He patted her on the shoulder before moving away. She heard the click of the kettle and a cupboard being opened. Tea. Jesus. The last thing she bloody well wanted was tea. Give her a glass of wine, a neat vodka. Anything to calm the confusion and pain filling her soul. She placed both hands on the table, palms down, and took a deep breath. Her skin was like paper and her chest felt empty like she'd been awake for days.

"What are you doing here?" she asked, twisting around to

look at him.

"I was on my way home, and I realised I passed by your house, so I thought I'd pop in and see how you were. I take it you located your wayward teen?"

Beth bristled. "Oh...yes."

"Great. I knew you would. But you did the right thing coming home." He turned from the cupboard, a mug in each hand and a grimace in on his face. "And I should have rung first. You're probably knackered. The last thing you want is me intruding. Or scaring you half to death."

But he was wrong. Having someone here was exactly what she wanted. She opened her mouth - ready to tell him as such, that she was glad he'd come around - but then she closed it just as quick, worried the outpouring of any emotion would open the floodgates. If that happened, she wasn't sure if she'd ever shut them off. Instead, she forced a smile. The best she could do in the circumstances. "I should apologise too," she said. "For almost staving your head in."

"God. No. It's understandable. You can't be too careful. I don't know what the hell I was thinking." He grimaced again and made a goofy face. "Listen. I should go."

"No. Please..."

"Well, can we start again?"

Beth laughed. The involuntary action brought with it a wave of relief, sharply followed by a barrage of guilt and then shame. "Fine by me," she replied, turning around and drawing in a deep breath.

The room fell silent as Dr Raul finished making the tea. Beth stretched her arms out over the table and yawned. Staring down at her from the wall was Freya's school photo from when she was ten. Beth had put her hair in plaits especially for the photo and even though she'd suggested to Freya that she smile with her mouth closed, she was grinning wide, exposing the gap in her front teeth where her adult ones were yet to appear. Poor kid. She looked so innocent. So free of worry. Little did she know that two years later, her entire world was going to cave in on itself in the maelstrom of her parent's divorce.

"Here we are." Beth looked away and wiped at her face as Dr Raul appeared and placed a mug of steaming tea in front of her. "I put some sugar in. Hope you don't mind. Hot sweet tea. Good for a fright. So they say."

Beth snaked her fingers around the mug. "Thank you," she said. "You're a good man, Dr Raul. I appreciate you caring about us."

"Oh please, call me Sammy. All my friends do."

Beth nodded and tilted her head to one side. She so wanted to tell him about Freya, about the phone call, about how absolutely desperate she felt, but she couldn't. She wouldn't.

Await further instructions, the caller said. But when will that be? Tonight? Tomorrow? Ever? Never? How the hell was she supposed to get any sleep tonight, or the following night, or any night until her darling baby girl was home safely?

Beth sipped her tea and Dr Raul – Sammy – did too, both of them exchanging awkward smiles over the rims of their mugs. It was one of those moments when you realise you don't actually know someone as well as you thought you did.

"Where was she then?"

"Pardon?"

"Your daughter. Freya, isn't it?"

She gulped back a mouthful of tea. It burned her throat, but she liked that. More penance. For what she was about to say. "Like we thought. She was at home all along." She stared into the beige liquid. "Apparently she had a tummy ache after I left, so kept herself off school." She tensed the muscles across her shoulders, the voice in her head crying out for forgiveness. "Then she switched her phone off so she could get some rest.

Don't worry, I've told her never to do that again. She's in her bedroom now, doing her homework."

She lifted her head and smiled her widest smile. Smiling because if she didn't, she was likely to burst into tears.

"Kids, hey?" Sammy said.

"Do you have children?" she asked, glad to change the subject.

He shook his head. "No. I want them. But I don't know if I'll get the chance now. You see, my ex-wife *did* want kids, but then decided she *didn't*. Only by that time, we were already married. Not a great position to be in. It wasn't the only reason we split up, but it was one of them."

"I'm sorry," Beth said. "I didn't know."

"Why would you?" He waved his hand over the table. "It's fine. It is what is it."

"Well, you never know. How old are you, thirty-four? Thirty-five? Plenty of time to find the right person and settle down."

He scoffed. "I'm thirty-eight next birthday. But thank you." He sat back. "I don't know. I just see people with their kids, like you and Freya. She's your friend too, right, as well as your daughter? I'd love that."

That was it.

Beth lifted her hand to her face and turned away, but there was no hiding it. The tears had arrived. Deep body-shaking sobs rained out of her as though she'd been welling them up for years. Maybe she had. She sniffed, tried to laugh it off, but it only came out as a loud snort of emotion that didn't even sound human.

"Oh, Beth, I'm sorry." Sammy shunted his chair around and placed his hand over hers. "I'm such an idiot."

"No," she wailed. "It's me. I'm such a terrible mother. I was horrible to her last night. She's so young and precious, and I take her for granted. All the time. She's had it just as hard as me since Adam left and I've been so selfish. I just want her to... I just want to... Oh, fucking hell!"

She yanked her hand away from Sammy's and gritted her teeth. Tears and snot were pouring down her face.

"I'm the worst mother in the world."

She wiped her hand across her face. She could feel Sammy's gaze burning into her cheek, could sense the nervous energy coming off of him. Poor man, he didn't need this.

"Is something wrong, Beth?" he said. "Has something happened?"

Yes! She wanted to yell. Yes, Dr Raul – Sammy - something has happened. Something terrible. In fact, the worst thing that could possibly have happened has happened. The second worst thing at least, and there was still time for the worst thing.

She stood. "I'm sorry. I need to get an early night. It's been a stressful day."

He was on his feet immediately. "Of course. My bad. I'll leave you to it."

They walked to the front door together. Beth tensed as Sammy opened it and stood framed in the doorway. If they were out there watching her, they'd see him. They'd know she'd met with someone. Would that be enough to anger them? For them to hurt Freya?

"I'll see you tomorrow," she said, grabbing the door's edge and closing it.

"Yes. Sure." He stepped out onto the doorstep as she forced him out. "And I am sorry, Beth. Me and my stupid knight-on-a-white-horse complex. You don't need me interfering. You're great. Umm... shit. Okay, I'm going."

She shut the door behind him and was quick to lock and bolt it. Then she leaned her back against the wall and sank to the floor as more sobs erupted from deep inside of her.

12

The room was cold and the blanket they'd given her was thin and provided little warmth. Freya huddled her legs up to her chest and wrapped her arms around her knees. They'd removed the restraints from her wrists and ankles, which was something. But the chilly air nipped at the cuts and welts where the hard plastic had rubbed at her skin. She'd felt exhausted for most of the day, but now alone with nothing to do but sleep, she was suddenly wide awake.

She sat up and felt for the salt crackers and glass of milk that were on the floor next to the mattress she was lying on. Her fingers found the plate, found the crackers. They'd removed the bag from over her head so she could now eat and drink, but a thick blindfold that dug into her eyes and pulled at the hair over her ears had replaced it. It was for her own protection, the man with the gruff East London accent had told her. The little she knew of them, who they were and what they looked like, the better.

What she didn't tell him was she'd assumed from the start he was the same man who'd snatched her this morning. The one with the kind face and the newspaper under his arm. She might have been mistaken, it was a possibility, but that's who she pictured when he spoke. He was tall, about the same size as her dad, with short grey hair and a little stubble. Not the most memorable of faces, but she'd recognise him if it called for it. Whether or not that was a good thing, she wasn't yet sure.

There'd been three men guarding her so far, doing it in shifts. But Newspaper Man was her favourite of the three if that could possibly be a thing. For an English assignment last year, Freya had to write about Stockholm Syndrome. But she didn't think this was that. Newspaper Man was just the 'best of a bad bunch', as her mum sometimes said. The other guards had strong foreign accents and a brusque way of speaking that made them sound perpetually angry. They also didn't speak to her much. Only to bark "Toilet?" at her twice a day.

She'd visited the bathroom twice since she'd been here. Both times they'd led her down a winding corridor that seemed to go on forever before being shoved into a room no bigger than a cupboard and the door slammed shut behind her. They'd told her under no circumstances to take her blindfold off, and she'd obeyed. But if she tilted her head back, she could see a sliver of the room under the bottom of the blindfold. A small hand basin stuck out of the wall to the right of the toilet cistern and on the opposite wall she could make out the edge of a small window. It was too small for anyone to climb out of and when she reached up to feel at the latch, it was sealed shut anyway.

Back in the main space, she heard the beep-click of the door and turned her head toward the sound.

"You still awake?" It was Newspaper Man. He pulled the door shut and walked to the centre of the room where Freya's mattress was lying.

She squeezed her legs tighter to her body as he got closer. "I'm too cold to sleep."

"Sorry about that." A chair scraped against the floor and

creaked as he sat down. "I'll see if I can get you a thicker blanket or something."

Freya didn't know what to say to that. Being polite had always been drummed into her, especially by her dad, so her instinct was to thank him. But it didn't seem right to. Because she wasn't thankful. She was scared and angry and confused and a million other emotions, but she wasn't thankful. She didn't have Stockholm Syndrome.

"What's going to happen to me?" she asked.

The man huffed out a sigh but didn't answer. She imagined him leaning back on the chair, arms folded and with his legs out in front of him.

"I don't understand," she tried. "What do you want with me?"

"It's not what I want."

Freya shifted on the mattress. "What do you mean?"

"Forget it." He sniffed back.

"Please. I'm cold, I'm scared. I'm only fourteen. I want to go home. I want my mum" The blindfold dug into her eyes; her tears instantly absorbed by the coarse material. "Why are you doing this to me?"

"I'm not doing anything, all right?" the man said. "I'm not paid to answer questions like that. I'm a hired hand, that's all. And I was put on this job by a fixer. You know what a fixer is?"

"Not really."

"It's a middleman, someone who hires people like me to people who need us. And that's so we never know who we're working for. So, I don't know why you're here or what's going to happen to you."

She sensed him lean toward her and instinctively she mirrored him, almost tumbling off the mattress and putting her hand out to steady herself.

The man lowered his voice. "All I know is your mum is in

play as well, somehow, and if she does as she's told, I'm to release you." He sat back and the chair creaked some more. "And I'll tell you this much, kid. There's big money on the table paying for my time and silence, so whoever is doing this, they aren't amateurs, and they aren't messing around."

Freya sat back, nodding as if she understood, but she didn't, not really. Her arms tingled with goosebumps, and it wasn't just from the chilly air. She lay on the mattress and put her back to the man.

"That's right," he muttered. "You get some sleep."

She didn't reply, but she knew sleep was a long way off. The way he'd spoken just now, all secretive and about her mum, it felt like he was giving her some sort of message. But she had no idea what it meant.

It seemed like forever ago when she'd been dragged into that other room and the phone shoved under her chin to speak to her mum. But it was only this afternoon. She'd give anything to hear her voice now.

Freya closed her eyes, imagining her mum in one of those police command centres. The sort she'd seen in the type of TV dramas she hoped to have a role in one day. She imagined the photos of herself up on a notice board, along with grainy CCTV stills of her being kidnapped, pictures of the men who'd taken her. Some of them were actual photos, others were featureless heads with question marks drawn on them. Yes. That's what would be happening right now. Her mum would be with the police, telling them everything she knew. There were probably teams of special officers already combing the streets for her, whilst those in the tech team traced the phone call.

It was going to be okay. The police were coming for her. Because that's how it worked, she told herself as her breathing deepened and she sensed sleep on the horizon. Give it a day and she'd be home safe. Back in her own bed. This was easily the worst thing that had ever happened to Freya, but she still had hope and she was damned sure going to cling onto that with everything she had. She was freezing cold, terrified, lying on a worn-out air bed in a dark room with only stale crackers to eat and a scary man watching over her.

Without hope, what else was there?

13

Beth sat upright in bed, knowing straight away something was wrong, but not remembering exactly what. A heavy sense of dread hung over her, so dense she could almost feel it weighing down on her.

"Freya," she gasped.

The remembrance knocked everything out of her. She narrowed her eyes at the alarm clock on the bedside table. It was a few minutes after six. She'd watched the hour turn from twelve to one, to two, but must have fallen asleep at some point. The wine had helped. Eventually. But now her head was fuzzy and her mouth and throat were dry, and that wasn't what she needed. This was going to be one of the toughest days she'd ever endured. She already knew that. But the kidnappers had been very clear with their instructions. She was not to change her routine and to carry on as normal. That meant she was going to work. She dragged herself out of bed and into the shower.

The journey to the Royal Farringdon Hospital was a surreal experience. Beth's lack of sleep, coupled with her paranoid, anxious state of mind, had her questioning every person she saw. On the train, she stared too long at people. She felt jittery; she didn't know what to do with her hands or face. It wasn't dissimilar to when she had a few too many wines after work with Louise or Carla and then got the train home. In those times, she found herself wondering whether her fellow passengers could tell she was a bit tipsy and how they could act so serious and po-faced when her own reality was deliciously skewed and rather giggly. This morning, however, her bewilderment arose in the form of a different question. How the hell did all these people act so normal when the ground had crumbled to dust and the sky had turned black? How did the man sitting opposite her, reading from his Kindle, not see what she was going through? How did he not pick up on the pain she carried? Everyone was so damn calm and polite, so unburdened by their existence. Didn't they know it was all pointless? It was all a sham.

Beth's phone was in her hand, ringer on full volume, ready for the next call. The one that would tell her what she must do next. She'd almost had a heart attack this morning, whilst gnawing at a burnt bagel, when the thing had rung. She was over to it in a moment, yanking the charging lead from the wall and answering it with shaking hands and voice.

But it was only Mia's mum, checking on Freya, asking if she wanted a lift to school.

"I know how busy you are," she'd told Beth in what she took to be a somewhat condescending tone. "We're happy to pick her up if it helps."

Beth had bitten her tongue. Told her it was fine. That Freya wasn't feeling well (a bad tummy) and was staying off school. She wasn't sure whether Jan bought it entirely, but she didn't care. Because something else had just dawned on her. She had to ring Freya's school. That call had been brief, but no less difficult. Once she'd been put through to the correct department, she ditched the bad tummy line and opted for a chest infection, hoping that meant they'd be fewer questions when she told them she was keeping Freya at home for a few more days. The woman on the phone was surly and unresponsive but didn't seem suspicious. So that was that. Job done. But now, as the train trundled across the river towards Farringdon, a fresh wave of anxiety overcame her.

She'd lied to the school. She was now a willing participant in whatever this situation was. Did that mean she was now implicated in her own daughter's kidnapping? When this was all over, would she be arrested, charged? Maybe deep down, that was what she wanted. What she deserved. She leaned her head on the window, the cold glass felt good against her skin.

The notion arose once more (although, really, it had never left her) that she should call the police. It wasn't too late. Whenever Beth watched a film or TV show where the character was going through a similar dark predicament, it always annoyed her when they never rang the police, and always did what the bad guys told them to, even against their better judgement. It always seemed so out of character, especially for a parent of a missing child. But when it was your own daughter's life on the line, it was very different. That distorted baleful voice had spelt it out to her repeatedly. Tell no one. If she did, Freya died. She had no reason not to believe they wouldn't carry out their threats.

After getting off the train, she walked the short walk to the hospital. The cool morning air revived her fuzzy head, and the brisk stroll got the blood pumping and her heart beating. Once through the security gates and in the elevator, the familiarity of her surroundings and the remembrance of the tasks still on her 'To Do' list were also welcome. By the time she'd got herself a strong coffee and was sitting at her desk, she hoped she might survive the morning without bursting into tears.

She switched on her PC and, as the machine whirred into life, she placed her phone next to the keyboard and drank back a large mouthful of coffee. It was bitter and hot but tasted good. Like normality. Beth's computer always took ages to settle down, so while she waited, she picked up her phone. She had a sudden impulse to read back over old messages between Freya and herself. The nice messages. The loving ones. The ones where they were sharing a joke or arranging to do something fun together. It was masochistic perhaps, but it was also her only link to her gorgeous little girl. So, when she found herself opening her recent call list and selecting Adam's number, she was rather perturbed. But she couldn't stop herself as she pressed call and held the phone to her ear.

"Hey there, this is Adam Lomax. I'm real sorry…"

"Prick," she snarled, as his recorded voice rumbled in her ears. This time she waited for the beep and said, "Adam, it's Beth. Listen, I need to talk to you about Freya. It's important. I know you're incredibly busy, but if you can ring me back when you get this, that would be helpful."

She hung up and slammed the phone down on the desk.

"Shit."

If you tell anyone about us, Freya dies.

What the hell was she doing? Adam was hot-headed. If he found about the kidnappers, he'd make her ring the police. But is that what she wanted? Was this her subconscious taking over?

She didn't have a chance to answer those questions because at that moment, Carla and Jaz entered the room in a flurry of chatter.

"Morning, boss," Carla bellowed with a cheery smile. "You feeling any better?"

"What? Oh, yes, thanks," she said, guessing Sammy had told them she wasn't well when he collected her bag yesterday.

"Excellent stuff." Carla sat down at the desk next to Beth's and placed her daily Starbucks (a white chocolate mocha-something or other) beside her Statue of Liberty snow globe. "You do look a bit pale," she added, slipping her coat off and over the back of the chair.

"Didn't get much sleep."

"Yeah. You can tell."

Beth shrugged. *Great. Thanks, Carls. I get it. I look like shit. On top of everything else.*

She peered around her computer screen as Jazmine sat down opposite. "I thought you were in late?"

Jaz grinned. "I managed to get an appointment first thing. Poor Sandy Bob. He's got some kind of stomach upset."

"Oh dear, well hope he gets well soon."

"Me too. Costing me a fortune in cat litter."

Beth was about to respond but Jaz already had her phone in front of her face and was sucking her cheeks in, using the front-facing camera as a mirror. Beth knew from experience it was pointless talking to her when she was in preening mode.

Searching for other distractions, she turned her attention to her computer, opening Outlook and being met with fifty-six unread emails. That's what happens when you miss a day's work around here. She scanned down the list, deleting any she knew to be spam. Halfway down was an email from Freya's school asking her to call them. She startled, her mind racing with possibilities. Did they know something she didn't? But then she saw the time stamp of yesterday evening. She'd already spoken to them this morning. She deleted this too and reached for her coffee. The other emails could wait.

She sipped at her coffee, catching Carla's eye as her eyes

scanned the office. She frowned at Beth, mouthing. "You sure you're okay?"

Beth shot her a smile in response. It seemed to placate her, but it was clear she was giving off negative vibes. That wasn't good. The last thing she needed was people asking questions. She thought of herself as a relatively resilient and headstrong person (she'd had to be these last two years) but with every hour that ticked by with Freya still missing she was closer to breaking.

Right now, she felt hollow and empty. It was as if the part of her that created feelings had withered away. It must be a self-defence mechanism. Her psychology protecting itself so she could function. But she also knew from experience it could only hold off the inevitable for so long. Then what? She breaks down, tells someone about the call, about Freya.

No. Couldn't happen. She was on her own in this nightmare, and that's how it had to stay. She checked her phone for the hundredth time that morning, checked the ringer was on, checked the volume was all the way up. The clock on the screen told her it was only 8.20 a.m.

"Ah, Beth, there you are."

She looked up to see Louise framed in the doorway. As Beth acknowledged her, she moved into the room and over to her desk.

"I've been looking for you."

"Oh? I've been here since half seven."

"No. I mean I came by yesterday afternoon. Needed to speak to you about something." She sat on the edge of the desk looming over her.

"I had to go home," Beth said, not looking up. "I felt really sick. Sorry, Lou, I should have told you, but I had to get out of here quick, get some air. It came on from nowhere."

As Beth raised her head, Louise kept her smile in place, but the skin had tightened around her eyes. "And you're feeling better now?"

"Much better. Thank you. Must have been a bug or something I ate. Nasty business." She pulled a face, hoping the subtext on display would close down any further questions.

Louise nodded, as though she was thinking about something important. Beth shifted in her seat.

"You wanted to see me?"

"Yes. Something important I want to discuss with you." She looked up, craning her neck to take in Carla and Jazmine. Although they were both examining their screens with real intent, Beth could tell they were listening in. Louise turned back and smiled. "But you know what? It can wait. You've no doubt got a heap of emails to get through this morning. We'll talk later. It's fine."

Beth frowned. "You sure?"

"Yes. I'll come and find you." She stood and rested her hand on Beth's shoulder. "Glad you're feeling better. I'll see you later."

Beth watched her boss as she sashayed out of the room and then looked at Carla and Jaz, who were both staring at her with puzzled expressions.

"I thought you had a migraine," Carla said.

Shit!

Beth shrugged. "It started with a migraine, then turned into sickness. Weird."

Carla didn't look convinced, but thankfully, her attention shifted quickly. She nodded at the door as Louise exited. "I'm telling you. She's after you, that one."

Beth shooed her away. Despite living in one of the most advanced and multi-cultural cities in the world, Carla still found the whole idea of same-sex relationships worth commenting on. She wasn't a bad person, just a product of her age and upbringing.

"Stop that," Beth told her. "You're a bloody HR officer for a start."

"Just saying," Carla said, holding her hands up. "I say go for it, kid. Take one for the team. You might even get another promotion out of it."

Beth shook her head. "You do know she's married?"

"To a man?"

"Yes!"

Louise's energy was rather masculine at times, but that was a good thing in Beth's eyes. It was why she could hold her own amongst all the uptight old men who comprised the board of trustees.

"What's her husband like?" Carla asked.

"I've never met him," Beth replied. "But he's quite a dish, from all accounts. And rich."

"Is he? What does he do?"

Beth wrinkled her nose. She did know, but she'd forgotten. "Something finance-y," was all she could come up with. "Investment banker, perhaps. Something along those lines."

"Well, good for her," Carla said. "Maybe she's a tiger in bed."

"Hey, I mean it," Beth said, wagging her finger. But they were all laughing now. Even Jazmine, who rarely got involved in joking around. After the anguish and torment of the last twenty-four hours, it was good to laugh. But any release provided by the laughter was swiftly countered by a sharp twinge of regret, or maybe shame. Regardless, Beth brushed these feelings away. Because this wasn't her putting her head in the sand or playing down Freya's plight. It was her staying sane, so she could do what she needed to do to get her back.

She was still chuckling to herself when her phone vibrated

on the desk next to her hand, followed by the melodic chime of her ring tone. The laughter froze in her throat as she saw the name on the screen.

Unknown Caller.

There was no number listed. Same as before. It was them. It had to be. She grabbed up the phone and headed for the door.

"You going to find your girlfriend?" Carla called after her. But Beth didn't turn around. She left the office and headed for the stairwell. If this was Freya's kidnappers calling, then it was time to get serious. The fun and games were over.

14

Beth yanked open the door at the end of the corridor and moved into the stark concrete stairwell. These doors, positioned in the same spot on every floor, were emergency exits and only supposed to be used in case of a fire, but staff often sneaked out onto the landing areas to make private calls or to puff on a vape. As the door sucked shut behind her, she swiped to answer the call, praying they hadn't rung off.

"Hello. Hello, this is Beth Lomax."

"Are you alone?" It was the same voice as before. Processed and distorted.

Beth glanced back the way she'd come, through the long rectangular porthole in the door. There was no one in the corridor beyond. No voices echoing up or down from the other levels.

"Yes. I am," she replied, keeping her voice low all the same.

"And you are at work?"

"Yes. You said to maintain my usual routine."

"Good. And have you told anyone about us, or about Freya going missing?"

Beth shook her head emphatically but pointlessly. "No! Of course not. You said—"

"Good. Well done."

The line went silent.

"Hello?" Beth rasped. "Are you there? What's going on? Is Freya okay? Can I speak to her?"

There was no response. Beth lowered the phone to view the screen, but she was still connected. The time showing the length of the call ticked away. She lifted the phone back to her ear as the voice came on the line.

"You will get your daughter back in due course. Once we get what we want."

"Fine," she said. "Whatever it is, I can get it. I can sort it. Just tell me your demands."

The line broke up into static, as though the person on the other end was laughing into the receiver. "We only have one demand, Ms Lomax," they said.

"One demand. Fine. Tell me."

The line went silent once more. Beth chewed on her lip. They were probably toying with her. Testing her tenacity. She had to hold her nerve.

"Are you listening carefully, Ms Lomax?" The voice sounded different now. It was still distorted and robotic, but the tone was higher. Possibly a different person. "In two days, Sir Gerald Hopkins, the British Prime Minister, is expected to visit the Royal Farringdon Hospital, your place of work. His people are currently making arrangements with your bosses."

Beth swallowed. "Okay." Maybe this was what Damien had been alluding to. *Something exciting.* Yeah right.

"We have it on good authority he will meet with you and your team," the voice continued. "You will have close access to him."

It wasn't a question, but Beth answered regardless. "Yes. I suppose so." Now she really felt sick.

"You are a good-looking woman, Ms Lomax. And it is no secret Mr Hopkins likes female attention. It is a weakness of his. When he visits your department, you will talk with him, make him feel relaxed. You will then orchestrate it so you are alone. Just you and him. Then you will kill him."

The words hit Beth like a tonne of bricks. Even though her mind had already been racing towards this outcome, hearing the actual words knocked her into a tailspin. She held her free hand over her forehead as a strangled laugh bubbled up from inside of her.

"Kill him?" she said. "The Prime Minister. Are you serious?"

"Of course we're serious, Beth," the voice snapped.

"But... Why?"

"We have our reasons. You don't need to know why."

"How can I?" she asked. "He'll have people with him, body-guards, police whatever. I'll never be able to—"

"You are an intelligent and assiduous woman, Beth. This is one reason why you were chosen. You'll come up with something. Because if you don't do this for us, you know what will happen."

"Freya."

"This is our demand, Ms Lomax. This is how you get your daughter back. This is how you save her life."

An involuntary shudder ran up Beth's torso. Like someone had walked over her grave. That's what her old gran used to say when that happened. Beth never really knew what it meant. Her mouth opened and closed a few times, but no words came to her.

What did she say to this?

What the hell could she say?

"Tomorrow you will go to a location at 4 p.m., where you will be given further instructions and the equipment needed to carry out our demand."

"But I'll be at work then," Beth said, immediately feeling stupid for saying so. Like that was any kind of excuse.

"Again, you're a shrewd woman," the voice told her. "You'll think of something. And I hope it doesn't need repeating that if you tell anyone about us, about Freya being taken, or what we are asking of you, we will kill her. Then we will kill you."

"I understand," Beth replied, but her voice sounded like it was coming from another room, from another time. Oh god, wouldn't it be wonderful if this was all just a bad dream? She wrapped her knuckles on the bony part of her chest, then pinched the skin on her forearm hard. She was still in the stairwell. Still living this veritable nightmare. "Where is it you want me to go?"

"The Isle of Dogs. We will text the exact address to your phone in due course," the voice said. "Tomorrow afternoon. Come alone. Tell no one."

The line went dead. Beth checked the screen. They'd gone for real this time. With her heart thumping against her ribs, she slipped the phone back into her pocket and slipped out of the stairwell. There was no one around as she hurried down the corridor and pushed into the female bathroom. Once there, she lurched over to the nearest cubicle, vomiting a semi-chewed bagel and two cups of strong coffee into the basin.

Gasping for air, she yanked at the roll of toilet paper, wrapping a few sheets around her hand before breaking it off and wiping it around her mouth. As she straightened up, dizziness hit her, and she feared she was going to faint. Taking deep breaths, she leaned against the door of the cubicle.

What the hell was she going to do?

For some reason, she'd thought the not knowing was the

hard part, and that when the kidnappers had told her their demands, she'd feel more empowered. The reasoning behind this was if she knew what she had to do, at least she'd have more control over the situation. But as it was, they only had one demand, and it didn't make her feel empowered or in control at all. Instead, she felt scared and terrified and unable to think straight. To save her daughter's life, she had to kill someone. She had to actually kill someone dead. And not just anyone, the bloody Prime Minister.

How the hell was she going to do that? She couldn't do it. She'd never even killed a spider.

And the implications of that had Beth bending over the toilet once more as a torrent of bitter coffee and bile filled her mouth.

15

"Why you not eat? You must eat. Stay strong."

Freya turned towards the voice. It belonged to one of her foreign captors. She'd now reached the conclusion he was Turkish, but he could just as easily be from Poland or some other eastern European country. It was hard to tell with just the voice to go off. And like the other foreign guard, this one was rather uncommunicative. If he spoke at all, it was staccato comments like these, barked at her like she was an unruly pet.

"I'm not hungry," she told him.

"You be sorry. You may not get anything for a while."

Freya shrugged. *So what?* She'd go on a hunger strike like the Irish men she'd been learning about in her history class. Starve herself to death. She'd be no good to these people dead.

It was an empty threat of course. She wasn't going to do anything of the sort, but the brief feeling of nihilistic power offered some consolation.

Freya had been awake since sunrise. She knew that because it was another bright day and the sunlight permeated even the thick cloth over her eyes. It also told her the windows in the room faced east. She didn't think it helped her, knowing the sun rose in the east each day, but there it was. Another useless fact she carried around with her. All that time she wasted in geography and history when she could have been pursuing things she really loved. Like acting, listening to music. If she was to die here in this room, at the hands of these faceless demons, she thought it all terribly unfair she'd wasted half her life attending boring lessons.

She leaned over the edge of the mattress and peered through the gap at the bottom of her blindfold, at the plate on the floor. Her breakfast comprised a small, rectangular pain au chocolate wrapped in cellophane. It looked disgusting, but her stomach was rumbling. Without speaking, she reached for it and tore the wrapper off before devouring it greedily in three bites.

"See," the man said. "I told you. It's good?"

Freya shrugged. "It's okay."

Drop dead, the voice in her head yelled.

She swallowed down the last mouthful and was about to ask for some water when the door opened. She sat up, not daring to move as she waited for whatever was about to happen. Next to her, the guard got up from his chair and walked over to the door. Once there, he spoke with whoever had entered the room. She listened but couldn't distinguish any words. Just two voices mumbling, and then what sounded like a whispered argument. She turned her head, pretending she was doing anything but listening to their conversation.

The men stepped out of the room, and the door shut behind them. Left alone, Freya shifted around and sat cross-legged on the mattress. She could still hear the men through the door. They were shouting at each other now. One of them sounded furious and from his inflexion and the fact he was doing most of the shouting, she guessed it was Newspaper Man. She leaned her head nearer the door.

"Someone should have told me. That's all I'm saying," he yelled.

The other man mumbled something she couldn't make out. His voice was low, and through the door, nothing but a bass rumble.

"No. I did not know that," Newspaper Man went on. "She's only fucking fourteen, for Christ's sake."

Freya stiffened. She held her breath as the other man replied. It sounded like he was saying, "They told us this. They told us."

"No. They bloody well did not. I thought she'd be eighteen, sixteen at least. That girl in there is a bloody child. I would never have taken the job if I'd known."

The other man made a growling noise at this, but it was clear he didn't agree with what was being said.

"I don't care, mate," Newspaper Man said. "Some of us have principles, yeah? *Principles*."

Freya gasped as the door flew open and Newspaper Man's voice filled the room. "Forget it. Don't worry about it, mate. I've got it from here."

"It will all be fine," the other man bellowed after him. "You want anything?"

"Nah. I'm all right." But he didn't sound all right. He sounded tired and annoyed and like he was about to crack. As he shoved the door shut, Freya heard him stomping over to the chair.

She waited until he'd sat down and finished huffing and puffing before she spoke.

"Hello," she said. "Is it you?"

The man snorted down his nose. Like people did when they

couldn't believe what they were hearing. "Is it me? Yeah, it's me. Last time I looked." The chair creaked as he adjusted himself. "How are you doing?"

Freya sighed the most pathetic sigh she could muster. She'd been playing this all wrong, she now realised. Stepping into the role of the warrior woman had been the right thing to do back when she wanted to stay calm and keep the bad thoughts at bay. But now there was a better role she could step into.

"I didn't sleep very well," she said, making her voice sound as youthful as possible. She didn't quite say *vewy well*, but she wasn't far off.

"Well, you shouldn't be here too much longer, from what I hear."

She sighed again. "I don't suppose you could remove my blindfold, could you?" she asked. "Just for a bit. I'll turn around. I won't look at you or anything. It's so very uncomfortable."

She'd actually gotten used to the material around her eyes, the way you always do with something alien. When she'd first had her braces fitted, she'd hated them and assumed they'd feel awkward and uncomfortable for the whole two years. But after a few days, she hardly noticed them at all. It was the same when she first started wearing a bra. If she remembered she had it on, it was annoying, but after a while, she forget to remember.

But whilst the blindfold wasn't too much of a problem, Freya had read on the internet that a clever trick to get someone to like you was to ask them for a small favour. The idea was that if they did the favour; they were communicating to their subconscious that they must like you, otherwise they wouldn't be helping you. It was called cognitive discordance, something like that.

But Newspaper Man wasn't falling for it. "Not a chance," he grumbled. "Can't risk it. For your sake, as much as mine. We aren't playing games here, kid. These are serious people you're dealing with."

"But not you?"

"Excuse me."

"You're not one of them?" She lowered her head, giving it the full Bambi-eyes behind the blindfold. "You said you were hired by a fixer. Does that mean you aren't really a part of what's going on?"

"Shit, yeah. I did tell you that, didn't I? That was stupid." He tutted. "But that doesn't make me any better than the people who are paying me. So don't get any ideas."

"But you aren't part of... whatever's going on. I mean, not really."

He breathed heavily down his nose. "Yep. I know nothing. The fewer questions I ask, the better. And the same goes for you."

But Freya could sense he was softening. She didn't have much (didn't have any) experience with boys her own age, but she'd been around enough older men to know how they operated. Not in a creepy way. Not like that. But with her dad's friends, her friends' dads, male teachers, she understood how to play to her strengths. And more importantly, how to play to their weaknesses. It seemed to Freya all men wanted to be a hero deep down. Even those who'd taken the wrong path in life.

"I'm only fourteen, you know," she said, well aware he knew. "Only by a few months, as well. I'm not fifteen until August. I'm one of the youngest in my class."

The man didn't reply but instead whistled through his teeth.

"Do you have children?" Freya asked him, her voice barely a whisper.

"Ah, no. No, no. Don't you dare."

"What? I'm only trying to make conversation. To pass the

time. It is rather boring being locked up here all day with nothing to even look at."

The man cleared his throat. "I'm not discussing this."

He said it like it was final and Freya accepted that. She shuffled back on the mattress and brought her knees up to her chin, hugging her arms around her legs.

"When will I get out of here?" she asked.

"I'm not sure. It depends, I'm told."

"What on?"

"Things you don't need to concern yourself with."

"Okay." She whimpered.

The man sighed and whispered, "Jesus," to himself.

He was troubled, that was clear. But so was Freya. She might have been a talented actor, able to lose herself in a role and find solace there, but she was also terrified and growing more so by the minute. The whimpering was real.

"Look, kid," Newspaper Man said, lowering his voice to a soft growl. "All I know is they're after something big and your mum's involved."

"You said that before. My mum? I don't get it."

"All I know is, by this point, they'll have contacted her. Given her their demands. That's how it works."

Freya didn't respond to this. It had thrown her. If they'd contacted her mum already, why hadn't the police shown up yet?

Her heart sank.

Goosebumps prickled up her arms and down her legs.

Of course, that's how it worked. *Don't tell the police or we'll kill your daughter.* That's what they'd have said to her. The realisation landed heavily on her shoulders, and she stifled a wail, pressing her face into her knees.

The police didn't know she was here

No one knew.

What the hell was her mum going to do? She couldn't save her. Freya loved her mum and even liked her most of the time, but she wasn't a warrior woman. She worked in an office. She didn't even go to the gym. There was no way she was strong enough, physically or mentally, to save her. Indeed, ever since the divorce, Freya had noticed her mother growing increasingly unwell. Mentally unwell. She hid it most of the time, but Freya had noticed.

Throwing herself into her work was one of her mum's coping strategies. Freya knew that, and she'd still given her a hard time about it. The last time they'd seen each other they'd rowed; Freya had told her to piss off (as well as saying a million nastier things to her in her head). What a horrible bitch she was to her. She shook the thought away. It didn't help. It was all too horrible to think about.

How was her mum supposed to cope with all this? Her only child had gone missing. She'd be distraught. In bits. No use to anyone.

The beep-click of the door snapped Freya from out of her thoughts. The Newspaper Man's chair scraped against the floor as a voice called out.

"Hey." It sounded like the other guard from this morning. "He is here."

Newspaper Man got up and walked over to the door, where the two men talked once more in hoarse whispers. Then he called back to Freya. "Be back in a minute. Don't you go anywhere, okay?"

The other guard let out a cruel snicker, but the way Newspaper Man had said it, Freya felt he was sharing the joke with her.

She nodded in response, held her nerve. Maybe she did have Stockholm Syndrome after all, but she also saw something in this man. Not kindness exactly, but humanity. To her, he was a real person, not a shadowy demonic figure like the others. If she was able to reason with him, she wasn't yet sure. But all she knew was if she was to see her fifteenth birthday, she had to take matters into her own hands. She had to escape. And this man was her only chance out of here.

16

After receiving the phone call, Beth didn't tick much off her 'To Do' list. In fact, for the rest of the day and most of the evening, she operated as though once removed from her life. She said the right things, acted the right way, did what she needed to do. But it was all done as if she was observing herself from above. Her watching this ridiculous Beth Lomax character as she attempted to negotiate a normal existence whilst struggling with a tsunami of panic which threatened to engulf her.

She had wondered about speaking to Louise about the imminent visit. But if it was still being finalised she might not know anything. And then how would it look, with Beth having inside information? No. She had to play this the way they'd told her. Say nothing. Wait for their text.

Once home she'd passed out fully clothed on the couch after one large glass of wine before waking and dragging herself to bed. After that, she had hoped she'd be able to get to sleep quickly, but in the quiet of her bedroom she'd tossed and turned, and when she eventually fell asleep, her dreams were plagued with dark images and unsettling tableaux. She saw Freya tied and bloody; her face wiped of all features except for an open mouth, which let out a perpetual scream of anguish, like in that nightmarish painting by Munch.

But fall asleep she must have done, because the next thing she knew, the incessant chime of her alarm was smashing her dreams into a million tiny shards, bringing with it the new day and everything that entailed.

"Here we go then, girl," she said. "We can do this."

She sat up and actually said the words out loud. Speaking to herself like some crazy person. It had happened a few times over the last twenty-four hours. She hoped it was just a way of settling her nerves, reassuring herself in the only way she could. But maybe that was why all the other mad people did it, too.

In the shower she turned the hot water up as far as it would go, letting the sharp heat spear her skin in the hope it might harpoon the lingering memories of her dreams and drag them from her soul. It didn't do that, but she felt more awake as she stepped onto the mat ten minutes later and wrapped a towel around herself.

She stared at her reflection as she ran the electric toothbrush around her mouth, eyes barely visible in the steamed-up mirror over the sink. She looked like she was lost in a thick fog, but that was how it felt too.

They wanted her to kill the Prime Minister. Her. Beth Lomax. They wanted her to kill Sir Gerald fucking Hopkins. She'd never had much time for the guy, but she didn't wish him dead. And she certainly didn't want to be the one who killed him.

She'd been obsessing over the kidnappers' single ominous demand ever since the phone call. Almost twenty-four hours later, it didn't seem any less surreal. Things like this didn't happen to people like her. And forget the whys and whats of their demand. *How* was she going to do it? She wasn't some worldly assassin. She was a slender white woman in her early forties who drank too much, exercised too little and operated mainly on a mixture of nervous energy, coffee and self-loathing. She was going to fail. She knew it. The Prime Minister's body-guards would intercept her, arrest her, and that would be it. She'd be thrown in jail and Freya would... The kidnappers would...

She spat violently into the sink, hoping it would get the thought out of her head. Then she twisted on the cold tap to wash it away and got dressed for work.

Carly and Jaz were already at their desks chattering excitedly as Beth got into the office. Her journey to the hospital had been uneventful. In fact, being here now, she had no recollection of the last forty-five minutes. It was like she travelled here completely on auto-pilot.

"How you are doing, doll?" Carla asked, turning from her screen to address Beth. Her face dropped. "Oh, hell's bells."

Beth stepped back as Carla got up from her desk and moved towards her. "What? What is it?" Her voice was shaky.

"Come here, you muck tub." Carla grabbed at the front of Beth's blouse, lifting it to show her the large coffee stain. "In a rush, were you?"

Beth scowled. "Shitting hell. That's all I need. I didn't even notice."

"Here, wait a minute." Carla shuffled back to her desk and lifted her bag onto her chair, returning with a packet of wet wipes. She dabbed roughly at the stain, a look of concentration creasing her brow. "That's about as good as it's going to get, I'm afraid." She stepped back and closed one eye.

"Thank you," Beth told her, fighting back tears. She turned

her head and laughed. "Sorry, my head's all over the place today."

Carla grabbed Beth's upper arm and squeezed it before glancing over her shoulder at Jaz, who was scrolling through her phone, probably on Instagram. When she turned back, her face was serious. She leaned in. "I know."

Beth stiffened. "You know?"

"Yes. I know."

"But how? What do you mean? You... know? About Freya?"

Shit.

What the hell was she doing? If Carla knew that meant she was in on it. Was this a test? Was this them seeing if she'd blab at the first opportunity?

Fucking hell.

Shut up, Beth. Shut up now.

You're being ridiculous.

Carla nodded conspiringly. "I know how hard it is bringing up a teenager as a single parent. And I know you and Freya have been through a lot."

Beth let out another laugh, louder this time. "Oh, yes. Sure."

Carla kept on talking as Beth walked over to her desk and removed her coat, telling of her own experience bringing up her twin boys after their father died. Carla had had it tough, and Beth empathised, but she couldn't focus on the words. She'd heard the story before, and right now her focus was on slowing her heart rate before she keeled over.

"Thanks for the clean-up job," she said as she lowered herself into her seat, hoping to put an end to the conversation. "I'm all over the place at the moment."

"Don't mention it," Carla said, sitting also and winking at her as she did. "But you can't be coming into work with coffee down your front when we've got VIPs visiting."

An icy chill ran down Beth's spine. "What do you mean?"

"I mean, none other than the bloody Prime Minister. He's coming here."

Beth cleared her throat. "I see. Do you know when?"

"In a couple of days, I think. Everyone's talking about it. From what Aga was telling me, he's being shown around the main bit downstairs and then a visit to the research department and then us admin lot last. Makes a change we get a look in doesn't it. You're excited aren't ya, Jaz?"

Jaz looked up from her phone. "What's that?"

"Never mind." Carla rolled her eyes at Beth as behind her the door opened and Damien and Louise entered the room.

"How are we all doing?" Damien asked, wringing his hands together. "I take it you've now heard the exciting news."

"Yes," Beth said, straightening her back. "Very exciting. And you want us to be involved."

"That's right," he replied but didn't look at her. "Sir Gerald will be visiting this floor to view the records department and the like. Probably with some photographers in tow. So, we want to present a strong front to the press."

Beth glanced at Louise. Her face was stern. No doubt she saw this for what it was. A little exposure for the trust and a lot more work for everyone else. And for what? Another cynical photo opportunity for Hopkins, him in scrubs and a surgical mask. In any other situation her face would have been as stern as her friend's, but this wasn't any other situation. She needed this to happen. She needed it more than air.

"I'm happy to meet with the Prime Minister and show him around," Beth told Damien. "I've worked here the longest and as head of HR I can—"

"Actually, I was thinking Jazmine here could do the meet and greet," Damien said. He still hadn't made eye contact with Beth.

Shit.

This was about her refusal to help him with the proposal paperwork. He was punishing her. At the worst possible time.

"Me?" Jazmine said, sitting up and placing her hands in her lap. "You want me to show him around?"

"Yes, why not. I know you'll make Sir Gerald and his team very welcome," told her. "It will be wonderful exposure for the great work we do here. Give him a tour of the Human Resources and Operations departments. You could even show him our records room. I bet he'd like that. Give him the lowdown on what we do here and twist his arm for some extra funding if you get the chance." He chuckled to himself, but no one else laughed. "Then a few photos for the assembled press. You are very photogenic, after all"

Beth swallowed her frustration. "But sir—"

"Don't worry, Beth," Damien snapped, eyes wide as he finally looked her way. "You'll all get a chance to meet with the Prime Minister. You'll all get a photo I imagine. I didn't think you liked the man anyway. From everything you've ever said."

"Yes...but... I just think as head of the department..." She trailed off, looking at Louise for assistance but getting nothing back.

"I think Ms Rahim will do a terrific job," Damien went on. "She's young and attractive and seeing as we're rather unrepresented at the Royal in terms of certain ethnicities, it'll be good optics."

And there it was. Beth couldn't hide her sneer, but it was worse than that. A ball of fear and anger had got caught in her throat and it felt like she was going to choke. She needed air.

"Well, if that's everything," she said, getting to her feet. "Louise, can I have a quick word?"

Louise nodded at Damien and gestured at the door. Beth followed her out into the corridor.

"Are you all right?" Louise asked as the door closed.

"Not really," she said. "I know I've sometimes been a little harsh on Hopkins, but I just think if the Royal Farringdon is being visited by the Prime Minister, I should show him around our department."

Louise shrugged. "It's Damien's call, doll. And it's not going to be a big deal, all this pomp."

Yes! Beth's inner voice screamed. *Yes, it is going to be a big deal!*

"Will you have a word with him?" Beth asked. "Please?"

"Yes, if it means that much to you. But I can't promise anything."

"Thanks."

"You will get a chance to meet him, you know. We all will."

Beth gritted her teeth. But how was she going to get him alone? She glanced over Louise's shoulder as Damien exited the office.

"I'm getting off," he told them. "Speak to you soon."

"Cheers Damien," Louise called after him, then back to Beth. "I'd better get back to it as well.

"One more thing," Beth said. "I've got a dentist appointment this afternoon. A root canal. It's been bothering me for months. I tried to arrange it for after work, but it was all they had. Am I okay to get off a bit early?"

Louise pouted and tapped her on the shoulder. "Course you are. Hope it goes okay. And chin up, all right. You are number one. Don't let Damien wind you up."

"No, it's not that..." she started, but Louise had turned around and was heading along the corridor to her office. She yelled after her, "You will speak to him?"

"Yes. Don't worry," she called back. "We shall all get our time with the gracious leader."

Beth squeezed her fists together until her hands drained of

blood. Then she took a deep breath and went back into the office.

Jazmine and Clara were laughing together as she entered.

"You'd think he'd have asked you," Clara said, perhaps catching her mood.

"It's fine. I'll make sure I get a few minutes with him. To tell him what I think we need in terms of government help, I mean." She looked up and smiled. "But you'll be great, Jaz. I'm sure of it."

"Thanks," Jazmine said. "I can't believe it. Wait until I tell my mum and dad. They'll be over the bleeding moon."

"Actually, that reminds me," Beth said. "I've got a dentist appointment this afternoon. Will you be able to cover for me? I've let Louise know and she's fine with it. But I know how busy we are at the moment?"

"No worries. We'll be fine," Carla said. "What time do you have to leave?"

Beth made out she was thinking, but she'd been meticulously planning her route all morning. Somewhere on the Isle of Dogs, they'd said. Considering London afternoon traffic, train delays and the amount of walking she had to do, she reckoned that wherever the meeting point was, it wouldn't take her longer than an hour.

"Two thirty-ish?" she said, meaning two-thirty on the dot.

"Two-thirty?" Carla's eyes widened

"Yes. What's wrong?" It felt like her heartbeat was audible to the whole room.

"You're going to the dentist at two-thirty?" Carla said. "Two-thirty. Tooth hurty. You know, like the joke."

"Oh, right, yes. Of course." She shook her head. "Sorry, as I said, my mind's all over the place."

Carla raised her chin. Now she was definitely eyeing her with suspicion. "You are out of sorts, aren't you?"

Beth nodded, biting her tongue, and digging her nails into her palms to stem the tears. "Just in a lot of pain," she said. "With my tooth."

"Sure. Well, you get yourself sorted. Me and Jaz will hold down the fort here. Won't we, kiddo?"

Jaz looked up and smiled. "No worries. Hope you feel better soon."

Beth sat back in her chair and sighed.

Yes. So did she.

The problem was there was only one way she'd ever feel better again. And it involved her murdering the most famous and heavily guarded man in British politics.

17

Beth remained on auto-pilot for the rest of the day, tapping out insipid replies to tedious emails, but with one eye on her phone at all times, waiting for the text. When it arrived, she slid her phone off the desk and into her lap to read.

Millennium Harbour. Car park opposite Bellgate Place. Come alone. Tell no one. Now delete this text.

Beth did as instructed, but not before noting that the text had come from an actual number rather than 'Unknown Caller' as before. For a moment she pondered on whether she should write it down somewhere, but she'd watched enough TV dramas over the years to know it would be from what they called a burner - a cheap phone used for criminal activities that were destroyed once the call was made.

She deleted the text and pocketed her phone before putting the address into Google maps and reassessing her journey time. Her estimation had been correct. Which meant she still possessed some semblance of logic and reason. That was good to know. The clock on her desktop told her it was 14:21. Might as well call it. She logged off and powered down her computer.

Carla was on a phone call and Jaz was over at the printer as Beth shuffled past on her way out. At the door, she waved at Carla, receiving a sharp salute in response. It felt apt. As if she was going into battle, or (perhaps more fitting) going over the trenches into No-man's-land.

She rode the elevator down to the ground floor and stepped out before the doors had fully opened. Right into the path of Dr Raul. He was walking towards her and reading from a clipboard so hadn't seen her. She veered to one side to avoid him, but it was too late.

"Beth," he called out. "How are you?"

Biting her lip, she stopped and turned, hitting him with her best smile. "Hi, Sammy. I'm fine. Thanks. In a bit of a hurry, actually."

"Oh, I see. Not to worry." But he was walking over to her all the same. Why couldn't he take a damn hint? "It's just, I wanted to apologise again for being such an idiot the other night. I don't know what I was thinking, coming into your house like that."

"It's okay," she told him, feet pointing towards the exit. "You don't need to apologise."

"I wonder if I might make it up to you. Take you for a glass of wine or something? Maybe this Friday if you're not busy. Just casual, after work. As mates, you know..."

Beth puffed out her cheeks. In her head, she was telling him to get lost, to get the hell out of her way. He was a nice guy, but she couldn't deal with this now.

"Yes. Maybe," she snapped, bouncing from foot to foot. "Can we talk about it later? Like I say, I am in a bit of a panic now. I've got a dentist appointment across town."

"God, sorry, of course. Don't let me keep you."

She gave him a polite nod and hurried over to the exit, pulling her ID card from her pocket and swiping herself through the security gates. Once on the other side, she headed for a side door, rather than the large revolving doors of the main entrance and pushed it open. It was ten minutes to three. She'd thought about driving into work, but she'd felt too nervy to negotiate London traffic so public transport it was. Her plan was to jump on a tube from Farringdon to Baker Street and from there get the Jubilee line down to Canary Wharf. With connections on her side, it would take her around thirty-five minutes. If not, it might be nearer sixty. It was going to be close.

As it was, the gods of time were smiling on Beth. She found a tube waiting at Farringdon and only had to wait three minutes at Baker Street. By the time she'd left Canary Wharf tube station behind and was walking the last half mile to Millennium Harbour, she had twenty minutes to spare. No sweat. Or rather, plenty of sweat. It was another remarkably warm day for the time of year, but that wasn't the only reason her brow was wet and her blouse was sticking to her back. With every step, trepidation grew.

She was on her way to meet with the vile people who'd kidnapped her baby girl. The same people who wanted to make a murderer out of her. Even knowing full well how dreadfully true both those statements were, it felt ridiculous to even think about them. Yet here she was in a secluded area of the city, surrounded by abandoned factories and old dockyards like it was the most normal thing in the world.

The area around Millennium Harbour was deserted as Beth made her way down Westferry Road, but she'd expected that. These people seemed like they knew what they were doing. They wouldn't meet her somewhere heavily populated. Despite the balmy day, a chill breeze blew in off the river, causing her to wrap her coat tight around her as she pressed on toward Bellgate Place. Here she took a right down toward the car park where they'd told her to meet them.

She wound her way down the narrow street, careful not to step on any of the discarded needles and broken bottles that littered the pavements. There wasn't another soul in sight. Not even a car. Not even a rat. Were they nearby? Were they watching her right now?

"Hello?" she called out. "I'm here."

She waited. Nothing. She pulled out her phone, angry with herself that she'd deleted the number. The time on the screen showed 16:05. Where were they? She walked over to the nearest building, but the main doorway had a large bolt across the middle, with an industrial padlock clamping it shut. She was about to walk around the other side to check if there were any other entrances when she heard a car engine behind her.

She spun around as a large black Ford Transit van appeared from around the corner on the far side of the car park. A shiver of fear ran down Beth's spine. The vehicle drove towards her, showing no sign of slowing down, but Beth stood her ground, unable to move even if she'd wanted. The windows in the van were made of darkened glass so she could see no one in the driver's seat, but she stared at the space where she supposed they were all the same. She didn't blink. Didn't take a breath. Was she pleading with them to stop, or defying them to carry on? At that moment, she wasn't sure what she was doing or indeed who she was. At the last second, the van swerved around her and screeched to a stop a few feet away. The engine remained running, but other than that, it was still. Beth remained where she was. Nothing happened for what seemed like forever. Above her head, a seagull squawked. Then the side door of the van shuddered and slid open.

As it did, Beth stepped to one side, to better take in whoever was about to step out. But the back of the van appeared to be empty. A black void of raw metal. Nothing else.

"Step closer. Slowly," a deep voice said. It echoed from inside the van. Whoever it was must have been concealed around the side of the hatch.

"It's Beth Lomax," she called out. "I'm here like you told me."

"We know who you are. Move over to the van."

She took two steps forward.

"Now turn around," the voice said.

Beth tried to swallow, but her throat was completely dry.

"Turn around," the voice snapped.

She did as instructed, holding her hands up to her face as if in surrender. Her body felt like it was going into shock. Is this how it ended? Were they going to shoot her in the back? She caught herself and sniffed. No, stupid. Of course, they weren't going to kill her. They needed her alive. She was the one who had to do the killing.

"Now take two steps backwards," the voice said and when Beth moved, "Slowly... Slowly... One more."

She felt the edge of the van against the curve of her calf muscle and stopped. She still had her hands raised, but it felt amiss to lower them now.

"Good," the voice said over her shoulder. From this proximity, the voice had less echo. It was a man's voice. Beth couldn't place any kind of accent, but he was well-spoken. She wondered if it was the same person she'd spoken to on the phone. "Sit down," he told her.

She did and the second her bottom touched the floor of the van; she sensed a presence behind her. A knee pressed in between her shoulders. She heard a swoosh and felt hands around her neck. The world went black. She had a thick hessian sack over her head. She sucked back a breath to scream, but the material entered her mouth, choking her so no sound came out. It wouldn't have mattered, anyway. There was no one around to hear. The hands around her throat moved under her arms and they dragged her into the belly of the van. She heard the door slam shut and the grinding of gears.

"We've got her," the voice said. "Drive on."

18

"Where are you taking me?" Beth cried once she'd come to terms with what had transpired. Once she could get her words out. "No one told me this would happen. What's going on?"

She sensed the man's presence beside her. Possibly he was sitting on the wheel arch. He didn't speak, only let out a low growl as if clearing his throat.

"I've done everything you told me to," she continued with wavering tones. "I've told no one. I've gone about my daily routine as much as possible."

"We know that," the man said. "That's why you and your daughter are still alive."

"Freya," Beth gasped. "Can I see her? Speak to her at least."

The man growled again. "No more talking. We'll be at our destination shortly."

Beth nodded and adjusted her position on the metal floor so her leg wouldn't go dead. As the van turned right, she slid to the side and felt the man's shoe against her knee. They'd already taken a right out of the car park. This was the second right turn. She envisaged them driving down Westferry Road, which ran all the way to the bottom of the peninsula before it turned into Manchester Road. She raised her head, breathing in some deep yogic breaths (she was no use to Freya in a state of panic) but the air in the sack was stuffy and it only made her feel worse.

An image flashed across her mind's eye. A scene from the nightmare she'd experienced last night, Freya bound and gagged and covered in blood, her eyes black with fear. In the dream she'd stared up at Beth, pleading with her for help.

Shush. No. Don't do that.

She forced the image from her mind, replacing it with a memory of Freya on the beach in Santorini two years earlier. Her giggling as Beth got flustered ordering drinks in Greek from an exceptionally good-looking waiter. It had been an expensive trip, but Beth had used some of the divorce settlement and they'd both needed the time away. They'd got along great that week. The days were spent sunbathing on the beach or by the pool and at night they'd stroll around the old town, eating delicious food in quaint tavernas. It was like old times for the two of them. They'd laughed so much together that holiday. Beth wondered if it was the last time they were truly happy. Would she ever be happy again?

She was snapped back to the moment as the van took a sharp left. Beth had lived in London all her life. And like most Londoners, she knew the twist and turns of the tube map like the back of her hand, knew every relevant bus route and number. As the van drove onwards, she plotted the journey in her mind as best she could. It might help her, it might not. But by focusing her mind on where they were, geographically speaking, it meant it couldn't focus on where she was mentally. Or that she had a sack over her head.

It felt like they'd been travelling on the same road forever. She pictured them travelling up the East side of the peninsula back towards Canary Wharf. But another right turn soon after told her they were heading back towards the river.

She sat back on her haunches. "Where are you taking me?"

"Didn't I say for you to keep quiet?" the man said. "We're here now." The van lurched over to one side and Beth felt it slow down before coming to a complete stop. As they switched the engine off, a heavy silence fell, broken almost immediately as the side of the van slid open and a cool breeze wrapped itself around her legs and arms.

The man in the back stood, and the van swayed and bounced as he jumped out. Beth heard mumbled talking from outside the van and counted three voices, all males.

"Where are we?" she called out. "Is Freya here? Can I see her?"

None of the men answered her. A hand grabbed her upper arm and pulled her out of the van. As she stumbled out, she felt rubble under her shoes and as she peered through the material covering her eyes; she made out the silhouette of a building, standing on its own, in front of her.

"This way, Ms Lomax," a far-off voice said.

The man gripped her arm tight, leading her across gravel and into a building. Once there, they walked across a lino-covered floor and came to a stop. The man holding her leaned forward, and she heard him tapping at a button and then the unmistakable sound of elevator doors sliding open.

"Inside."

They shoved her into the metal box and all three men got in after her. The elevator rattled and shook as they went up and Beth counted four floors before they came to a halt and the doors slid open again. Without a word, she was led down a long corridor that seemed to stretch on forever.

"In here," the man said, squeezing the flesh on her arm.

She sensed a door open to her right, and the man pushed

her through into the next room, where he walked her over to a chair seemingly a few feet from the door.

"You sit," the man said, manoeuvring her around the side of the chair and pressing her shoulders down until she was in place on the seat.

Once there, the sack was whipped off her head, and she cried out as a bright light hit her in the face. The swift change from dark to light was disorientating, and she screwed up her face and leaned to one side. She had to get away, had to flee this painful source of intense brightness and heat. Her eyes burned; her lungs felt like they were full of ash.

She tried to stand, but a hand on her shoulder pushed her down.

"Please remain seated, Beth," a voice boomed. It was the same distorted voice from the phone call, the same digital filtering. "You'll get used to the light momentarily."

She lowered her head, panting for air as the adrenaline subsided, and her faculties returned. "Do we have to do this? Like this?"

She heard the door open and footsteps leaving the room. Possibly the men who'd brought her here.

"Please," she said, not looking up. "My husband, Freya's dad. He has his own company. We can get you all the money you want. You can use it to hire someone else. Someone who can do what you want much easier than me. Please let Freya go. I can't do what you're asking of me. I can't. I'm sorry. Please..."

She trailed off, knowing it was useless. Somewhere behind the light, she heard movement, and the voice said, "Enough."

She squinted in the speaker's general direction but could see nothing but black beyond the light.

"You don't want to see my face. That would be bad for you."

Beth nodded her head, gazing into her lap. "Okay. Sorry."

She felt exposed and so vulnerable and tiny sat here. Like a child being told off by the headteacher.

Only this wasn't a headteacher. This was someone with power and drive who wanted the Prime Minister dead. Someone willing to kill her daughter to get what he wanted. But for her, the question was valid. Why her? Why not hire a professional? These thoughts had been flapping around her psyche for the last twenty-four hours, like a vampire bat in a feeding frenzy. She was yet to come up with any kind of answer that made sense.

"Try not to panic, Ms Lomax," the voice continued. "The calmer you remain, the better for everyone. Your daughter most of all. You are so close to getting her back. Once the terms of our ultimatum are met you will be back together."

Beth tensed. The way they said *ultimatum* jarred. *Ulti-mart-um*. It sounded odd and, for a second, a part of her wondered if she recognised the voice. Even under the processing and distortion, there was a hint of something familiar.

Before she had a chance to consider what this meant, she heard more footsteps behind her and then a box was placed on her lap. She sat up to take it in. It was one of those metal brief-cases people used for the safe transport of delicate or expensive items. She imagined it filled with black foam, with areas cut out in the shape of whatever was stored inside. An expensive camera and lenses, perhaps. Or like in the movies, a disassembled rifle.

No.

Surely, they didn't expect her to shoot him. She'd never shot a gun in her life. She'd never even held one.

"I can't..." she started, but her voice was croaky and she didn't know what else to say.

"Open the case."

With shaking hands, Beth found the clasps on the front and pressed down. Metal locks flicked open off heavy springs. Carefully she eased open the lid, terrified of what she would find inside but not able to take her eyes from it.

Inside were just two items, resting snuggly amongst a rectangle of black foam as she'd imagined - a small syringe and a vial of clear liquid. She let out a sharp breath. This was it? This was how she did it?

"Cerberin," the voice said. "A deadly toxin derived from the kernels of India's Pong-Pong Tree. Otherwise known as the 'Suicide Tree'."

Beth stared down at the innocuous vial of liquid. "You want me to inject him with poison?"

"Correct. The poison acts in a similar way to the toxin found in our own Foxglove, blocking calcium ion channels in the heart muscles. It will stop his heart instantly. But while foxglove poisoning is well known to western toxicologists, Cerberin poisoning is not and will be undetectable in a post-mortem. Given Gerald Hopkins' age, body mass and lifestyle, they will not deem a heart attack suspicious. You will not be under any investigation. No one will ever know."

Beth closed the briefcase. She didn't want to look anymore. There was movement over her shoulder and a gloved hand reached over and placed a mobile phone on top of the case. It was one of those old-style flip-phones. A burner.

"From now on we shall contact you via this phone," the voice said. "Keep it charged, keep it on, keep it with you."

"Of course," Beth said. "And can I call you? If I need to."

"There is one number stored on this phone," the voice went on. "When you have done what we have asked, you will ring it. Not before."

Beth closed her eyes tight. "But I ask again, why me? Why not hire a professional hitman? They must do these sorts of things all the time. They could make it look like a complete accident. No one would know."

The person on the other side of the spotlight let out a throaty chuckle, the digital device feeding back as they did. "You are an intelligent woman, Ms Lomax. And that path has been considered. But your hospital specialises in heart disease, does it not? If he dies there, it will appear the doctors have done everything for him and there will be zero doubt that his death was nothing but a terrible tragedy. With no foul play involved. We also have operatives already placed in the hospital who will take over once you have fulfilled your part of the operation."

"The operation?" Beth said, unable to withhold her disdain. "You say it like it's a medical procedure. Saving someone's life, rather than taking it."

"By removing Hopkins, we are saving many lives. He is a cancer at the heart of this country and needs cutting out. By killing him, you will make the world a better place. Ending suffering. Literally."

Beth frowned at the cryptic response. It sounded like a lot of nonsense. Them justifying their actions as if it was some moral crusade.

"What if I won't do it?" Beth asked. "Or what if I can't? What if I fail? What you're asking of me is going to be difficult."

"Your job is to get Hopkins alone and inject him with the poison. Do that and your daughter will live. Fail and we've already made it clear what will happen."

"But I—"

"You are an intelligent woman, Ms Lomax. You will figure it out."

"I've not been put in charge of showing him around. It's going to be hard for me to get close—"

"You are an intelligent woman, Ms Lomax. You will figure it

out," The voice repeated the words with a rising tone, adding, "You will have to."

"Is Freya here?" Beth asked, leaning forward. "Can I see her, please? Just for a second."

"Beth! You need to stop this."

She raised her head, finding her voice as she cried. "Freya. It's me. I'm here, baby. I'm going to save y—"

A rough hand grabbed her around the mouth and yanked her back in the seat. Before she could yell out again, the hessian sack was shoved over her head and the material pulled tight around her throat.

"Don't be stupid!" the voice boomed. "You are so close, Beth. Don't mess this up."

She struggled to breathe, clawing at the sack around her neck. As the material loosened, she sagged forward on the chair, coughing and spluttering.

"Hopkins will visit the Royal Farringdon Hospital the day after tomorrow," the voice said. "You have forty-eight hours to make your plans and get your mind focused. Now take her away."

19

Freya sat upright and lifted her head. She'd heard something just now. It sounded like they were calling her name. It sounded like her mum. She strained to listen, closing her eyes for concentration despite the blindfold still tight around her face.

"Did you hear that?" she asked.

Newspaper Man groaned. "What?"

"Someone was calling my name. Freya. I'm sure of it. I think it was my mum. Is she here?"

"Calm it down, kid. If she is, you aren't getting to see her."

Freya gave it a beat, shifting back into the role of a helpless child. "Are they going to hurt my mum?"

"Facking hell," the man muttered under his breath. Then, louder, to Freya. "No. They aren't. Like I told you already, I don't know what's going on or what my employers want. But from what little I have heard, your mum's going to do something for them. In return for you being delivered back to her safely. That's why you're here. That's why I am too."

"What is it she's doing?" she asked. "Is it bad? Will she get hurt?"

"I don't know."

Freya fell silent, her brain whirring at a million miles an hour. She had to get out of here. Before they forced her mum to do something dangerous or illegal, or both. Newspaper Man was her only lifeline. She was certain of this now. If she could just twist him a little more.

"What's your name?" she asked.

"Oh, no. Not a chance."

"Just so I can call you by your name when we talk."

"No. Not happening."

She shifted on the mattress. "Okay. Well, can I please take the blindfold off? Just for a minute or two. It's really rubbing at my eyes. I promise I won't tell anyone what you look like."

The man growled under his breath, but it sounded to Freya like he was struggling with the request rather than it angering him.

"I'll tell you what I'll do. I need to go take a piss, anyway. Once you hear the door close behind me, you can pull down the blindfold, air your eyes or whatever you need to do. When I come back, I'll knock before I open the door. I want you to have it back in place before I enter. That make sense?"

Freya nodded. "Thank you."

"But I swear to you, kid. If you mess with me, there'll be trouble. I won't bother asking you to not look out the windows because I know you will do, but it won't matter, anyway. There's no one around. But don't be getting any silly ideas. I mean it."

"I promise."

"All right. You've got about five minutes."

She tensed as the chair creaked, and the man got to his feet. Five minutes. She was unsure what she was going to do in that time but getting her vision back would help. Plus, he'd succumbed to one of her requests. That was a good start.

The man strode over to the door, and she listened for the

beep click of the door being unlocked. "Five minutes," he said again. "You behave." Then he opened the door and left the room.

Freya waited all of two seconds before pulling the blindfold from her eyes. Red and grey spirals swirled in front of her face, and she had to blink a few times before they cleared. When they did, she saw she was in a square room with raw stone walls and a concrete floor. Exposed pipes and metal girders crisscrossed above her head, giving the place an industrial feel. Freya had hoped there would be more furniture here, perhaps with drawers or cabinets that might contain something she might use as... a weapon? Maybe. But regardless, except for the air mattress and chair she already knew about, the room looked empty.

She got to her feet and hurried over to the wall opposite the door, where two large windows looked down on the Thames below. The coldness roused her as she pressed her cheek against the glass, peering left and right, looking for a landmark she recognised. One Canada Square (the tower block non-Londoners often mistook for Canary Wharf) was over to her right, but it was a long way away. There was another building adjacent to the one she was in, but this one too appeared derelict, the two buildings standing away from everything in the middle of a vast concrete wasteland. The late afternoon sun cast long shadows over the area, giving the dilapidated surroundings a post-apocalyptic feel. Like in one of those zombie films her friend Lauren loved so much. Over the river, Freya could see cars and people passing by, but they were too far away for her to get their attention.

She moved from the window and walked briskly around the perimeter of the room, eyes fixed on the ground, searching for inspiration. Anything. In the corner next to the door, she stopped. Here the concrete floor had been chipped away, leaving a mass of rubble and dust. But there was something else, too. Kneeling next to the rubble, Freya brushed some of the dust away and lifted a piece of concrete to reveal a thin length of metal. It was bright orange with rust and was about thirty centimetres long. She lifted it out to inspect it. Metal furrows spiralled around along its length, making it easier to grip and there was a good weight to it. Holding it up in the light, she also saw one end was sharp where it had been snapped off.

A shiver ran through her. She gripped the metal bar tight as her imagination ran wild with possibilities, each one twisting at her stomach, making her feel like she was going to throw up. She might have been playing the weak, innocent child to gain Newspaper Man's sympathy, but the reality wasn't far off. Could she actually use this weapon when the time came? Could she hit someone, stab them? Kill them, even?

She jumped to her feet at the sound of footsteps in the corridor and rushed over to the mattress. Stuffing her newfound treasure underneath, she sat down on top of it and pulled the blindfold up over her eyes.

There was a knock on the door. "You ready in there?"

"Yes. The blindfold is back on," Freya called out.

The door beeped and clicked, and Newspaper Man entered. "Feeling better?" he asked her.

"A bit." She sniffed.

"Yeah. Bit of a stupid question, that." He moved over and resumed his position on the chair. "I suppose it's all relative, though, ain't it?"

He let out a humourless laugh, and Freya shifted on the mattress. It had been full of air and bouncy when she first arrived here, but over time the air had depleted, so it was now only half full and she could feel the metal bar under her bum.

Its presence there was reassuring. Not that she knew what the hell she was going to do with it. In fact, the thought of doing anything with it filled her with a crushing sense of fear. But it was there. She had her way out. All that she needed to do now was wait for the right moment, and hope that when the time came, she'd have the courage to do what she needed to.

20

Beth stared down at the syringe and vial of liquid in her lap. Here in her office, in the surrounds of the hospital, they appeared almost mundane, but they had the potential to cause so much chaos, so much pain.

Yesterday evening, after the men had dragged her back into the van, they'd driven in silence all the way back to Wandsworth, dumping her in an alley a short distance from her house. They'd told her to keep the bag over her head until they'd driven away, and she'd complied, listening until the sound of the engine had all but disappeared before pulling it off and gulping back mouthfuls of the cool night air. Then she'd trudged back home with tears rolling down her face and shivering from what she told herself was the cold, but knowing, deep down, was more likely terror.

Once home, and with the doors all locked, she'd taken a long hot shower before sitting at her laptop with a towel still wrapped around her. It was there she'd run a search of Sir Gerald Hopkins, discovering that as well as the wife she was aware of, he also had two daughters and a son. They were all grown up, but still. Whatever she thought of the man and his politics, he didn't deserve to die. His wife and children didn't deserve to lose their husband and father.

Back at her work desk she shook her head and carefully rehoused the syringe and poison into the leather make-up bag she'd used to transport them here.

So much chaos. So much pain.

That was putting it mildly.

And this was before you factored in the damage to the country caused by the death of a sitting Prime Minister. There'd be a bitter leadership battle, probably a general election. It wasn't what the UK needed right now. Not after everything.

She glanced at the clock. 8:20 a.m. It already felt like she'd been in the office forever. It was so quiet. So still. She switched on her PC, glad of the whirring hum that permeated the silence as the old machine sprang into life.

Beth had woken with a start at 4:30 a.m. knowing what she had to do if she was going to make this work. She couldn't get back to sleep after, so it made sense to get ready and go to the office early. That way she could hide away the syringe and poison before her colleagues arrived. There had been a scary moment as she passed through security, but her assumption that they wouldn't check her make-up bag had paid off. The guards all knew her well, so the checks were always rudimentary, anyway.

As her screen flashed on, she opened out the top drawer of the pedestal cupboard next to her desk and placed the make-up bag under a pile of cardboard files. It wasn't the best place to hide it, but it would keep it close to hand. No one ever looked in Beth's drawers except for her and if they did, all they'd see was an innocent make-up bag.

Sliding the drawer shut, she leaned back on her chair. A deep sigh escaped her, taking her unawares. Normally at times like this, when pent up stress flooded out from deep within her soul, it was a freeing experience, but today she burst into tears.

"Shit."

She hunkered down behind her screen as the door to the office swung open. Hiding behind her screen, she wiped at her face, hoping not to smudge her mascara.

"Beth?"

It was Carla.

"Morning," she replied, staying hidden as she pulled a tissue from the box on her desk and dabbed at her cheeks some more. "How are you?"

Carla stepped around the side of Beth's desk and pulled a face as she saw her there. "What's wrong?"

Beth shook her head, smiled. "Don't. I'm fine." She sat up and wafted her face. "Time of the month."

Carla pouted in acknowledgement, thankfully satisfied with that explanation. "You're in early."

"Yeah," she said, placing her hand on the top drawer of her pedestal, making doubly sure it was closed. "I woke up early and couldn't get back off. So, I thought I'd get a head start on a few things. It's a busy time."

"Don't I bloody well know it?"

"I don't suppose you also know what time Louise is in?" Beth asked. "I need to speak with her."

"Actually, you're in luck," Carla replied, pulling her chair out. "I've just seen her in reception. She seemed a bit harassed, though. Probably getting her fanny in a knot over the Prime Minister's visit."

Beth had assumed any mention of the forthcoming visit would send her spiralling or at least send a shiver down her spine. But as it was, she remained unaffected. Maybe it was the sheer mental exhaustion that was numbing her fear response or the fact her stress levels were so high, they couldn't take in any more input. But she suspected it was because somewhere between having a sack put over her head and being deposited unceremoniously in the dark alley, her resolve for what she had to do had strengthened. This was Freya's life on the line. Beth could wrestle with the rights and wrongs of what she was being asked to do until she was blue in the face, but the reality was simple. Would she kill someone to save Freya's life? And, of course, the answer was yes. Every time. It didn't matter if it was the British Prime Minister or The Dalia Llama. She had to save her daughter's life. It was what a mother did.

So, she'd ignore the niggling voice in her head that told her she couldn't possibly do this. The same one that asked her how she'd ever live with herself knowing she'd murdered someone. She'd ignore, too, the growing unease in her belly that this was a political move by someone who gained to profit from the chaos and would thus be terrible for the country. She ignored all those things because somewhere her little girl was tied up and terrified. Most likely wondering why her mummy wasn't doing anything to help get her home.

But I am, Freya.

I promise I am.

She looked up, grabbing hold of the edge of her desk with both hands as Louise passed by the door of their office, her blurred outline recognisable even through the frosted glass.

"Back soon," she told Carla, not waiting for the response.

She was over to the door and had it open before Louise disappeared around the corner at the end of the corridor.

"Lou?"

The Director of Operations turned around, flicking her wiry brown hair over her shoulder and smiling as Beth scampered up to her. "Beth. Everything all right?"

"Yes. It's just... Can I have a quick word?" She gestured down the next corridor, towards Louise's office. "In private."

"Oh, yes. Of course. Come this way." They walked side by side down the corridor, Louise with her key card already in her hand and a large Starbucks. She swiped at the electronic lock and shouldered the door open, making sure not to spill her coffee.

Once inside the room, she elbowed the light switch on and beckoned for Beth to sit. "What's going on?" she asked, placing the coffee down and moving around the desk.

"Umm... It's about the Prime Minister's visit."

Louise continued settling herself, taking off her coat and hanging it on the stand in the corner of the room. "Oh?"

Underneath the long coat, she was wearing an unflattering dark purple trouser suit and a pastel blue blouse. The sort of attire female politicians might wear. Normally, Louise opted for basic office attire. Black trousers, white shirt. Possibly this new outfit was inspired by the imminent visit. The fact her friend was trying so hard to impress would normally have been endearing to Beth, but today she only noticed in passing. There were too many other things racing through her mind. Not least the speech she'd been going over in her head since she woke up.

"I've been thinking a lot about the visit," she started. "I know Damien is set on Jazmine being involved, but I wonder whether that was a bit impulsive of him. Jazmine is lovely, we know that, and she would look better in the photos. But I'm wondering, would she be able to answer all the questions he might ask her? She's good at her job, I'm not saying that. But we don't want to miss an opportunity to big up our research or push our need for funding. Do you know what I mean? I just think... Well, you know..."

She trailed off and gritted her teeth. This wasn't going the way she'd planned.

"What is it exactly you're asking, Beth?" Louise asked, sitting down opposite her.

Beth sucked in a deep breath. Always one to get straight to the point was Louise. Some people disliked her for her curtness and no-nonsense approach, but Beth had always appreciated it and often defended her to people like Carla. A man in the same position, with a similar attitude and personality traits, would have been commended for being abrupt and plain-speaking. It didn't make Louise a bitch; it made her good at her job.

"I think I should be more involved," Beth said. "In the visit. I think it would be good for the head of HR – for me - to meet with the Prime Minister. I should be the one who shows him around the department."

Louise sat back in her chair as a frown creased her brow. But it was the sort of frown that was put on for the other person's benefit. A gesture to elicit Beth to explain further.

"I know what Damien said, but we both know he was pissed off at me and I'm hoping now with a bit more perspective he can see the need for a senior member of staff present on the tour. And yes, I have been dismissive of Hopkins in the past, but the more I read about him lately, the more I like what he's about. This is a good thing for the whole hospital. But the success of the Royal Farringdon doesn't rest solely on the shoulders of all the amazing doctors and nurses we have, does it? The HR team, the Operations team, we do good work here and we should be acknowledged. So, I'd like to meet him personally and show him around, so I'm certain he understands how important our role is."

Louise smiled. "I see."

Beth gulped back a mouthful of air. That was more like what she'd been hoping to say. She'd got the part in about being wrong about the Prime Minister too. That was good. They'd assured her there was no way she'd be implicated in his death, but it wouldn't hurt to let people know she liked the guy. That she had no reason at all to want him dead.

"So... What do you think?" she asked.

"I think you're right," Louise said. "And I think Damien will agree with me too once he's had time to think properly about it. But are you sure you want to do this? It's more work and pressure on you."

"Yes. No. I mean, I do want to do it. As I say, I see how good this would be for the hospital and I think I should do the tour."

Louise beamed. "Good. I'm glad about that. I think you'd be a wonderful advocate for what we do up here on the sixth. I'm sure Damien will agree once I've spoken with him. Poor Jazmine, though, we'll have to let her down gently. Maybe we'll still let her jump in on the photo."

Beth smiled, holding her face rigid, hoping she wasn't shaking as much as she imagined. "That's a good idea."

"That settles it then. I'll let the relevant parties know you'll be the one showing the PM around. I'll have to give Downing Street your full details for clearance purposes and all that shit. You okay with that?"

Beth sat upright. "Yes, of course."

"Just procedure, don't worry," Louise added, leaning down to switch on her PC. "Is there anything else you want to talk about?"

She looked up and for a second, Beth wanted to scream, *Yes! Yes, there is something else. My baby girl has been kidnapped and the only way I can get her back is by doing something absolutely terrible.*

But she didn't say of that. Instead, she smiled and shrugged and told Louise thanks, and that she'd see her later. Then she walked the short way back to her office.

Despite her continuing worry - that she wouldn't be able to kill Hopkins when the time came – she was now in position. She had access to the Prime Minister, and she had the murder weapon. Now it was just about waiting for the right moment.

21

The rest of Beth's day flew by in a frantic blur of activity and chaos. As well as her typical tasks, she also had to deal with a barrage of calls and emails about the visit, from Downing Street and the Prime Minister's press office, but also from most of the major UK news corporations. Word had got around about Hopkin's visit, and they wanted access. With every newspaper or TV station that requested a press pass, Beth's unease grew. How the hell was she going to get Hopkins alone to administer the poison with hundreds of extra people around?

That part of the kidnappers' demand had been vague. She assumed they didn't know exactly how she would carry it out, either. That bothered her a great deal. Their only stipulation was she had to do it. Because if she didn't...

It was these thoughts that had her heading straight for the wine rack the second she'd closed the front door behind her. She ran her fingers along the six bottles that lay horizontal in the steel rack and selected a Merlot. She'd have preferred a Chardonnay or something white, but there were none chilled.

Plus, the Merlot had a screw-top, and the last thing she could face right now was to struggle with a bleeding corkscrew.

Bottle open, she grabbed a glass from the cupboard and glugged out a large serving. She was well aware of how unwise this was the night before the fated day, but there was no way she'd get any sleep if she didn't self-medicate in some way. She had sleeping pills upstairs, prescribed to her after the divorce when she was at her lowest ebb, but they always made her drowsy the following day. Tomorrow, she needed her wits about her. A slight hangover was better than feeling like her head was full of cotton wool.

She drank half the glass down in one go. It tasted sharp and vinegary, but she wasn't drinking it for enjoyment.

"Come on, Beth," she said to herself out loud. "You've got to get through this. For Freya."

For Freya.

Those same words had been going over and over in her head all day, like a mantra. A way of keeping herself on track. Tomorrow was going to be the scariest, most troubling and fucked up day of her entire life. Her actions were going to have a dramatic and terrible effect on so many people. She was going to kill someone, for fuck's sake. She was going to murder the Prime Minister. Her. Beth Lomax. A murderer. Probably a terrorist too, if she thought about it, so she quickly pushed that thought from her brain.

For Freya...

All of this for Freya...

Her entire world had been flipped onto its head. Nothing felt real and yet over the last few days she'd sensed the weight of a thousand suns on her shoulders, casting everything in a sombre light.

She took another drink of the wine, almost finishing the glass before placing it down on the island. Her hand was instinctively reaching for the bottle when she heard a phone ring. It was the burner. Where the hell was it? She peered around the room but couldn't see it anywhere. The ringing sounded muffled, and she followed the sound out into the hallway and to her coat, which she'd flung over the end of the bannister on her way to the kitchen.

She yanked the phone out of the pocket on its third ring, flipping it open to answer.

"Yes. I'm here," she gasped as she accepted the call. "It's me."

"Mum..."

The voice was muffled and weak, but it was her. Her baby girl..

"Freya! Are you all right?" A million conflicting thoughts crashed into each other in her brain. "Where are you?"

"Umm, not sure," Freya said. Her voice was quiet and wavered with emotion. "They brought me to a new room to speak with you. It's bright. All I can see is light. Even through the blindfold." She let out a whimper and Beth's heart broke in half.

"Are you hurt?" she asked.

"No. I'm okay. Just hungry and tired. And I just want to come home..." She sobbed.

"Oh, darling, I know you do. I'm doing everything I can to get you home, I promise you. It won't be long now, Frey. Hang in there. Be brave. Yeah?"

"I'm trying. I am." But she was still sobbing, her pitch rising and falling as she struggled to get the words out. "They told me to tell you they're looking after me, but... But that will all change if you don't carry out their demand."

Beth bit her lip, turning to see herself in the hallway mirror. "Don't worry, baby. That's not going to happen. I'm going to do what they're asking." She raised her head, meeting her gaze in the mirror. She hardly recognised the woman staring back at her. "If you're listening, whoever you are, please don't hurt her. I'm going to do what you want. But then you have to let her go. Do you hear me? You have to let her go!"

Freya's sobs were louder now. Beth was crying too.

"I love you, mum."

"I love you too, darling. Please try not to worry. I'm going to see you very soon. I promise. I love—"

The line went dead. Beth glared at her reflection, knuckles whitening around the phone as she fought the urge to smash her fist into the mirror. Instead, she marched into the kitchen, poured the bottle of wine down the sink, and switched out the light.

She knew what they were doing. The call just now was a warning. A reminder of what she would lose if things went wrong tomorrow. But she couldn't let that happen. She wouldn't. She checked the front door was locked and headed upstairs. Whether she would be able to sleep tonight, she didn't know, but tomorrow was the most important day of her life so far. She had to stay clear-headed.

22

Beth straightened her back as the man, (what did he say his name was? Mike? Mark?) continued his briefing.

"...now, the Prime Minister is already downstairs meeting with doctors who I'm told are some of the best heart surgeons in the country." He looked around the room, perhaps expecting a round of applause, but none came. "He'll be coming up to the sixth floor straight after. We're planning on being here no longer than twenty-five minutes. I know that's not long, but the Prime Minister is a busy man, and he has lots going on today. He's going to arrive on this floor via the elevator, and Mrs Lomax, you'll meet him on the main landing..."

He continued talking, but Beth's attention was stuck on those six words. 'No longer than twenty-five minutes'. That was a small window. The first ten of those minutes would be him doing the rounds, shaking hands and offering a jolly 'Good job' and 'Thank you for the great work you do' to all he met. Then she was to show him around the department, the records room, explain a little about the work they did up here (a scripted piece Louise had prepared about the importance of strong foundations and support), then they'd do a few photos, smile for the carefully selected members of the press who were accompanying him into the hospital, and he'd be gone.

Beth had no idea when she might get her chance but knew also if she got too up in her head about it, she could blow the whole thing. Overthinking is the scourge of innovation. It was something Adam used to say. She hated that his words were a help. But he was right. The calmer she remained, and the more level-headed, the more likely she was to see an opportunity. Or even create one if she needed to.

It was, for this reason, she'd set her alarm for 5 a.m. and followed an old yoga DVD before getting ready for work. She used to love yoga but had let her practice slide since the divorce. As she'd stretched and focused on her breath, she'd made a pact with herself that she'd take it up again once this was all over. Because it would be over, she told herself. Very soon. Positive thinking was important too.

But as Beth had sat alone in the office, watching the clock tick by from seven, she'd realised the composure provided by the yoga session and subsequent guided meditation had only really levelled her out to her normal demeanour. Normal that was in the sense of who she was before Freya went missing (slightly anxious, a little stressed, more angry at the world than she was happy to admit) - what normal was for her right now was anyone's guess. After what she'd been through these last few days, she wondered if she'd ever feel 'normal' ever again.

As Mike (definitely Mike) droned on, she slid her hand slowly into her jacket pocket, careful so as not to spike herself. Her fingers rested on the cylindrical body of the syringe. She'd purposefully worn a jacket with large pockets so she could store the syringe and burner phone safely on her person without them showing. After filling the chamber of the syringe with the poison, she'd wrapped the needle in tissue and placed it poison-end down along the edge of her pocket. Her fingers rested on the cylindrical body of the toxic weapon as she nodded along to the briefing, making all the right noises but eager now to get on with it. To get it over with.

She glanced around the room. At all the people here. Everyone had come into the office for this, even those who mainly worked from home. Along with her usual office staff, there were Joe and Ben, the off-site IT guys, Mary from payroll, plus Rita and Simon from Louise's team. A murmur of anticipation filled the air. Everyone seemed very eager to meet the visiting dignitary, to maybe get in the papers and tell their friends and relatives they'd met the Prime Minister. Right before he died.

Beth caught Carla's eye and flicked up her eyebrow. Even she was grinning like an excited schoolgirl at a pop concert.

Jesus. If only they all knew.

A flurry of activity over by the elevators caught Beth's attention.

"Shitting piss," Mark spat. "They must have decided to start the tour on this level. Why am I always the last to know?" Then, to the room. "Okay everyone, the Prime Minister has arrived. Can we all get in our positions, please? Thank you." He grabbed Beth by the arm and pulled her towards the door. "Do you know what you have to do, Mrs Lomax?"

Beth stared back at him.

Was he part of this?

But then he rolled his eyes like he thought she was thick. "You know... Welcome, Sir Gerald... Show him around." He spoke sharply, teeth gritted under a forced smile as he led her through the corridor towards the landing. "Like we've been discussing for the last twenty minutes."

"Yes. Of course," Beth answered as they swerved around the people milling around. Walking up on her toes, she could see someone wearing a green scrub cap with a shock of white hair sticking out at the sides. Below this, the red bloated face of the man himself, Sir Gerald Hopkins. As they got to the landing and the crowds parted, she saw he was flanked by tall men wearing dark suits and impatient expressions, who she assumed to be his security. Her heart dropped into her stomach. There was no way she was going to manage this.

"This is Beth Lomax, Prime Minister," Mike said, a sharp thumb digging into her flesh as he guided her forward. "Head of HR here at Farringdon."

Hopkins turned to take her in, watery blue eyes looking her up and down and a wry smile spreading his thin lips. "Beth, is it?" he bellowed in that way he had that some people found charming. "How lovely to meet you."

"And you, Prime Minister, sir." She held her hand out for him, angry at herself for the involuntary curtsey she wilted into as he took it in his grip.

"And you keep all these talented people in line, do you?" he asked, playing to the crowd, who all chuckled along politely. He didn't let go of her hand as two photographers stepped forward and clicked away at them.

"I try," Beth replied.

"I bet you do." The way he said it, coupled with the twinkle in his eye, made her want to throw up. She held her nerve, kept her smile on. This was it. She was smack bang in the middle of the mission. No going back.

For Freya...

She breathed in and tilted her head to one side. "It's very good of you to come visit us. I know how busy you are. Would you be interested in a brief tour of the department? I can show you what we do here and provide more detail on the Trust and our world-beating research department." She leaned in closer, mirroring his energy as she whispered. "It's all very dry and boring, I'm afraid. But I'll try to jazz it up a bit. And it won't take too long."

He patted her hand, finally releasing it from his clutches. "That sounds wonderful, my dear."

Beth raised her head to the assembled crowd. "I'm going to show the Prime Minister around," she said, addressing the men in suits and the two photographers and trying to control the tension in her face. "But as this is the HR department and there's the risk of data breaches, we will have to ask you to give us some privacy whilst we walk around. We'll be back in a few minutes.

She tensed as Mark dashed forward and whispered something in the Prime Ministers ear. Damn it. It had been a long shot, she knew. But then, to her relief, Hopkins (stepping into that stage-managed persona he often employed, that of bumbling free-spirited libertarian) shooed the aide away with a dismissive wave of his hand.

"We'll be fine," he muttered. "Bloody protocol."

"But Prime Minister—"

"Stop fussing, man!" He turned to Beth, the glimmer in his eye even more apparent. "Beth here isn't going to pounce on me. Are you dear? This is the HR department, after all."

Another ripple of laughter went around the landing, and Beth felt a prickle of nervous energy zip up her spine. Mark backed away, eyes darting between the two bodyguards. Their expressions didn't shift.

"Shall we, then?" Beth asked, walking toward the door on the far side of the landing and easing it open.

"Absolutely. Lead the way, my dear."

Beth was aware of every step she took, every microscopic

movement she made as the door swung shut behind them and they made their way along the corridor. A security camera blinked its one red eye at them from the ceiling. There were a few of them about. She had to step carefully.

"Have you worked here long?" Hopkins asked as they turned the corner, heading for the staff lounge.

"Ten years," Beth told him, slowing to take him in. He was walking hunched over like he usually did, with shoulders raised and hands clasped together over his stomach. She fingered the syringe in her pocket. "It's a great hospital. We do so much important work. Not just the surgeons and doctors but everyone, us up here, our extensive research department, the strategy and fundraising teams. The list goes on, but all with a common goal. I always say to people, I couldn't work anywhere now unless their mission was the same as it is here: to improve people's lives."

This was the truth, but she didn't know why she was telling him. For starters, this old fool didn't care what she thought. She'd always suspected Sir Gerald Hopkins to be one of those typical types of career politician, in it to make as much money for himself and his cronies as possible, and everyone else be damned. Up close, those suspicions hadn't changed. But that didn't make what she was about to do any easier. He was a human being. He had a family.

For Freya...

"That's quite the speech, my dear," he told her, letting out a throaty chuckle before fixing her in the eye. "I get the impression you don't like me very much, do you?"

The comment shook her. Her fingers closed around the syringe, her thumb finding the plunger.

"I don't know you," she said, not stopping as they entered the staff lounge. "I didn't vote for you, but I respect that you've come here today."

He chuckled some more. "Good answer. You know what, I like you, Beth. You're a good woman. Honest. Ballsy."

"Thank you," she told him. "And for what it's worth I'm starting to think I was wrong about you."

As they walked on, Beth's gaze landed on the door to the records department over on the far side of the space. Beyond was a large room with rows and rows of filing cabinets and dusty files stacked up on high shelves. It was the sort of dusty window-less room that made one feel ill, but it was also impressive if you liked admin and data and interesting in an antiquated kind of way. It was also one of the few places she could think of without security cameras.

"Would you like to see where we store patient records?" she asked, already leading him over there. "I can't show you any in particular, but the filing system is the same one used for over a hundred years and—"

"Hang on a minute, will you?"

She stopped and turned around, realising the Prime Minister hadn't followed her. "Is everything all right?"

A grimace twitched at his lips. "That all sounds absolutely terrific," he started. "But the thing is... I don't suppose it could wait a few minutes... I just need to shake hands with the unem-ployed, as it were." He gestured to the bathroom door to his right.

"Oh?" she said, stepping over to him. "Of course."

This was it. This was her chance.

"Won't be a tick," he said with a wink. "Must have had too much coffee."

"No problem. If I can just..." He stepped aside and she leaned around him, swiping her key card over the lock. "Just through there."

"Thank you, my dear."

He shuffled past her, and the door swung shut behind him.

But not entirely, as Beth had jammed her foot against the frame. She cast her gaze around the room. The only security camera in view was in the far corner overlooking the lounge. The bathroom door was in its blind spot. Perfect.

She took a deep breath, slipped the syringe out of her pocket, and entered the bathroom.

23

Beth could hear the Prime Minister muttering to himself as she padded along the short hallway, which opened out into the communal bathroom, complete with showers and lockers. Peering around the tiled wall, she saw he was in one of the cubicles and had left the door hanging open. He was standing with his back to her, legs splayed and head lolling back as he urinated noisily into the bowl.

"That's the bloody ticket," he said.

Beth raised the syringe, thumb tense on the plunger, breath tight in her chest.

Just lunge forward. Jab him in the neck while he's indisposed.

She gritted her teeth, screwed up her face. Why wasn't she doing it? She needed to do it.

For Freya...

For Freya, for god's sake!

She readied herself to advance on him, but before she had a chance, he flushed the toilet and began shaking himself. Beth slipped back around the corner where she was out of sight, then peered back around to watch as he waddled out of the cubicle and shuffled over to the sinks, tucking his shirt into his trousers as he went.

Fucking hell, Beth. Do it.

Do it now!

As Hopkins got to the sinks, he stopped and did a double-take. "Bloody hell," he muttered to himself, shaking his head. "Still wearing the blasted hat."

He reached for the scrub cap and pulled it from his head, placing it on the edge of the sink unit as he attended to his unkempt hair. Beth winced as he spat on his hands and battened down his unruly locks. As he leaned closer to the mirror for a better look, he knocked the scrub cap onto the floor.

"Bloody hell." Grabbing hold of the sink unit, he lowered himself down to pick it up.

And Beth saw her chance.

Stepping into the main space, she was over to him in two strides. She didn't make a sound as he struggled to pick up the fallen hat, fat fingers brushing against the papery material but not making purchase. His lack of agility was clear and, coupled with his age and size, meant Beth didn't have to rush. She held her breath; the syringe poised and ready.

You can do this. Then it's all over. Then you get your baby back. You get your life back.

"Prime Minister? Are you in there?"

Beth froze as a loud banging echoed in the room. Someone at the door outside. She stepped back and placed the syringe behind her back as Hopkins lifted his head.

"Sir Gerald. Are you there?" It was Mark. "Will someone open this door, please?"

Hopkins got to his feet, his eyes meeting Beth's in the mirror. "Beth? What's going on?"

Her eyes widened. "I don't know," she stammered. "I mean, I needed the bathroom, which is why I'm.... I'm sorry... I don't know why... What he's..." She trailed off as the door burst open and Mike stumbled into the room, followed by the Prime Minister's brusque security detail.

"Sir, you need to come with us. Now."

Hopkins spun around, more graceful than Beth had ever seen him. He didn't seem fazed by her presence. That was a good thing. But what was happening now, that wasn't good at all. It felt like her entire world was slipping through her fingers.

As the men hustled into the room, she backed away, still holding the syringe behind her back.

"What is it, Mike?" Hopkins asked.

"We need to leave, sir."

"What? Now?"

"Yes, Prime Minister," Mike shot Beth a look of concern. "It's of a delicate nature. I'll brief you in the car."

"Mike, just spit it out will you, what's happened?"

Mike huffed out a long breath. "I can't say with civilians present. Other than it involves some of our troops in the Middle East being where they shouldn't have been. This could escalate if we don't act now. You need to get back to Downing Street. We've got a call waiting with Al-harbi you can take in the car, and President Anderson has asked for a video call. She's eager to speak with you."

Hopkins paused before giving Beth a weary look. "Sorry about this, my dear," he said. "Duty calls."

Beth went to reply, but Mike and the security guard were already bundling Hopkins out of the room. As the door closed behind them, she slipped the syringe back in her pocket and moved over to the sink. She could feel her heart beating heavily against her rib cage. She didn't know whether to laugh or cry or scream.

"What do I do now?" she asked the wild-eyed woman staring back at her from the mirror. "What the fuck do I do now?"

24

Beth wrapped both hands around the polystyrene cup as she stared without blinking into the hot coffee. She'd been sitting like this in the staff canteen for some time. How long, she wasn't certain. Around her, the room buzzed with heightened chatter, the Prime Minister's visit, and abrupt exit, the talking point of the day. Beth took a sip of the strong sweet drink and lowered it back to the table. Her face was rigid, she felt numb. She stared into the dark liquid, seeing so much more than just coffee, things she didn't want to see. Things no mother should think about.

My little Freya.

She'd had one chance, and she'd blown it. She'd failed. Her attention flitted once more to the burner phone in her pocket. She pulled it out and flipped it open, hoping somehow this would make it ring, or that there'd be a message that had arrived without her noticing. But there were no notifications. Scrolling through the phone's old-fashioned console she found the call list, the one number stored on the phone. Her thumb trembled on the call button. They'd told her specifically not to call until the job was done. But she had to let them know what had happened. That it wasn't her fault. She glanced around; suddenly paranoid people were watching her. She made eye contact with a woman queuing for the coffee machine and quickly looked away. No. She couldn't call them from the staff canteen. She'd go home. Call from there.

She slipped the phone back in her pocket and took another sip of the coffee. It tasted vile. But would anything she drank taste any different right now? Would anything ever taste nice again? Would she ever smile? Would she ever feel happy? Would the sun ever rise?

"Penny for them..."

She looked up. "What? Oh..."

Sammy was standing on the other side of the table. "Hi there. Sorry, you looked deep in thought. Is everything okay?" He was carrying a tray containing a shallow coffee cup and a piece of chocolate cake.

"I'm fine," Beth lied.

"Do you want some company? I've got the afternoon off." He shunted the seat opposite with his hip, an eager smile parting his lips. "May I?"

Beth sighed, perhaps too loudly. But as she glanced around the room, she saw most of the other tables were occupied. Everyone from the higher levels was down here in the canteen, it seemed. But that was probably to be expected. They'd been planning for a grand visit and their plans had been thrown out the window.

"Yes. Sure," she said, gesturing for him to take a seat. "I'm leaving now, anyway.

"Ah, that's a shame," he placed his tray down and sat, leaning over the table as he did. "What a carry-on hey? No one seems to know what's going on."

"I do," she said. "Hopkins got a call when I was with him. Something about British troops in the Middle East. He had to speak with President Anderson." Her voice sounded like a robot's, all the energy and personality wiped away. She coughed and forced a smile. It hurt her to. "So he cut his visit short."

Sammy frowned. He was one of those men who were good at holding eye contact. Usually, Beth thought it to be a pleasant trait. But not today. "Is it that bad?" he asked. "I didn't have you down as a fan of his."

Beth stifled a laugh. If she didn't, she knew it would quickly turn to sobs. "I'm not," she told him. "But, you know... It was a good thing for the hospital, him visiting. People had put a lot of effort in. And now it's all for nothing... Sorry!" She turned her head, her hand darting to her face to wipe at her eyes.

"Beth. What is it?" Sammy whispered.

She glanced at the queue for the coffee machine. The woman was no longer there. "Leave me alone. Please. You just need to leave me alone. I'm not good company."

But Sammy wasn't having it. He pushed his chocolate cake to one side. "What's wrong, Beth? Let me help."

The kindness in his voice was all she could take. A wave of emotion shuddered up her torso and left through her mouth in a loud wail.

"I'm sorry," she stammered. "I've just had a really shitty week. I'm so sorry."

"Hey, hey, it's fine." He moved his chair around the side of the table and put his hand gently over hers. "We all have shitty weeks now and again. It's nothing to be ashamed of. Let it out, I say."

Beth shook her head, unable to speak as the tears fell. She'd been holding it together so well since Freya went missing, but she'd had to. She'd had a mission, something to give her attention to. But now all that had crashed and burned, and she was doing the same. The sky had fallen.

"I'm so fucking sorry," she snivelled, saying it to Sammy, but also to Freya and to herself, too. She hadn't experienced sorrow and despair like this. Not even when Adam told her he was leaving. Hot, salty tears ran down her cheeks, mixing with the streams of snot from her nose.

"Oh heavens. Here." He offered her a napkin off his tray, and she snatched it from him, dabbing at her eyes before opening it out and blowing her nose.

When she could see again, Sammy was still looking at her. He smiled. "Come on, let's go somewhere quiet where we can talk. Or not. Up to you. But let's get out of here." He got to his feet, waiting for her to do the same.

But her legs didn't feel like they belonged to her. "I can't," she whispered. The phone lay on the table, its blank screen mocking her with its lack of notifications.

"Let's go to my office. I've got a decent coffee machine in there. Better than the stuff they serve here."

Beth glanced up and saw him stiffen as he scanned his gaze around the room.

Shit.

She remembered something the kidnappers had said.

We have operatives already placed in the hospital who will take over once you have fulfilled your part of the operation.

Was it Dr Raul? Was he part of this?

Was he going to take her somewhere and kill her?

She caught his gaze but could only see kindness in his eyes. Surely not. It was Dr Raul. Sammy.

He smiled and placed his hand on her shoulder. "Come on," he said again. "Let's get out of here. Somewhere less chaotic."

This time Beth agreed, scooping her phone up and slipping it into her jacket pocket as she stood. If Sammy was involved, then perhaps this was their way of sending her a message. And if that was the case, she needed to talk with them, explain what had happened. She needed to tell them it wasn't her fault and plead with them not to hurt Freya.

She sniffed back. "Okay," she said. "But not your office. Is there anywhere else we can go?"

"My apartment isn't far away. I've got even better coffee there" He glanced at his watch. "It's almost lunchtime. What time do you need to be back?"

"I don't. I've taken the afternoon off as well."

"All right then. My apartment it is then."

"Sounds good," she told him, swallowing back a mouthful of cold coffee, along with most of her emotions. She picked up her bag and slung it over her shoulder. "You lead the way."

25

Beth had wanted to walk to Sammy's place in the hope some fresh air might help her spiralling mood. But in the end, Sammy insisted he should drive, explaining that whilst his apartment was relatively near, it would still take them forty-five minutes on foot. Beth was in no fit state to argue by this stage, so after taking the elevator down to the basement car park, they jumped in his shiny silver Audi and sped away from the hospital.

Beth watched him as he shifted gears and swerved in and out of traffic toward their destination. His face was stern and his jaw stiff, a look of steely determination in his eyes. He saw her looking.

"What?"

Beth shrugged. "Nothing." But it had thrown her a little, seeing him like this. Tense, but in control. In action-mode. Did that mean her suspicions just now were correct? There was certainly more to this man than she'd first realised. But was he really part of the conspiracy?

"Come on, you..." he muttered to himself, slowing down at a

set of lights. He lifted his chin, one hand on the gearstick, the other gripping the wheel at arm's length. He turned to see Beth still staring at him and tilted his head, a grin twisting at his lips. "Yes, I know. I get a bit full-on when I'm driving. I can't help it."

"No, it's fine," Beth replied. "I think."

He shifted the car into first gear, and they set off once more down Liverpool Road toward Islington, the Audi purring softly beneath them. They drove along in silence for a minute more before Sammy took a right and slowed the car to a stop alongside a large area of green space.

"Here we are," he said, nodding to a three-storey apartment block overlooking the green. "Home sweet home."

Sammy's place was on the first floor. Beth followed him up the stairs and onto a long landing that looked out over a small courtyard. It seemed like a nice place to live. But was it the home of a kidnapper? Or a killer?

Once Sammy had unlocked the door, he stepped aside for Beth to enter. A shiver ran down her arms as he beckoned her inside, but she went in regardless. She'd come too far. She had to know.

As soon as he'd closed the door, she rounded on him. "Are you one of them?" she asked.

"Pardon me?" He froze, halfway through taking off his jacket.

Beth stepped closer, intense indignation trumping any fear. "Are you part of what's going on? Do you know where she is?"

"Whoa, Beth, what are you talking about?"

"Freya!"

She yelled her name and then burst into tears. It was too unbearable.

She'd failed.

They'd told her in no uncertain terms what would happen if she failed.

164

"Your daughter? What about her?" She sensed he wanted to come to her, to comfort her, but he remained where he was. "I don't know what you're talking about. What's happened?"

Beth sniffed. "You're not part of it, are you?"

"Not part of what?"

She stared deep into his eyes and all she saw was concern and compassion. "Can I trust you?" she asked.

He frowned but stepped closer. "Of course you can."

"Okay," she said. "Sit down and I'll tell you everything."

It took Beth less time than it took Sammy's expensive-looking coffee machine to warm up to fill him in on all that had happened in the last five days. With a wavering voice, she explained how Freya had gone missing, about the first phone call, and how Beth herself had been blindfolded and dragged into a van. Then she told him about their demand, what she had to do if she ever wanted to see her daughter again.

She had been expecting Sammy to be shocked, sceptical even, but he seemed neither of those things. Instead, he listened to what she had to say without comment, just nodding along or frowning slightly at key points.

When she was finished, she leaned back on the couch, exhausted and trembling. She hadn't taken her eyes off him the whole time she was speaking, waiting for him to baulk, to tell her she was crazy, or an idiot. But he remained still.

"You don't seem shocked," she told him. "The Prime Minister, Sammy..."

"No, I am. It is shocking. Very shocking. I'm just so sorry you've had to go through this alone. I can't even imagine how hard it's been for you."

She sat up and swallowed. "It has been hard. But all I'm

thinking of is Freya. You understand that, don't you? I didn't have any choice. I had to. But now it's all gone wrong." She huffed out a breath, an attempt to keep the sobs at bay. "Do you think they'll have done what they said?

"No. We can't think like that." His hand came up to his chin, and he rubbed at his stubble. "Do you still have the syringe? The poison?"

Beth patted the side of her leather bag. "I was able to squirrel it away in all the commotion."

"Okay. Good."

"Do you think I should have gone to the police?" When he twisted his mouth to one side, she took that as a yes. "Oh, god. I'm such a fool. I was just terrified and confused and didn't know what the hell to do."

"It's fine. You did what you had to."

She leaned forward. "Why aren't you freaking out more?"

He got to his feet. "I am. I've just learned to internalise these things over the years. After I graduated, I worked for Doctors Without Borders for a year and then for two years as a doctor in the Peace Corps. I was in Sudan at the start of the civil war. I saw a lot of horrible things. A lot of scary things. I was kidnapped, actually."

"Really?"

"Me and two of my colleagues. But it was just desperate kids. They returned us after a few days in return for medical supplies and some food. But I know what you're going through, the stress, the not knowing. It's crippling."

"Wow. You're quite the enigma."

He smiled, but it travelled little further than his mouth. "Not really. I enjoyed the work though, even the hint of danger. It tends to focus you."

"You're telling me."

"Oh, shit. I'm sorry, I didn't mean…"

"It's fine. What made you leave?"

His eyebrows rose and fell. "I met my wife. My ex-wife. She convinced me a life back in England was more preferable. And profitable – but that was always her thing. For a while, she was my entire world. So, I came home, married her, and specialised in anesthesiology."

"It must have been a relief, to get away from warzones?"

"From one warzone to another." The eyebrows went again before his face fell into that same serious expression she'd observed on the ride over here. "I've just thought of something. Tell me again about where they took you. What did you see? What did you hear?"

Beth screwed up her eyes to better think. "Not much. They took me from Millennium harbour on the west side of the Isle of Dogs and into a mid-level building somewhere over to the east."

"Mid-level, what does that mean? How many storeys, roughly?"

"Five, maybe."

Sammy stood and Beth watched as he paced up and down in front of her. Telling him had been a big risk, but it seemed to be paying off. He was taking this seriously. He wanted to help her.

Damn it, Beth.

She'd been an idiot to suspect he was anything but a good man. But not only that, he was a good person to have on her side. It had been such a relief to finally tell someone, but it wasn't only that. Dr Raul was somewhat of a dark horse. She already knew he was dependable and kind, yet as he prowled up and down, a scowl darkening his fine features, it struck Beth how strong and forceful he was.

"Could you hear birds of any kind, seagulls?"

"Maybe. It was very near the river; I could smell it. Through the blindfold, I could see two buildings silhouetted against the sky. There was nothing else around from what I could make out."

"Got you," Sammy said, holding a finger in the air. He hurried away through a door leading off from the open plan living room and reappeared a few moments later carrying an open MacBook. He placed it down on the coffee table and sat beside her, leaning into it and opening up Google Maps. He tapped something into the search field and tilted the laptop her way. "Here, what do you think?"

Beth narrowed her eyes at the screen. It showed the east side of the Isle of Dogs and a red marker pin in the bottom-right section.

"It's called Cubic Wharf," he said. "My ex-wife is an estate agent. She was working with the developers on the project before it all fell through. It was one of those typical situations, bought up in the early two-thousands by people looking to make a quick buck, then abandoned when the recession hit. There are a lot of derelict buildings like that around the city. But it's got to be one of those buildings. Do you think that's where they're holding Freya, too?"

Beth stared at the screen. "I'm not sure."

"But it's a possibility." Sammy was over by the door, putting his jacket back on. "Come on. We need to get over there."

Beth got to her feet. "What?"

He grabbed up his keys from the sideboard where he'd placed them, eyes scanning the room as he did. "I know what they told you, Beth, but the situation has changed." He reached for her, beckoning her to follow him.

"But these people are dangerous. We can't."

"We're just going to have a look, see what we're dealing

with. Okay? Once we know for certain, we can have a rethink. But if you ask me, we need to act. Now."

Beth glanced at her hands. Then back at Sammy. His expression was all the reassurance she needed. "Okay," she told him. "Let's go."

26

Beth followed her new ally down to his car and they set off across London. Sammy driving in his now familiar manner, foot down, weaving around other cars, trying to gain distance at every opportunity. Normally this would have given Beth cause for concern, but today she was thankful for the speed and her companion's confidence. She clung to the door handle, leaning into the car as it swerved and jolted, not slowing down for a second. She was surprised, also, at how determined she felt, how clear-headed and focused. It was more than likely adrenaline rather than bravery or resolve, but who the hell knew anymore?

"Thank you so much for helping me," she told him as they zoomed along Dalston Road towards Hackney Wick. "I don't know what I'd be doing right now if you weren't here."

"Don't mention it," Sammy replied, not taking his eyes from the road. "Listen, I've been thinking. There's one aspect of all this we haven't talked about."

"Oh? What's that?"

"The why. Why are these people doing this? Why do they want Hopkins dead?"

Beth peered out the side window. The thought had crossed her mind, but with nothing to go on, she'd not considered it too deeply. She was mainly concerned about the how. As in, how did she get her daughter back?

"What are you thinking?" she asked.

Sammy pouted his lips. "I've got a few ideas. You know he's about to sign a big deal with Braxxon Kleiner?"

"I heard, yes. They're an American company."

"Oh yes. Big, bad U.S. Pharma. It's a massive, multi-billion-dollar deal, and no one is that clear yet on the ramifications. It could be bad for British pharmaceutical companies."

"And you think they might be behind this?"

"I don't know. It's a theory."

They were in the heart of the east end now, with Fish Island on their left and Bow over to their right. Up on the horizon, Beth could see the distinctive shape of One Canada Square. They weren't far away.

"Would you really kill someone over a business deal?"

Sammy turned to her with raised eyebrows. "Over money, Beth. A lot of money. Often, that's more than enough reason. I know it's not a particularly controversial statement, but if you ask me, most of the world's ills are caused by greed and money."

Beth didn't know how to respond to this. Instead, she looked out the window as they travelled through Blackwall Basin, heading for the docks.

"How was Freya?" Sammy asked as they pulled up to traffic lights. "When you spoke to her, I mean."

"The first time she sounded scared but also sounded like herself if that makes any sense. But the second time... I don't know. There was genuine terror in her voice."

Her voice broke, and she turned to the window to catch a stray tear. There was no real reason to do this. Sammy had seen her crying once already today. But to hide it from him was to hide it from herself as well.

"From everything you've told me, she sounds like a clever girl, and resilient too," Sammy said. "Don't give up on her."

"She's so small," Beth wailed, unable to stop herself. "She's my baby."

"And we're going to get her back."

"Are we?"

He didn't answer as the lights changed to green and they set off over Aspen way onto Canary Wharf. Beth found a tissue in her coat pocket and blew her nose as Sammy put his foot down and they sped past the south docks onto the Isle of Dogs.

They were now on a long road that spanned around the edge of the peninsula and as they got closer to their destination, an eerie silence fell over the car. Beth was still scared and unsure about what the hell Sammy expected them to do when they got there but understood his reasoning. At least if they knew they had the right place, they could form a plan. If that involved calling the police, she didn't know. But as Sammy had said, they had to act. They had to do something. She stuffed the tissue back in her pocket and felt the outline of the burner phone. It still hadn't rung or vibrated or done anything. She pulled it out and checked the battery and volume controls for the tenth time that day. All in working order. Why hadn't they got in touch?

Please get in touch.

"Look, there."

She raised her head, following Sammy's finger as he pointed over to the right where two buildings stood alone about fifty metres apart. Each perfectly square structure stood on barren wasteland and neither looked inhabited. Beth's heart sank as she surveyed the scene. Was this really where they'd brought her darling child? It had all sounded so plausible sitting in Sammy's apartment. She'd even allowed herself to feel hopeful. But seeing these bleak buildings silhouetted against the grey London skies, she wasn't so sure. Even if she had been here, the kidnappers' plan had failed. She'd failed. They could have packed up and left by now, worried their cover had been blown. Freya could be anywhere by now. She might never see her again.

Oh, God, no.

The very thought she'd been pushing away ever since Freya went missing now hit her hard and without warning. But it was true. She might never see her again. Perhaps it was time she faced that fact. Overwhelming nausea washed over her and she worried she was going to be sick. Gripping hold of the handle above the side window, she inhaled and exhaled to try to calm herself. It did little good.

"Hang in there," Sammy said as he slowed the car. They drove alongside both buildings, the two of them peering out of Beth's side window as they passed. Sammy veered the car around in a wide arc, approaching the first building from the south side and coming to a stop at the edge of the sprawling wasteland that surrounded it. Up close, the building looked even more derelict and uninhabited and as Beth cast her gaze up the side, she saw no lights or sign of life on any of the floors. Her heart broke a little more.

"It's useless," she said. "Isn't it? What the hell do we do now? I'm sorry for dragging you into this, Sammy. But I don't think we've—"

"Wait. Look over there," he said, cutting her off and leaning over the steering wheel. "Can you see?"

"What?" Beth raised herself off the seat, craning her neck around the side of the building. "Oh, bloody hell, yes, I see it!"

There it was. Parked up between the two buildings, sitting

there like a black shiny beast. The same Ford Transit van she'd been in two days earlier. It was them; she was sure of it. They were still here. And if that was the case, maybe Freya was, too.

27

Freya Lomax might have possessed a certain amount of what her dad called 'innate street-smarts', but she had scant experience of real life. Indeed, she hadn't needed to delve too deeply into her acting toolbox to portray an innocent and vulnerable girl. Yet even she could tell things had gone sour.

It had started late morning, with phones ringing and hurried footsteps in the corridor, then all three guards raising their voices at each other. Once alone with Newspaper Man, she'd pressed him for answers but like always, he'd told her to be quiet. Told her she should keep her head down and if she did that, all would be well. But then she'd heard him speaking in hushed tones to someone on the phone. Asking, "What the fucking hell is going on, then? What do we do now?"

But it wasn't these comments that had brought the fear bubbling up inside Freya. That was when he'd walked over to the furthest corner of the room and lowered his voice even more into the phone.

"What about the girl?"

She couldn't help letting a yelp of anguish escape from her

throat when she heard him say that, but had tried to pass it off as a cough. When he'd finished on the call, she'd asked him what he'd been talking about, believing it would be better to know her fate. But once again, he'd been non-committal. He said it was all going to be fine and that she shouldn't worry. But the atmosphere had definitely shifted and as the tension in the room grew, so did the dread inside of her.

What about the girl?

What about her?

Had these evil men changed their minds about whatever it was they were planning on doing with her? Was it now only a matter of time before they dragged her away to kill her, to slice her up, or worse?

She shook her head, trying but failing to shake the terrifying thoughts from her mind.

After Newspaper Man left, the older of the two foreign guards took over. This was the guard she hated the most. He was gruff and rude and was constantly snorting back phlegm and spitting it across the room. Every time he did it her stomach turned over.

Today was even worse. He had done nothing but snort and grumble ever since he sat down. He stank too, worse than usual, a sour chemical stench that reminded Freya of the smell of ammonia or her mum's morning breath when she'd stayed up late drinking wine. Freya had never drunk alcohol herself, but she knew what a hangover was. She knew they gave you headaches and made you act carelessly.

"What's going on?" she asked the man once there was a lull in the snorting and spitting.

"Shut up."

"Has something happened? Are you going to hurt me?" She didn't know where she was going with this line of questioning, and she didn't expect an answer. All she knew was this was zero hour, and she had to try something.

"You talk too much, you know that."

Freya giggled. The sort of phoney laugh some of her classmates did whenever they had English with Mr Chaplin and he made a lame joke. It was fake and girly, and Freya hated them for it.

"Really? Do you think I do?" she asked, tilting her head to one side.

She was grasping at straws. Desperate. Over the past few days, especially when Newspaper Man had been guarding her, she'd fallen into a feeling of – not security, exactly - but like she was going to be okay if she held her nerve and played the game. But now she sensed her safety ebbing away fast.

She shifted on the mattress; the metal bar was still there underneath. She had to get to it, but any sudden movement would alert the guard. If he was hungover, then he wouldn't be as watchful or responsive, but he was still a grown man, hired specifically to make sure she didn't escape. He was still scary. What chance did she have?

She snapped her awareness back to the moment as the guard burst out coughing. It was harsh and loud, and made the chair he was sitting on creak beneath him. He got to his feet.

"Oh, fucking hell," he moaned between more coughs. "Oh, Jesus."

Freya heard him shuffling around and grumbling some more. She didn't speak. She didn't move. The metal bar was under her right foot on the mattress. If she rolled over now, she could slide her hand under and pull it out. She pictured the man bent over. She pictured herself rising up and smashing the makeshift weapon down on the back of his head, knocking him unconscious. Only in this imagined scenario she was six feet tall and had no fear of anything. The reality was rather different.

"Fuck me," the man spluttered before another coughing fit sent him reeling. "You have water?"

Freya shrugged. Newspaper Man had brought her a bottle of water along with the crappy cereal bar which comprised her breakfast, but she'd already drunk it. "I don't think so."

"All right, don't do anything." The man was stumbling over to the door, his voice still strained and husky. "I be back in a moment."

Every muscle in Freya's body tensed as she heard the door open and then close. But the man hadn't shut it properly. For the last few days she'd been listening carefully to the sound of entrances and exits, the noise the door made each time. She guessed that the wood of the door was slightly warped because everyone who came in had to close it manually, with a loud *thunk*.

She straightened her back and pulled the blindfold down off her face. Yes. The door appeared to be shut, but the lights on the electronic swipe-lock showed two green lights and one yellow rather than the three red ones that had been on when Newspaper Man allowed her to remove the blindfold.

It was now or never.

She jumped from the mattress onto her feet and reached underneath for the metal bar. Standing, she gripped it in two hands, getting a feel for it before raising it above her head. It was heavy, but not so heavy she couldn't swing it with some force. Whether that was enough force to stop a grown man, she didn't know, but it was all she had. With every muscle rigid and her skin tingling with nervous energy, she padded over to the door and tried the handle.

She was right.

It was unlocked

This was it.

Carefully, she eased the door open and peered around the

side of the frame. The corridor was dark and stretched out in both directions. To her left, she made out three doors standing at intervals, but it was so dark she couldn't see to the end of the corridor. Craning her head to the right, she saw light emanating from around the corner at the far end. That way seemed the best option. She could sense static in the air coming from that direction as well, something electrical, which she hoped was the elevator. As she left the room and headed towards the light, she heard footsteps around the corner and the coughing bluster of the guard.

No.

Please no.

She was so close.

With her heart racing and every cell in her body throbbing with anxious tension, she retraced her steps back into the room and closed the door behind her, making sure she heard the click of the lock. Once inside, she stepped around the side of the door and pressed herself against the wall.

This was it.

Now or never.

A second went by, then another. She heard the guard on the other side of the door muttering to himself. The door handle rattled, and she stifled a yelp, catching it in her throat before it could give her away. The door rattled some more, and her eyes shot over to the chair. Had he left his key card here? If he had to go get help, she was done for. There was no way she'd ever make it past two of them. She clasped the metal bar in front of her; her knuckles burning from the tautness of her grip. It felt like time had stopped. On the other side of the door, the man coughed. But then he gasped in a way that sounded like relief.

"Ah shit, here you are..."

She heard a key card being slid down the lock mechanism and waited for the beep. When it came, she straightened up to her full her height and raised the metal bar over her shoulder like she would do a rounders bat.

Come on, motherfucker

The voice in her head didn't sound like hers. But that was because it wasn't her. This was the voice of the warrior woman. The role she needed to take on if she was going to survive this ordeal. The warrior woman was bold and brave. She was angry as hell and ready for war.

She could do this.

The door opened, and the man stumbled into the room, coughing as he went and holding a large wad of tissue paper up to his mouth. He strode into the room, past where Freya was standing, and stopped. The door was hanging open. She could slip out now and run for her life, all the way to the elevator. But even in the warrior woman's shoes, she was unsure she'd make it. The guard may have been unwell, but he was almost three times her size. She adjusted her grip on the metal bar. It had to be this way. He had his back to her but was still wiping at his nose and mouth and making pathetic snivelling noises. He was yet to notice she wasn't on the mattress.

And this was it.

This was her chance.

Letting out a scream, she launched herself at him. His upper body stiffened at the sound of danger, but before he could turn around Freya swung the metal bar, smashing it into the side of his head. It made a dull thud, and the metal juddered against her palms, but she kept hold, too full of adrenaline now to notice pain. The man yelled out and staggered forward, his hand going to his head. But the blow didn't knock him out as Freya had imagined. He didn't even fall over. As he twisted around to face her, she swung the weapon over her head and brought it down on the side of his forehead.

Then she ran.

Out the door and down the corridor to the right, pushing off from the corner as she headed out onto a wide landing. Two doors stood in front of her. One metal, which she assumed to be the elevator, the other painted white with a small window centre top. Above this one was a sign, *Fire Exit*. She paused, jumping from foot to foot as she assessed the situation. In her head, she'd planned on making her escape via the elevator, but it was slow and might take time to arrive. Behind her she heard movement, then a voice.

"Get back here. Stupid bitch." Then, much louder. "She's attacked me. She's loose."

That settled it.

Freya ran for the fire exit and burst through the door. In front of her was another, smaller landing and a stone stairwell that spiralled down to the ground floor. Grabbing the handrail, she set off, taking the steps two, three, four at a time and skidding around the landing on each level, hauling herself along with the handrail. She'd been on the top floor, and she counted four below her. Behind her, she heard the man again, shouting something she couldn't make out. If he was calling the lift, that meant he'd have to wait for it arrive. She'd be free before he got down there.

She sped across the third-floor landing and jumped down the next flight of stairs, all ten of them. As she landed, her ankles seared with pain, but she didn't lose her pace, reaching for the handrail and pulling herself along. She still had the metal bar in her other hand and was bracing herself ready to use it. She had the fire inside of her now. She was no longer Freya Lomax, young, naïve schoolgirl. She was one hundred per cent the warrior woman. Fierce, daring, savvy. Nothing could stop her. She ran along the next landing and headed down the next set of stairs. Two more flights to go. She could see the ground floor. She could see the door leading out to the main space.

"She's here. In the stairwell. Get here." The guard's voice echoed down from the fifth floor, followed by the sound of heavy footsteps on the stairs. But she'd put too much distance between them. There was no way he could catch her.

She jumped down the last few steps and charged at the door, falling through into a large open plan entrance hall. Fifty metres in front of her, she could see the main doors of the building. Three glass doors stood in a row: two of them were boarded up, but the third looked useable. The glass was grimy, but the metal surroundings had buckled so it didn't shut properly. It was her exit to freedom.

With the man in the stairwell gaining on her, she set off at pace towards the exit, but she hadn't travelled more than a few steps when Newspaper Man and the other guard appeared from another door next to the main entrance.

"Shit," Newspaper Man spat. "You are joking."

Operating fully in survival mode, the warrior woman swerved to one side as the other guard lunged forwards, his arms outstretched, trying to grab her. She swung the metal bar wildly but found nothing but air as she continued on her path. The guard righted himself and gave chase, snarling with rage behind her. She was almost at the doors when she felt a hand close around her arm.

"No!" she screamed. "Get off."

The guard kept hold, and the momentum sent the two of them spinning around like they were involved in some terrible dance. Freya slammed the metal bar onto the man's hand, trying to get him to release her. But he held on tight. This wasn't fair. She was so close. So close...

The room spun even faster as something heavy slammed into them. Now the guard let go and Freya stumbled backwards to see it was Newspaper Man. He glared at her, his face rigid with anger, his eyes wide.

"Go," he yelled.

She didn't need telling twice. Turning, she set off, almost falling over her feet but righting herself in time. She ran for the exit. But as she got up to the door, a loud bang filled the air. Twisting around, she saw the guard pointing a gun at Newspaper Man who was clutching at his stomach, a look of puzzlement wilting his stern expression.

Freya went to cry out, but her throat was so dry no sound came out. She stared wide-eyed as the gunman moved his aim towards her. But she'd come too far now. She wasn't going to stop. Turning, she grabbed the door handle, ready to throw all her weight back to get it open. But before she had a chance, another gunshot cracked through the air. She tensed, searching her body for pain. But as she glanced back over her shoulder, she saw the guard has his gun aimed at the ceiling.

"Stop or I kill you."

But Freya didn't stop. A cool breeze hit her in the face as she yanked the door open. This was it. Now or never. As the man screamed after her and another warning shot permeated the air, she fell through the door and out to freedom.

28

Two seagulls as big as vultures circled over the bleak wasteland as Beth and Sammy got out of the car.

"Which building do you think it was?" he asked, leaning against the car door.

Beth stuck out her bottom lip. She had no idea. The one closest to them was nearest to the road, so possibly that one. She closed her eyes, trying to remember her journey in the back of the van. She remembered the ground becoming uneven as they drove across broken concrete. But where the van was parked up, they could have dragged her into either building from there.

"What are we planning on doing?" she asked, opening her eyes and looking across the car roof at Sammy.

He met her gaze, and the serene determination on his face that had so buoyed her in his apartment suddenly riled her. Why wasn't he talking? What was he thinking?

"Sammy?"

"If she's in there, Beth, she's probably well-guarded." She shook his head. "I think we need to tell the police. They'll know what to do."

"They told me no police, or they'd hurt Freya. I've told you

184

that. Shit! I've already messed everything up. And now I've got you involved too. What an absolute idiot"

"The police won't storm in all guns blazing, Beth. They'll have tactical units. Ways of approaching these sorts of situations?"

"Yes, and what if the people inside get spooked and kill her?" She felt the tears rising again, but she didn't care. "What if she's already dead?"

He looked at her with a concerned frown. "Have you heard from them?"

"Oh shit, of course. Maybe I should check." Sarcasm was never really Beth's forte, but today she just sounded nasty. She also didn't care. "No, Sammy, they haven't been in touch. I've checked the phone every two seconds."

"All right. Fine. Just asking." He smiled. "Hey, I'm new to all this as well, you know. Just trying to figure it all out."

"Yes, I know. I'm sorry. I'm just terrified and stressed."

Sammy's nostrils flared. He turned his attention back to the buildings and so did she. Away from the cut and thrust of the city, the only sounds were the chirp of the gulls and the dull hum from faraway traffic. It was too quiet. It made her queasy.

"Do you think the main people are in there?" Sammy asked.

"Do you?"

He shook his head. "Doubtful. I'd imagine they've got people guarding Freya, but the real culprits are probably lounging in some penthouse somewhere. Or in Russia."

"Yes, well, I don't care. All I want is my daughter back. They can do whatever they want. Kill the entire government. I don't care. Just let me have Freya back."

"You don't mean that," he told her. "We can't let them get away with this, Beth. What they're trying to do is... Wait. Look. Over there."

She followed his gaze over to the far building. One of the

main doors had swung open and as she looked on, a lone figure stumbled from the building. It was a young girl with dark hair, wearing a school uniform.

"Freya?" She narrowed her eyes, uncertain at first. But it had to be her. She stepped forward. "Freya!"

From this distance, she couldn't make out the girl's features, but it was clear she was terrified. She looked feral. Her lank, matted hair whipped across her face as she peered about her.

Beth yelled again, and this time the girl looked her way.

"Mum!"

It was her. It was really her. Leaving the car behind, Beth broke into a run, eyes fixed only on her baby girl. There were over a hundred yards between them, but the distance felt like nothing at all. Freya was free. Her little girl was coming home.

"Beth," Sammy cried out after her. "Wait!"

But she couldn't wait. Her sides ached and her eyes stung, but she kept going, even as Sammy caught up with her and grabbed at her arm.

"Stop! Look!"

He yanked her towards him and as she slowed down, through a haze of tears, she saw two men running from the building. One of them was tall, the other broad, but both were fast and they were heading after Freya.

"They're armed," Sammy yelled. But Beth had already seen the guns in their hands. She screamed, but the noise that came out of her sounded like a desperate animal caught in a trap. A primal scream of hopelessness. She struggled against Sammy's clutches, trying to get away, to get to her daughter.

As she watched on in despair, the taller man caught up with Freya and grabbed her around the waist. He scooped off her feet and jammed a gun into the side of her head.

"NO!" Beth cried, the force of the scream ripping at her parched throat.

"Mum, help me," Freya yelled. She looked petrified. Tear tracks ran down her grubby face. "Help me. Please."

Beth wrenched her arm out of Sammy's grip, gasping for air. "I need to get her—"

"Stop right there or I kill her here and now." The man holding Freya jutted his chin, regarding Beth with wide, unblinking eyes. "I mean it. Stay back."

She stopped and held her hand out. "Don't hurt her."

The second man moved around the side of his colleague and raised his gun, waving it between Beth and Sammy. "Get back. Now."

"Please..." Beth sobbed. "She's terrified. She needs me..."

"Get back."

The man holding Freya was dragging her back towards the building. He'd pocketed his gun and had his hand around her mouth as she struggled and tried to scream. As they got to the door, Freya stared at Beth, a look of abject fear in her eyes. Then the man hauled her into the building and the door closed behind them.

"No," Beth whimpered. "Please, no."

The other man backed away, gun still trained on her and Sammy and a sharp sneer twisting at his lips. "Stupid bitch."

"Beth, leave it," Sammy whispered, stepping over to her. "Not like this." He wrapped one arm around her shoulder and gripped her arm with his other hand, holding her back in case she decided to charge. But she wasn't going to do that. She couldn't. Her legs didn't feel like they belonged to her.

As the gunman got to the entrance of the building, he lowered his gun and gave her a stern nod, then he was gone.

As the door swung shut, Beth wilted in Sammy's arms. It was if she'd been holding onto so much emotion it had grown too heavy to bear. "My baby," she whispered. "They've got my baby."

Sammy hugged her tight. "I know. But we've got to get out of here. Do you understand? We can't stay here. It's bad for us. It's bad for Freya too."

He was trying to stay calm, maybe for her sake, but she picked up on the fear in his voice all the same.

"What are we going to do?" she asked, as he led her back to the car.

But he didn't answer. Maybe because he was too shaken up, maybe because he didn't have an answer. He just opened the car door and climbed in behind the wheel. And at that moment, Beth lost all hope of getting her daughter back.

29

It could have taken them twenty minutes to get back to Sammy's apartment, or it could have been three hours. Time had lost all meaning to Beth as they left the concrete wasteland behind and drove into the city. She'd rested her head against the side window, watching but not seeing as they sped through the late-afternoon traffic. Every so often, her eyes would fall on her reflection in the wing mirror and every time it shocked her to see the woman staring back. She looked like a ghost. She had red rings around her eyes and her hair was stuck to her face with tears. But so what? What did it matter what the bloody hell she looked like? Nothing mattered now, and nothing would ever matter again.

"Here we are," Sammy said, as he pulled into a parking space opposite his building.

Beth snorted down her nose. She knew he was only saying something to break the awkward silence, but his words sounded so banal she wanted to scream.

"Let's go inside," Sammy said, clicking off his seatbelt. "I'll make us a drink."

"I don't want a drink."

"Let's go inside, regardless. We can't sit in the car."

He got out and slammed the door shut. It made Beth jump. She waited another few seconds and then unfastened her seat belt and climbed out. Sammy waited for her to join him on the roadside before remotely locking the car. Together, but in silence, they crossed the street, entered the apartment block, and climbed the stairs to the first floor. Once safely inside Sammy's apartment, he switched on the coffee machine.

"Have you got anything stronger?" Beth asked, walking into the lounge and slumping onto the couch.

"I guess so. But is that wise?"

"I don't bloody know. But it's needed." She was being a bitch, and it wasn't helping, but she couldn't stop herself.

She watched as Sammy placed both hands on the kitchen island and lowered his head. He looked like he was in deep prayer. Then he looked up and sighed. "Okay. Fine."

Beth sat back on the couch and stared at the stark white wall in front of her. It was strange; she felt nothing. She had no thoughts. All she was certain of was that life as she knew it had shifted. Is this what going crazy felt like? A minute passed by and it felt like forever.

"Here you go."

She looked up as a glass of amber liquid hovered in her eye-line. When she didn't take it from him, Sammy placed it down on the coffee table. The couch pitched as he sat down beside her.

"This is thirty-year-old scotch," he said. "My brother bought it for me when I qualified as an anesthesiologist." He paused, swallowed some of his drink, and sighed. "Sorry. I just don't know what to say."

Beth reached for her glass and drank back a mouthful without looking at it. It tasted horrible and burnt her sinuses. "What am I going to tell Adam?"

"Adam?"

"My ex-husband. Freya's dad. How am I going to tell him that his daughter is gone, and it's my fault?"

"Beth. No. Don't talk that way." His voice was stern, unwavering. "I mean it. You're talking like it's all over. It isn't. We can still get her back."

She turned to face him and there it was again, that determined expression, the eyes alert and ready. "How?" she asked, feeling some of her life-force return.

He grimaced as if in concentration, or annoyance. "Things didn't go to plan this morning with Hopkins. But you said they've got other operatives inside the hospital. They'll know it wasn't your fault. Plus, they're most likely in disarray right now. Not knowing what to do. It might be the perfect time."

Beth adjusted herself on the sofa. "For what?"

"I think it's time we involved the police. I know what you think, and what they told you. But I don't see any other way."

"These operatives that are supposedly working at the hospital." She narrowed her eyes at him. "Do you think that's possible?"

He leaned back. "You don't still think I'm involved, do you?"

"No. I don't know. But I don't know what I think. I'm exhausted and my nerves feel like they can't take any more."

Sammy took the glass from her and placed it alongside his on the coffee table. When he turned back, his expression was kind but serious. Beth imagined this was the face he used when talking to patients. All doctors had one.

"Freya's still alive and we know where they're keeping her. And they know we know that. I don't think they're going to hurt her while you're still 'active'. They've got too much to lose."

Beth frowned. "While I'm still active?" It was things like this that made her suspicious of him.

"Sorry. I read too many spy novels. All I mean is you know too much for them to force your hand by doing something drastic. And yes, maybe contacting the police is a dangerous move. But time is of the essence here. Those men we saw today were hired thugs. They had to be. They won't do anything without an order from the top dogs. The people paying their wages. Who, as I say, will have been chasing their tails since their plan failed. And that's not down to you. They'll understand it wasn't your fault." He reached for her hand, laying his other reassuringly on top of hers. "But if we act now, maybe we can catch them off guard."

Beth chewed her lip. "But what if the police storm into that building and something goes wrong? It happens, doesn't it?"

"What's the alternative?"

She looked down, her eyes drifting over to the glass of scotch as a shiver of indignation sharpened her resolve.

"Sorry, I don't mean to sound brutal," Sammy added, tilting his head, trying to make eye contact. "I'm just trying to be realistic, that's all. If these people are spooked, that's a good thing. But we need to get the police involved. Before they—"

Beth's head shot up, the two of them locking eyes as the burner phone chirped in her pocket. She scrambled to get it out and flipped it open.

"Yes, yes! I'm here," she stammered as she pressed the phone to her ear. "Are you there?"

The line was silent except for a low hum. She looked into Sammy's expectant face and shook her head. A crackle of distortion filled her ear, and she moved the phone away. Then a voice boomed out.

"That was idiotic, Beth Lomax."

The caller was using the same digitally altering device as before, but it was a different person. The underlying tone was a little higher.

"I did everything you told me to," she replied, spitting the words out in rapid staccato. "It wasn't my fault. I was there. I was ready. But his people came in. They took him away."

"You should not have come looking for your daughter. You should not have involved anyone else. We told you what would happen if you did either of those things."

Beth let out a cry. "No. I'm sorry, I'm so sorry." She placed her hand over her mouth to stem the sobs, which were seconds away from erupting. "Please don't hurt my baby."

"Freya is safe. For now. She will be moved to a different location. If you try to find her again, we will kill her." The line went quiet. "Do you understand, Beth?"

"Yes."

Sammy held his arms out, mouthing, "What is it", but she waved him away.

"What do I do now?" she asked. "How do I get Freya back?"

There was no answer. The line went quiet, same as before.

"Are you still there?" she asked. "Please. What do I do?"

A crackle of static came over the line. "Keep this phone close and await our instruction," the voice told her.

"Yes. Okay. Thank you."

Tears were rolling down her cheeks. A part of her was angry for feeling so grateful, but she couldn't help it. The world had spun off its axis.

"But Beth," the voice continued. "If you or your doctor friend say anything to the police about this, if you say anything to anyone, then Freya *will* die. Do I make myself clear?"

Beth looked into Sammy's eyes. "Yes. You do. No police. I promise."

"Good. Then await another phone call."

A high-pitched squeal came down the line, and then it went dead. Beth lowered the phone from her ear.

"No police?" Sammy repeated.

She sniffed. "No. We can't. They know. They know about everything." She reached for the scotch and tipped it down her throat. It burned all the way down.

"That means we have to find another way," Sammy told her.

Beth bit her lip. "They saw you. They know about you. You're in danger too now, Sammy. I'll understand if you don't want to help me."

He tilted his head to one side with a frown. "Of course I want to help you. I'm part of this now." He picked up his glass and stared off into the middle distance. "Don't worry Beth. Whatever it takes. We're going to get Freya back."

30

Freya didn't dare move as the men yelled at each other in broken English. Not that she could have moved much, even if she wanted to. The second they were back inside the building, one guard had shoved the thick black sack over her head, whilst the other bound her wrists and ankles with more painful plastic ties. The drawstrings of the sack were so tight around her neck she could hardly move her head. If she moved even a fraction of an inch in either direction, the rough material pressed on her windpipe and choked her.

But she'd seen her mum. Her beautiful, brave mum. She'd come for her. That was the only explanation Freya could come up with why she was there. She'd come to rescue her. And if she knew where she was being held, then surely it was just a matter of time before she succeeded. Freya didn't recognise the man she was with, but her hope was he was a police officer, someone else brave and strong who would help them.

"You facking idiot. You let them get away?" The taller man was yelling. "I thought you were going to grab them."

"No one told me to. This is not part of the plan. No one told us to do this."

The taller man stepped forward. It looked like he was going to hit the other one. "And now they know where we are. You idiot. Where the girl is. Shit. We have to let everyone know. This is very bad. You are a moronic man you know this?"

Freya listened as the guards continued to argue. Seeing their faces up close just now, she knew now the taller man was dark-skinned and looked Turkish or Arabic. In contrast, his partner was most likely Eastern European if his colouring, accent and facial features were anything to go by. She presumed they were the same men who'd grabbed her off the street, but in her memory, those men were just dark sinister outlines with red demonic eyes. But that made sense to her, and she understood why her imagination had created them that way. As she'd stared into their eyes, she'd seen no semblance of humanity at all. Rather, these ogres, with their big, grabbing hands and scars on their faces, seemed like embodiments of hate and anger and greed. And they were completely terrifying.

"You are a very stupid girl, you know this. Make us look bad. Mess everything up."

Freya flinched. It was the Eastern European guard talking to her.

"I'm sorry," she whispered, as the last of the warrior woman energy left her body. "But I just want to go home. I just want my mum. Why are you doing this?"

The man huffed angrily. "You fuck everything up. Make us look like fools."

"Is the other man dead?" she asked.

"The *other man* is a fool, too. And he paid the price for that foolishness. You will too if you try running away again."

Freya nodded. It hurt her neck. The guards carried on talking to each other, but in hushed tones now. She listened, trying to pick out any words or phrases, but she got nothing. The conversation went on for a few minutes until she heard the tall one say, "Okay, I go and call them and explain what has happened, ask them what they want us to do."

A shiver ran down Freya's spine. *Someone walking over her grave.* A whimper of emotion followed the thought, the memory of her gran and her strange sayings bringing no joy with it today. In fact, right now, the phrase only sounded worryingly prophetic. But if they were going to kill her, she had to try something. Anything. She coughed out the sorrow as best she could, remembering something Newspaper Man had told her.

"I know you're just hired hands," she said. "And that someone else bigger and more powerful is paying you to do this. But you don't have to do it. You don't have to be a bad guy."

The man sneered. "You don't know what you're talking about. You don't know who you're talking to."

"That's right," she said, some of the warrior woman energy flooding back. "I don't know who you are. I don't know your names; I hardly saw your faces. I couldn't pick you out of a police line-up."

It was a phrase she'd heard in some movie, and it was also a total lie. These men were no longer black outlines, with demonic eyes, part of her overactive imagination. They were real. Very real. Indeed, she suspected she'd be seeing their scarred, surly faces whenever she closed her eyes for as long as she lived. But if that was the case, she'd also like to test that theory well into old age.

"You can let me go and you'd be safe to go too," she went on. "I won't call the police. I won't let my mum call them. Ever. Just open the door and I'll run. I won't stop."

The man laughed humourlessly. "Easy as that, huh? And what happens to me then? You think those who have paid me would be happy about that?"

"You can run away too," she said, her voice rising as more ideas came to her. "My dad, he's really rich. I mean, really rich.

He'll pay you double what they're paying you. Triple. With all that money, you can go to a different country. Get away from this life."

The man was silent now. Freya waited. Was he considering the offer? She didn't dare take a breath, didn't dare speak in case she jinxed it.

But then the guard let out a gruff chuckle. "Too late for that," he told her. "Things have happened. Too much mess. My bosses are angry and worried. Your mother has one more chance and then our orders are to clear the field of all players."

Freya's shoulders sagged and her heart turned to dust. "What does that mean?" she asked in a wavering voice.

"You aren't that stupid. I think you know what that means."

She did. And it made her feel like she was going to throw up. "One more chance?" she said. "What does she have to do?"

"Something she has already failed at once. I'd suggest you prepare yourself."

"No! God! Please!"

"Enough talking."

Footsteps across the other side of the room announced the arrival of the second guard. As he got closer, the one she'd been talking with grabbed her arm and pulled her to her feet.

"What did they say?" he asked.

"As we thought," his partner replied. "We are to take her to the other place immediately and await further instructions. And no more fuck-ups. You understand?"

The man squeezed Freya's arm. "Of course. We go now?"

"I checked outside. There is no one around. We take her now and I'll come back to clean up."

The man shifted his grip under her shoulders, and the other grabbed her legs. As they walked her across the room, Freya gave them no struggle. She was done. She had no more fight in her.

The other place.

That same memory as before – from the Netflix documentary about abductions – arose from the dark swirling thoughts in her head.

If you're snatched and taken to a single location, it means your captors are probably waiting for a ransom. But if they take you to a second location after that, it means you're most likely going to be...

Freya screwed up her face to stop the thought from forming. It was no use. As the stuffiness of the building ended and cool air enveloped the bare skin on her arms and legs, she sobbed.

Clear the field of all players.

This was it, all right. They were going to kill her and then kill her mum. As she heard the van door slide open, she felt the warrior woman leaving her for good. Then she was thrown inside, and the door closed with a loud slam.

31

Beth could sense people's eyes on her as she and Sammy arrived at the hospital together and signed in at the security desk. Maybe in the past, this would have bothered her, but she was past caring what other people thought.

"Check your bag, Mrs Lomax?"

Shit. She froze. The syringe was in there, primed and ready.

"Oh yes, of course." She handed over the leather shoulder bag.

"Everything okay?" Sammy asked, appearing beside her and placing the lanyard connected to his ID badge over his head.

"Yes. No problem," she replied, not taking her eyes off the guard as he opened up the bag and simply glanced inside. Her shoulders relaxed as he handed it back to her with a smile.

"Have a nice day."

"Yes, you too."

She clutched the bag to her as she hurried across the foyer towards the elevator. Her heart was racing, but that was probably just as much to do with the strong coffee she'd just consumed, that and the fact her precious child was still being held by those evil bastards.

She was glad she'd had a shower, though. It had made her feel a little more normal. That and the change of clothes. After the phone call yesterday, she'd been too distraught to be on her own, so Sammy had insisted she stay at his. Ever the gentleman, he'd put her in his bed while he took the couch, but a part of Beth had hoped he might have joined her. Not because she had any ideas on him (God, how could she even think about sex!) but it was the closeness she'd yearned for. Someone to hold her and tell her everything would be well.

As it was, she tossed and turned in his enormous bed all night, half the time in fits of worry and the other half with a bitter-sweet smile on her face as she scrolled through old pictures of Freya on her phone. When morning came, she was clammy and sticky, and her hair looked like Helena Bonham Carter's in one of her more kooky, gothic roles. So, she'd been glad when Sammy suggested they call at her place on the way to work so she could freshen up. It also allowed her to call Freya's school and put them off for a few more days. This time the woman on the phone sounded annoyed, speaking to Beth like she was an overprotective simpleton. They'd need a doctor's note now, she told her. For Freya's records. But if getting one of those was all Beth had to worry about, then that suited her just fine.

"Are you sure you wouldn't rather take the day off?" Sammy whispered as he joined her in front of the elevator doors and pressed the call button. "I've got a consultation at ten, but I've got time before to run you home."

"No. Thank you. I need to keep busy." Before he could further convince her, the elevator pinged, and the doors slid open. No one was inside and Beth felt a pyrrhic sense of relief as she stepped inside and pressed for her floor.

"I'm going to be in surgery for most of the afternoon with my phone off," Sammy told her as the doors closed. "But if you need me, leave a message and I'll come and find you the minute I'm done."

The doors sucked shut and the metal box lurched into life. As it ascended the building, Beth resisted the lure of the large, mirrored wall to her left. She knew what she looked like, even after washing her hair and reapplying a little make-up; like someone who'd not slept properly in days, like a member of the undead. Her nerves were brittle, and her skin felt like paper. As the elevator arrived at her floor, she closed her eyes and took a deep breath. She had to stay focused. Had to keep it together.

"Oh, there she is," Carla called out, walking past with a steaming mug of coffee as Beth stepped out onto the landing. "You heard the news?"

Beth followed her down the corridor and into their office. "What news?" She half-expected her to come back with some pithy comment about her and Dr Raul. Gossip travelled fast in this hospital.

Carla pointed at her computer screen. "An email's just come around from Louise, it's back on. Tomorrow morning."

Beth placed her bag down on her desk and stepped around to see. "What is?"

"What's-his-face, Hopkins. He's coming back. To finish his visit."

"Really? For definite?" She squinted at the screen, at the internal memo from the Operations Director. There it was, in black and white.

The Prime Minister, Sir Gerald Hopkins, will recommence his visit to the Royal Farringdon Hospital tomorrow at 11 a.m. More to follow.

"When did this arrive?" Beth asked her.

Carla pulled her chair back and sat. "Twenty minutes ago?"

"Great. Thanks."

Carla said something else, but Beth wasn't listening. She

was already heading for the door. She strode down the corridor and across the landing to the Operations department with her fists clenched and her throat the same way. As she approached Louise's office, she saw the door was open and her colleague was sitting with her hip up on her desk, reading a file. As Beth got nearer, Louise glanced up and saw her, beckoning her forth with a big grin on her face.

"Did you see my email?"

"Yes. That's good. Do you still want me to be involved?"

Louise lowered the file she'd been reading and shunted her weight off the desk. "Do you still want to be?" she asked, walking over to the water cooler in the corner and yanking a blue plastic cup from the stack. "Water?"

"Yes. I want to be involved," Beth told her but waved away the offer of water. "I was having rather a good chat with Sir Gerald, to tell you the truth, telling him about all the good work we do here, about the trust. I was explaining how helpful it would be if we received more government funding when he was dragged away..." She shut up and gasped for air. She was over-doing it. "Sorry, Lou. Bit highly strung today, for some reason. But yes, I'd love to be part of the visit, if that's okay."

Louise chuckled. "Absolutely. He seemed rather smitten by all accounts. I'd say if anyone can convince him to put in a good word for us, it'll be you." She glanced Beth up and down and scrunched up her nose. "Are you okay, though? You look... different."

"Do I?" she asked.

Different how? Like I've had no sleep? Like my heart has broken a million times in the last week? Like I'm one more stressful situation away from totally losing my mind?

"Probably just the lighting in here," she added. "Not the most flattering things in the world, these fluorescent lights."

Louise stuck out her bottom lip and nodded in agreement.

"You always look good, though. Ignore me. I'm talking nonsense. So, then. Tomorrow. First thing. The itinerary is going to play out the same as before. I'm still waiting to hear full confirmation from Downing Street, but that's what they've suggested. Easier that way."

"Right. Great," Beth said, stepping away. "I'd best get back to it to then, do a bit of prep and all that."

"Good stuff. If you need anything, let me know."

Beth was already in the corridor. "Will do, thanks." As she marched out of the Operations department out onto the landing, she pulled her phone from her jacket pocket. She was calling Sammy's number as she pushed through the door onto the fire escape.

"Hey, it's me. Can you talk?"

Sammy cleared his throat. "For a minute. I take it you've heard?"

"Yes, I've just been in with Louise. I'm still part of the visit."

"I see." He didn't sound pleased. "What are you thinking?"

"What do you mean, what am I'm thinking? I've got to go through with it, Sammy. There's no other way."

"What if there was?"

"There isn't."

He was starting to annoy her. What did he expect?

"Okay," he said finally. "I've got to go. Speak to you later."

She hung up and growled at the phone. What the fuck?

What if there was another way?

Didn't he realise she'd been asking herself that question ever since these people told her their demand? If there was another way, she'd take it. But there was no other way. The Prime Minister would be back here in less than twenty-four hours. She had one more chance to get her baby back, and she would not let it slip away a second time. She had no choice.

32

It was 3:37 p.m. when the call came. Beth knew the exact time because she'd been staring at the clock all afternoon, watching the minutes tick away. Until that point, the day had passed by in a total blur. She'd done her best to engage with her work, had answered an email from a recruitment agency, took a call from a training company, but her mind was spinning so fast she could hardly concentrate.

She slipped away from her desk with the burner phone still ringing in her pocket and answered the call on her way to the fire escape.

"Are you alone?" the voice said.

She glanced back the way she'd come and then along the corridor in front of her. "Yes."

"Good. We'll make this quick. By now you will know that the Prime Minister's visit has been rescheduled for tomorrow. Are you still in play?"

"Absolutely, I went in to see my boss and—"

"Yes or no will suffice."

"Yes."

"Good. And you still have the equipment we gave you?"

"Yes."

"Then you know what to do. And Beth, know this. We have gone easy on you and your daughter up to now, but this is your last chance. Fail tomorrow and Freya will turn up under a bridge somewhere along the Thames with track marks in her arm and enough heroin in her body to kill a grown man."

Beth swallowed, doing all she could to stay calm.

"I tell you this to stress the reality of your situation, and show how serious we are, and how serious you should take this. Do you understand?"

"Yes."

"Get it done. Once he is dead, we shall contact you."

———

After that, Beth was good for nothing else. It felt like she was floating above her body as she made her way back to her desk and by 5 p.m. she admitted defeat, telling Carla and Jazmine she had a migraine and was going home to bed. It wasn't far from the truth. The best thing for her now was to make something healthy to eat and try to get some sleep. Or at the very least, lie in a dark room. Somewhere quiet and warm, where she could be alone with her thoughts.

On her way out, Sammy called, asking if she wanted to stay at his apartment. She'd be safer there, he said, and they could discuss the situation. But Beth told him no. She wanted to be in her own home, where photos of her beautiful daughter hung on the wall and where, if she went into Freya's room, it still smelled of her. Besides, as far as was she concerned, there was nothing to discuss. Tomorrow she would get the Prime Minister alone and would inject him with deadly poison. After that, she didn't know. But she couldn't think that far ahead. Couldn't bring herself to dream of what it would be like to hold her little Frey-

Frey in her arms. That was tempting fate, and she needed fate on her side.

Of course, one always feels so much braver and self-assured in the daylight. The second Beth got home and locked the front door, she regretted turning Sammy down. She'd wanted quiet and warm but with just her in the house, it was too quiet and even after turning the thermostat up she still found her teeth were chattering.

She turned the TV on, boiled the kettle, made herself some pasta. But nothing she did could take her mind away from her plight. Her skull felt like it was being crushed by a thick black cloud. She was jittery and jumpy and a nervous wreck.

Screw it

She'd put it off for as long as she could. She marched over to the wine rack and slid out the first bottle she laid her hands on. A basic Cabernet, but it was alcohol and that's all she cared about. She twisted off the cap and swigged from the bottle as she walked over to the sink and picked a glass from off the draining board. She poured herself a full glass and went upstairs, drinking as she went and carrying the bottle in her other hand. The idea had been to go to her en-suite and run a bath, but she walked straight past her door and along the landing to Freya's room.

She eased the door open and flicked on the light switch with her elbow. The room was still exactly as Freya had left it on that morning. Beth scanned her eyes around the space, a poignant smile twitching at her lips and an entire lifetime of sobs simmering in her chest. She shook her head at the pile of creased clothing and underwear on Freya's chair. Beth was always telling her to put them away, but she never did. She took another large gulp of wine and moved over to the bed. Blue Rabbit was sitting in the corner, staring at her as if to say, "Where is she?"

Beth placed the wine bottle down on the bedside table and reached over for him.

"I'm sorry, Blue," she whispered. "I'm trying my best. You miss her too?"

Blue looked up at her with one black eye and the other that was scratched and chalky after a session in the washing machine a few years ago.

"Do you think she's scared?" she asked him before laughing bitterly at herself.

Of course she's bloody scared. She's a fourteen-year-old girl.

But that wasn't Blue talking. He continued to stare up at her with an expression of stoic support. He was like that was Blue, always had been. For a long time, Beth had done his voice, making Freya giggle with the nasal way he'd say things. Then, when Freya was a little older, she'd taken over, delighting in giving her blue rabbity friend a multi-layered personality. He'd been a good friend to Freya, but he hadn't talked in many years.

She placed him back and finished her wine before pouring herself another large glass. Getting to her feet, she held the bottle up to the light. Already only a third left. It never seemed to last that long these days.

She was walking over to Freya's desk to open her laptop when she heard the muffled sound of her phone ringing. It was downstairs. In the kitchen. Why the hell hadn't she brought it up with her?

"Wait, wait, I'm coming," she yelled, racing along the landing with the glass of wine and bottle held high and scurrying down the stairs as fast as she could without spilling anything.

The phone was on the kitchen island, vibrating itself towards the edge of the worktop as she got there. Placing the wine and bottle down, she snatched it up to look.

Caller Unknown.

The same thing it had said when they first called her. Why weren't they ringing on the burner?

She swiped the phone open and answered. "What do you want?"

"Wow. Is that how you answer the phone these days?"

"Adam?"

"Good evening, Beth. Is everything all right?" The way he said it, all sarcastic and condescending, was typical Adam. He wasn't enquiring about her well-being.

"What line are you calling on?" she asked, her mind bouncing from one idea to the next before she could properly get a grip on any single one. "It said Caller Unknown."

"I'm in San Francisco on business, calling from my room. They mustn't list their number."

It sounded plausible.

"What time is it there?"

He laughed. "You sound paranoid, Beth. Are you sure everything's okay?" When she didn't respond, he sighed. "It's just after eleven."

Beth reached for the wine glass. "What do you want?"

"I thought I'd better return your call. You sounded stressed. Have I missed a payment or something?"

"Piss off."

It was her instinctive response but as she spat the words down the phone, she looked up and caught sight of her reflection in the glass front of the oven. What a state! Bent over her wine glass with a face creased in anger. She couldn't help herself. She burst into tears.

"I'm a terrible mother," she sobbed. "I've failed her. I'm so sorry..."

"Beth, what are you talking about?" He sounded impatient. "Are you drunk?"

She stared into the wine glass. "No. I'm not drunk."

"What's happened? Where's Freya? She's not texted me back. Can I speak with her?"

"No." She straightened up. No, he couldn't speak with her, and neither could she. She sniffed. "She's at Mia's house."

"And is she okay?"

Her lip trembled. She so wanted to tell him. To put some of this horrendous burden onto his shoulders. But what good would that do? He was hundreds of miles away and would just tell her to ring the police, chastise her for not doing so sooner.

"She's fine," she lied. "I'm sorry. I've just had a hard week. I needed to vent. We're okay. Both of us."

Adam sighed, as though he wanted her to sense his irritation. The subtext being *not this again.* "Well, I've got to go."

"Yes. Sure."

"Tell Freya I love her, and I'll see her soon."

"Of course." He hung up, his last words echoing in Beth's head. "I hope so," she whispered.

She finished the wine and walked over to the sideboard, where she picked up a silver-framed photo of her and Freya. Adam had taken it, on their trip to Dubrovnik six years ago. It showed Beth and Freya sitting on a section of the ruined walls of the old town, legs dangling over the side. The sun was shining and the eight-year-old Freya was grinning overzealously into the camera, resting her head on Beth's shoulder. They looked so happy, the two of them, so close. This was back when they used to tell each other they were best friends. Before the divorce and high school. Before Beth's promotion left her with less time and even less patience. She sniffed back to stifle more sobs. Freya could be a royal pain in the bum, but it wasn't just her fault they'd grown apart. Beth had told anyone that would listen that the reason she'd applied for the promotion was the extra money. But that wasn't true. The maintenance allowance from Adam more than covered the mortgage and any extra expenses that might arise. No. Beth had gone for that promotion because there was now such a gap in her life, she was scared she'd go mad if she didn't fill it with something.

She ran her finger over her daughter's smiling face. "My baby," she said. "My best friend. What happened to us? How the hell did we get here?"

She placed the photo back on the sideboard and continued to stare at it. She was resolute now. More than she'd ever been since Freya went missing, even more so than she had been in that communal bathroom, inches away from injecting Hopkins in the neck. She was going to do it. Tomorrow she'd leave all her emotions and fears at home and get the job done. Get Freya back. Then, when she was safely home, she'd do everything she needed to get her best friend back, too.

It was time to get some sleep. After two large glasses of wine, she was woozy enough that she hoped it might come easily for once. She'd already set two alarms within fifteen minutes of each other, just in case. The plan was to get up early, have a cold shower, do some yoga, centre herself as best she could. She switched off the kitchen light and was heading into the hall when a loud knocking on the front door startled her and she let out a cry. She stepped back into the kitchen to see the clock above the oven showing 9:44 p.m. Who the hell was calling at this hour?

"Hello?" she called out, despite knowing they wouldn't hear.

She peered around the doorframe, but with the hallway light on, she could see nothing behind the stained glass of the front door.

The knocking went again. More frantic. Beth picked up her empty wine glass and went to answer it.

33

"Who's there?" she asked, gripping the stem of the wine glass tight. What she was planning on doing with the glass if this was someone who'd come to kill her, she didn't know. It was probably the flimsiest weapon anyone had ever brandished. Still, if some big scary man was standing on the other side of the door ready to murder her, maybe it was fitting she died with a wine glass in her hand. Someone might find it funny. Adam, perhaps.

"Hello?" she tried again, as she got closer. Her hand shook as she reached for her keys from off the side table. "Who is it?"

"Beth, it's me. Are you okay?"

"Sammy." Her shoulders dropped. She grabbed the keys and moved over to the door, unlocking it with the swiftness of someone who hadn't just downed two-thirds of a bottle of wine. "Thank god."

She opened the door to reveal his kind, caring face illuminated in the hallway light. He looked to be glowing. Her prince had come to save her. But on seeing the wine glass gripped in her hand, he frowned.

"Sorry," she said. "I didn't know who it was. I was scared."

"Can I...?" he asked, gesturing to come in.

"Oh, yes, of course." She stepped back to allow him to enter and shut the door once he'd passed by.

"Thanks, it's freezing out there."

Beth locked and bolted the door and then stood with her back against it. Sammy turned and smiled. She smiled back. It felt weird.

"Listen, I'm sorry for turning up announced. I know you said you wanted to be alone, but I thought—"

"No, no, I'm glad you're here," she said, not letting him finish.

He smiled again. "I thought it might be good for us to talk through a few things. I might have an idea how we can get Freya back without you having to— Oh, Beth, don't do that. Come here."

She'd been trying to hold it in, but the relief she'd felt when it was Sammy at the door had caused the floodgates to burst open. He reached out and pulled her to him as she bawled.

"I'm so scared," she told him. "So bloody scared."

"I know, I know, you must be. Come on, let's sit down." He walked her through into the front room and they sat on the sofa. The light was off, but that didn't matter. There was nothing worth looking at in this room but grim memories of a life she thought would last forever.

"You know we'd had an argument," she said. "Me and Freya. I mean, I've talked to her on the phone since then, but the last proper conversation we had was an argument. I was horrible to her. I was angry, tired, like always. Sammy, I don't remember the last time I hugged her. And now I might never get the chance."

"Don't talk like that." He put his arm around her. "But about tomorrow... Did they indicate how many of their people they had in the hospital, or who they were, which department?"

She shook her head. "No. But does it matter?"

"Maybe. I've been thinking—"

"Will you hate me?" she asked, cutting him off.

"What do you mean?"

"If I go through with it. If I kill Hopkins. Will you hate me?" She shook his arm away and twisted around to face him. "They said there'd be no trace of any poison, that it was some rare type that wouldn't show up, but what if they were lying? What if I get Freya back only to be arrested for murder and thrown in prison?"

"Beth," Sammy said, placing his hand over hers. "I need you to calm down. I've got something I want to run by you."

Beth screwed up her eyes. "I can't calm down, Sammy. I have no bloody idea how to calm down. I'm a fucking mess. I feel like whatever I do, I'm going to lose everything. Why me? Why Freya? It's not fair, Sammy. It's not bloody fair."

She was sobbing again; the tears blurring the good doctor's face as he tilted his head to one side. "No. It's not fair. At all. But for what it's worth, I don't hate you. And nothing you could do would make me hurt you. You're in a terrible situation and—"

He shut up as Beth's lips found his. She kissed him hard, desperate for some release, to feel something other than despair. Sammy resisted for a second, then kissed her back, his soft lips opening to receive her as they grabbed at each other. Beth closed her eyes, falling into his warm embrace as the fuzziness provided by the wine transported to a place of comfort and security, a place where everything was good. She shifted forward, her hands snaking up his chest, undoing the first button on his shirt.

"No. Beth." His hand closed around her wrist, and he pulled away. "We can't. We shouldn't." He held her at arm's

214

length, not breaking eye contact. It made her feel like a stupid kid.

"Why not?" she asked. "I like you; you like me. I need this, Sammy."

He frowned, mouth widening into a concerned smile. "Not like this, Beth. You're not thinking straight."

"Of course I'm not. But I don't want to think about anything. I want to lose myself for a while."

He looked like he might be faltering, but then he got to his feet. "I should go."

"No. Please. Stay." She reached for him, but he was too far away. "I'm sorry. That was stupid. You're right, I don't know what I was thinking. But don't go. Please, Sammy. Don't leave me alone. Not tonight."

The tears were falling again, but even as they did; she knew right now they were for herself. And not just that, they were for him. So that he'd feel sorry for her.

The knowledge of that made her hate herself even more.

"Why don't you try to get some sleep," he said. "It'll help. I'm not going to pretend things will look any better in the morning, but you might deal with them better after some rest." He held out his hand for her and she took it.

"Will you stay?" she asked, as he helped her to her feet.

"I will. On the sofa. Let's get you up to bed." He led her through to the hallway and up the stairs. She still felt like a little kid, but one that was being looked after and cared for. It felt nice.

After showing him which room was hers, he helped her inside and over to the bed. "Are you okay with taking it from here?"

She nodded. "Yes. Thank you. I'm going to get up early, try to get my head together before... You know..."

"That sounds like a good idea. I'll set an alarm for 5:30. How does that sound?"

"Thank you."

"Night, Beth." He was almost out the door when she remembered something. "Sammy. Am I going to get Freya back?"

He turned around, one hand on the door frame. "Yes, you are." He smiled. "Why don't you get some sleep. I'll be downstairs if you need me."

Beth shifted her legs up onto the bed. "Thank you - for being here. For being you."

"Don't mention it. Good night and I'll see you in the morning." Sammy backed out of the room, closing the door as he went.

And then she was alone. She lay back on the bed and huffed out a deep sigh. This was it. No turning back. In twenty-four hours, it would all be over. She'd be a murderer, but Freya would be free. That was all that mattered.

It was all that mattered.

34

The room was chilly, and Freya could hear the drip, drip, drip of water coming from another room. But except for these miserable characteristics, she had no clue what her new prison looked like or even what time of day it was. All she knew was it had taken them a long time to get here in the van, and her captors were taking no more chances. The black sack remained over her head and her wrists and ankles were still bound with the uncomfortable plastic ties. She'd not struggled as they'd carried her up two flights of stairs or when they'd placed her in the room and slammed the door shut. This was partly out of fear, but also because she knew there was no point. Any chance she had of escape was gone. There was no Newspaper Man to talk to. No mattress to lie on. Worst of all, there was no hope.

She leaned back against the cold, hard wall and put her legs out in front of her. It was strange, but sitting here in total darkness, she realised she didn't feel scared anymore. She just felt numb. There were no tears left to cry.

Voices outside the room pricked her attention, and a moment later, the door opened. She counted two sets of footsteps entering the room and heard metal chair legs scraping against the floor. Then one set of footsteps left the room and the door slammed shut.

Freya raised her head, sensing a presence in front of her.

"Hello, Freya."

She flinched as the person approached. They loosened the material from around her neck and yanked the sack off her head. She blinked into the gloom and blew her hair off her face. A man was standing over her. He was slim and tall and wore a dark suit. As he stepped back and sat on the chair facing her, she saw he was about the same age as her dad, with grey, swept-back hair and tanned skin. Women her mother's age might have found him attractive (he looked a bit like a movie star) but for Freya, he was just another bad man, another demon. Albeit a well-spoken one.

"Don't worry, my dear," he said. "Soon this will all be over."

He smiled, and the skin around his eyes crinkled up. Freya drew back a sharp breath as something dawned on her. He'd allowed her to see his face. According to that same documentary, this was another sure-fire sign you weren't ever going home.

He leaned forward, elbows resting on his knees, and his hands clasped together.

"Are you scared, Freya?"

She didn't know what to say to this, so she just nodded.

"I know, and I am sorry." His voice was deep but gentle. He didn't seem like a child killer. "We didn't want to involve you, or indeed anyone innocent. Yet there is a greater good to our mission and we had no choice."

"But you do have a choice," Freya whispered. "You can let me go."

"And we will," he said. "Don't worry. Your mother is going to free you. Once she does what we have asked of her, we will honour our part of the deal. Tomorrow morning, my associates

218

will take you to another location, where they will wait for the news. Once we have confirmed the Prime Minister is dead, we shall inform your mother of this location and release you to her."

"What?" She frowned, uncertain she'd heard him correctly. "The Prime Minister?"

The man chuckled. "You didn't know? I assumed your friend would have told you everything."

"My friend?"

"The dead man. The one we had to shoot for... what would one call it, gross insubordination? Although to be fair, I'm not sure he knew the full story. Silly bastard. I mean, what sort of mercenary goes and does something like that? Shoddy work, Freya. Very shoddy."

She didn't respond. He was playing with her. She saw that now. Enjoying himself as she shivered in front of him.

She met his gaze. "I don't understand."

"The Prime Minister, Freya. Your mother's going to kill him. That's how she gets you back."

"But why?"

"Because he's an absolute pain in the arse and we need shut of him. Because he's made a very bad decision." He sat back and crossed one leg over the other. "You see, I work for some very dangerous people, Freya. I can't say who for obvious reasons, but if I tell you they're Russian, you might get some idea of the extent of the situation. You see, amidst the post-Brexit chaos, your corrupt, self-serving Prime Minister is about to get into bed with a crooked US pharmaceutical company and grant them exclusive rights to the UK market for the next fifteen years. Do you know how much that's worth, Freya? Billions. Billions of dollars in revenue. And my employers own large stakes in a rival pharmaceutical company over in the States. This means if Hopkins signs that exclusivity deal, they stand to lose a lot of money. They don't want that."

Freya's head was spinning. She understood some of what he was saying. "You're going to kill him over money."

"No. Your mum's going to kill him." Freya's throat tightened, but she forced herself to keep looking at him. The smug expression on his face made her feel sick. "But don't worry, my dear, no one will ever know it was her. He will die and she'll get away with it. Then, once all this awful mess is over, you can go home."

"My mum would never hurt anyone."

"She might if your life is at stake, don't you think?"

"Maybe."

The man uncrossed his legs. "There we go. See? And once Hopkins is no more, all we need do is orchestrate a leadership bid and get our own man into Downing Street. Which will actually be the easy part."

"Why are you telling me all this?" Freya asked.

The man stuck out his bottom lip. "I thought you might want to know why this is happening to you."

"It's because of you."

The man tutted. "I'm just a piece on the game board, same as you."

"I've seen your face."

"Yes? And? What are you going to do? Who would you tell? And more importantly, what would you say? Your mum might have killed Hopkins to save your life, but that won't stop her from being a murderer. Your silence buys her freedom. That's if all goes to plan tomorrow, of course." He got to his feet and fastened the buttons on his suit jacket with one hand. "If it doesn't, well, I'm sorry Freya, but you won't be telling anyone anything. Because you and your mother will both be dead."

At this, she crumbled. She couldn't help it. Her tired, aching body shuddered with desperation.

The man whistled sharply, and the door opened to reveal

the taller of the two guards. He stepped over to Freya and picked up the sack, placing it roughly over her head. The last thing she saw before everything went black was the man in the suit striding out of the room.

"Goodbye Freya," he said. "Best of luck."

35

Beth and Sammy left the house together but travelled separately to work, Beth taking the tube and Sammy going back to his apartment to get changed then driving in from there. It was a few minutes after eight as Beth passed through security and called the elevator.

The Prime Minister's visit was scheduled for 11 a.m. and she'd arranged to meet Sammy in his office at 9:30. After that, she and the other people involved in Hopkin's visit were to be briefed by his team and get into position. It meant the timings were going to be tight, but it was doable.

Up on the sixth floor, Beth headed straight for her desk and hunkered down behind her computer screen. With Sammy being at the house this morning, she hadn't been able to do her yoga practice, but she hoped a little deep breathing might go some way in levelling her out. But as she closed her eyes and tried to clear her mind, she realised how nervous she felt. She was physically shaking. More so than she had been on Hopkins' first visit. But maybe that was because she knew what to expect this time around. Plus, there was more at stake. Much more.

The next hour passed quickly once Carla and Jazmine and

the other admin staff had arrived. Like last time, they'd drafted the home workers into the office to make the place look busier and more industrious. But unlike last time, the atmosphere was listless and morale low. People were subdued rather than chatty, and there was a resignation in the air that this was simply a work event they were being forced to engage with, rather than something special or exciting.

At 9:15 a.m. Beth reached into her bag and removed the leather make-up case that contained the syringe and vial of poison. Getting to her feet, she coughed for attention.

"I'm just going to make a quick call and then I'm going to go to the bathroom to freshen up," she announced, waving the make-up case in the air. "Might even put on a bit of lippy before the briefing."

She'd rehearsed the speech twenty times in her head over the past few minutes just in case the words came out wrong and her colleagues became suspicious, but why would they? Neither Jazmine nor Carla batted an eyelid as Beth slunk out of the office. Once clear, she hurried along the corridor towards the landing, glad when the elevator pinged its arrival the second she hit the *Down* button. She mouthed a silent 'thank you' into the ceiling tiles as the doors opened to reveal it was empty.

She jabbed her finger on the button for the first floor, bracing herself as the stuffy metal box descended the building, telling herself to stay calm. Everything was taken care of. All she had to do was follow the plan.

On the first floor, she was straight out of the elevator and following the network of corridors around the side of the building towards the consulting rooms and the offices of the second level doctors, the anaesthetists and radiologists rather than surgeons. The ones you addressed as Dr rather than Mr.

She knocked on the door to Sammy's office and waited, glancing both ways down the corridor. No one was around. A second later, the door opened up to reveal a stony-faced Sammy framed in the doorway. He didn't say a word, but stepped aside and waved her into the room. Once she was inside, he closed the door.

"Do you have it?" Beth asked, whispering for no good reason.

Sammy nodded and flicked his eyebrows at a small box on his desk. It was like he thought the room was bugged and a cloud of paranoia swooped down on Beth.

"Give me your phone," he said, holding out his hand. "Your personal one, not the burner."

"What? Why?" She pulled the phone from her pocket and handed it over.

Sammy took it and held it to her face to unlock it before stooping over the screen and tapping away. "I'm downloading an app that links our phones and locations," he said. "It uses the latest tech GPS 3 technology, meaning it's accurate to around 1 to 3 metres. So, we'll know where each other is at all times." He moved next to her and held up the phone. "See, that blue dot is you and the red one is me. All you have to do is keep the app open."

"Thank you." Beth took the phone from him and pocketed it. "Is everything set? Do you know what you're doing?"

"Yes. Don't worry about me. I'll make sure I'm where I am when I need to be."

Beth looked at her feet. Her breathing was shallow and sharp. She drew back a more conscious breath, holding it in her lungs for a few seconds before exhaling. "Are you going to be all right?" she asked, glancing up to meet his eyes. "These are bad people, Sammy. Willing to kill to get what they want. There's still time to back out, you know. I won't hate you or even think badly of you."

He shook his head. "I want to know who their mole is,

which doctor here is willing to kill someone. The pathetic creep." He lifted the box from off his desk and held it up it with a solemn expression. "It's all in there."

He handed Beth the box and she held it to her stomach.

"You can do this," Sammy told her. He placed his hand on her shoulder and smiled as he gave it a gentle squeeze. At that moment, she wanted to hug him so much. She wanted to tell him again how great he was, and how thankful she was that he'd fallen into her life and was helping her. But she didn't do any of that. She couldn't. Not now.

Instead, she gave him a curt nod. "I have to do this," she told him. "I've no other choice."

Then she turned around, opened the door, and retraced her steps back to the elevator. She sensed Sammy watching her as she walked away, but she didn't turn around. As she got to the landing, the clock above the elevator showed 9:48 a.m. She pressed the *Up* button for her floor. It was time for the briefing. Time to meet the Prime Minister.

36

It was Mike, the same man as before, who had been tasked with briefing Beth about the Prime Minister's visit. Like before, his voice was clear but monotonous and he went about the whole procedure (telling her what to expect, what to say, what not to ask) as if he'd never met her before, never mind the fact he'd recited these exact words to her just two days previously. Once finished, he held her gaze with concerned eyes and raised eyebrows.

"Is there anything you don't understand?" he asked. "Questions you want answering?"

Beth gave him a thin-lipped smile. "No. All good," she said, glancing at the clock. "And he'll be here at eleven?"

Mike twisted around to follow her gaze, then checked his watch. "Yes. Any minute now." He turned to the assembled throng. "Okay, people. The Prime Minister will be on his way up here, so please get ready. Remember, no photography or recording equipment. At all. If the secret service people see you with a phone, they will take it from you."

This was it. Beth straightened up and made a face like she'd forgotten something. She grimaced, sighed, let out a groan. "Oh, shit," she whispered. "I've forgotten my jacket. Am I okay to nip back?"

Mike turned to her with a heavy scowl. "He's on his way."

"I know," she said. "And I'm sorry. In all the rush, I forgot to grab it. But I need it. I want to wear it for any photos." She lifted her bare arms. "I've not been on holiday or to the gym for a while. A woman of a certain age and all that." She met his eye, fixing him with a look she hoped said, *question me at your peril.*

Mike sighed. "Fine. Be quick."

"It's only down there, thirty seconds." She left him and scurried back to her office, thanking the cosmos once again that she'd had the foresight to leave it there earlier. In the elevator, up to the briefing she'd had a hunch that security might have been stepped up this time around so had left her jacket and the contents of its deep pockets hanging over her chair before meeting with Mike and the Prime Minister's close security personnel. The relevant parties had already searched and approved her and she hoped that would be the end of it. Once in her office, she headed for her desk and grabbed up the jacket, slipping it on as she headed back to the landing. As she went, she felt at the pockets hanging by her hips, feeling like a wild west gunslinger on the way to a duel; her phone along with the burner in one holster; the syringe in the other. She was ready. There was no turning back.

"There you are," Mike hissed as she joined him. "He's here. You need to get into position."

Beth lifted herself on her toes to see Sir Gerald Hopkins, red-faced as always, standing shaking hands with Louise and members of her team. Like last time, he was flanked by two men in dark suits, both wearing earpieces and stern expressions. On seeing them, a shadow of doubt crept up on her. What if they didn't leave him alone this time?

She shook the thought away and put on a big smile. One

step at a time. No point fretting about things until they happened.

With her chest out and her head up, she marched over to the welcoming committee and took her place beside Louise.

"Prime Minister," she cooed as he turned to face her. "So good to see you again."

He regarded her with narrow eyes, wagging a crooked finger in the air. "I want to say, Gwen?"

"Beth. Beth Lomax."

"Beth! Of course it is. How could I forget? You know my children's nanny was called Beth. A fine girl." He looked misty-eyed for a moment.

"Beth is going to finish showing you around," Louise said, leaning in. "You're in excellent hands, Prime Minister."

"I'm sure I am," he said, shooting Beth a wink. "Shall we then?"

He gave the assembled crowd a triumphant wave, playing up for the select members of the press like always. But as Beth led him down the corridor towards the research department, he leaned into her and lowered his voice.

"Let's get this over with quickly, can we?" He sounded hurried and irritable, the convivial manner of which he was so famed nowhere to be seen.

"Is everything all right?" she asked him as they got to the first set of doors, and she glanced back to see the two security guards behind them.

"No. Not really," he said. "I've got a bastard headache, and nothing seems to be clearing it."

"Oh, I'm very sorry to hear that," she said, as they pushed through into the next corridor. "What have you taken for it?"

He waved her away. "Don't worry about me. Let's just get this done so I can go. Once around the block to show willing and then I'll be off. Nothing personal, you understand."

"Of course. But that is a shame," she said, her mind spinning faster than she could deal with. "Last time you were keen to see our records department, I believe."

Hopkins gave her a withering look. "Maybe some other time."

"Are you really not feeling well?"

"I'm afraid not. I've had indigestion all morning and now this. A bit of advice, Beth, don't get old. It's bloody awful. You know, when you get to my age... Well, I sometimes wonder if I'm too old for this lark."

"You? No. You look so well," she lied. Sweat was pouring down his face and his breath was coming out in short, rasping gasps. He looked like he might keel over any second. Maybe she didn't need to kill him after all.

"Bloody hell." He stumbled and steadied himself against the wall. "I'm sorry, my dear, we may have to rearrange. Or cancel altogether."

Beth's heart sank. What could she do? Her eyes flittered around the space, searching desperately for inspiration.

"That is a shame," she told him, taking him by the arm and leading him onwards as best she could. "The records room is such an amazing space and so extensive. We could..."

She trailed off as they turned the corner. In front of them, at the end of the corridor, stood the door to the old service elevator.

"Hmm. Wait a minute."

"What is it?" Hopkins asked as she stiffened.

"I was just thinking. What if I knew a way out of here so you can make a quick getaway - without all those interfering reporters bothering you?"

At this, Hopkins pulled a face. But it was a curious expression, rather a discouraging one.

"I know it's rather naughty," she whispered, hoping to appeal to his famous rebellious nature. "But if you're feeling under the weather, you don't want to deal with those awful people, do you?"

He smiled and leaned in, placing one hand on her forearm. "And we can do this?"

"If you know the right people." She tapped her nose flirtatiously. "See the door at the end here? It's the old service elevator. It still works, but it's not used anymore. Not since we started outsourcing our linen service. It goes all the way to the ground floor and comes out at the back of the building. You could get your people to bring your car around and you'd be able to make a swift exit."

She watched him intently as she spoke, every cell in her body willing him to go for it. He raised his head to regard his bodyguards. "Bit of a change of plan, chaps," he called over, falling back into his usual blithe manner. "Beth and I are going to sneak out via the laundry chute."

One of the bodyguards stepped forward. "What exactly do you mean, sir?" There was a world-weariness to his voice, but that was another factor Beth had been relying on. It was well reported that Hopkins hated rules and procedures and often went against the wishes of even his most trusted aides. He was his own man, a populist renegade who marched to the beat of his own drum.

"We're fleeing the bastille by the tradesman's entrance," he replied with a chuckle.

The bodyguard scowled. "Excuse me, Prime Minister, I still don't understand what you're saying."

"It's a service elevator that the linen service staff used to use," Beth explained. "As the Prime Minister isn't feeling well, I thought he could leave via the back exit, to avoid the crowds."

The man didn't look at her as he addressed the Prime Minister. "I don't think this is a good idea, sir. We have a protocol to adhere to."

"Yes, I know that, Simon," the Prime Minister said with a wave of his hand. "But I've got a splitting headache and a bit of a hot flush. What with everything else going on today, I'd like to sneak away unencumbered by protocol and without having to deal with the hoi polloi outside."

Beth held her nerve, resisting the eagerness rising inside of her. She couldn't have planned this any better. Hopkin's feeling unwell was the perfect set-up for what was to come next. But she couldn't get complacent. It wasn't over yet. Not by a long chalk.

She tensed as Simon held his hands up, appealing to Hopkins. "Prime Minister, we have not planned for this eventuality. We can't change our route at this stage. It could be dangerous."

"Oh phooey," Hopkins replied. "What the hell is going to happen between here and the ground floor?"

"We can't guarantee your safety, sir."

"Simon! Leave it. Okay?"

"Prime Minister I—"

Beth tutted loudly. "The Prime Minister isn't well! He needs some fresh air. And he doesn't need people getting in his face." She stared at Simon, nervous energy bristling under her skin. "Why are you being so difficult?"

This was risky, she knew that. But it was her only option and she had to go for it.

For Freya...

She turned to Hopkins, placing her hand over the one he had resting on her arm. "What would you like to do, sir? You are the Prime Minister, after all."

He smiled. "I want to get out of here."

"Right then. Follow me."

She led them down to the end of the corridor and called the elevator. As the old mechanism whirred and clanked behind the metal shutters, she turned to the two bodyguards. "It's a small space, only room for two at a time."

Simon frowned. "Sir, this is very unorthodox."

Beth squeezed Hopkins' hand. "No, it's rather cosy as I remember."

He shot up a flirtatious eyebrow, but the headache seemed to get the better of him. He grimaced. "I'll be fine, chaps. Don't worry. Beth is a good woman. A real trooper."

The bodyguards exchanged a glance. "Where does the elevator come out?" the one called Simon asked.

"The ambulance depot on Saffron Hill," she replied. "The back entrance of the hospital. If you head down to reception, there's a door marked 'Employees Only' that will take you straight there."

Neither Simon nor his partner looked convinced. He tried again. "This is against procedure, Prime Minister."

"Yes, well, I'd rather change procedure if it means I can get out of here with no more bloody fuss."

"But Prime Minister I—"

"For Heaven's sake! He's not well!" Beth cut in, her voice rising sharply. "Can't you see that? Have a bloody heart. Jesus Christ!"

Was she over-doing it? She couldn't tell. But the bodyguards appeared to get the message. As the elevator bell dinged behind her, they stepped away and one of them spoke into his cuff.

"Change of plan. Repeat, change of plan. Big Chief is on the move. Taking the service elevator to the ground floor. Bring the cars around to the rear of the building. Saffron Hill. Ambulance depot."

Simon held his finger to his ear and then nodded to his partner. Beth swallowed. If there were people on the inside, they'd hopefully get wind of this change. If not, this could all be for nothing.

She reached for the door to the elevator and wrenched the metal shutter with a shriek of rust on rust. "Here we go, sir," she said, stepping inside and making space for him. "It is a little cramped, I'm afraid."

The truth was, it was smaller than she'd remembered. As Hopkins shuffled inside, she pressed herself against the wall, drawing her phone from her pocket and holding it down by her side to conceal it from the bodyguards.

"Not a problem, my dear," Hopkins whispered. "What was the word you used? Cosy? Yes. I'd say so."

He gave a half-salute and chuckled to himself as Simon grabbed hold of the shutter. "We'll head straight down to the depot," he said as he slid it closed. "And the car will be waiting."

"Good man," Hopkins called after them. As the door clicked shut, he blew out a sigh. "What a bloody fuss."

"They're just doing their jobs," Beth told him. But her voice caught in her throat as the reality of what was about to happen hit her in the guts. She glanced down and tapped out a brief message to Sammy before pocketing the phone. Then she reached into her other pocket and closed her fingers around the syringe. As she reached over and pressed the down button, she pulled it from her pocket. The elevator was old and rickety and would take around a minute to reach the ground floor. But that was perfect. One minute was all she needed. She held up the syringe, going over everything Sammy had told her about intravenous injection and where to aim for. Then she held her breath, leaned all her weight against the Prime Minister, and plunged the needle into his neck.

37

Hopkins was gone by the time the elevator reached the ground floor, but with his sizeable bulk hunched in a sitting position in front of her, Beth couldn't slide the shutters open.

"Help!" she screamed, bashing her fist against the metal wall. "Help us, please. He's collapsed."

She heard a commotion coming from the other side, and a second later the doors were yanked open. As the Prime Minister's lifeless body slumped through the door onto the raw concrete beyond, Beth looked up into Simon's eyes.

"What happened?"

She shook her head, mouth flapping, but no words coming out. Simon knelt next to the Prime Minister's side and held his fingers to his neck.

"Is he dead?" Beth asked. Then, before he answered, she stepped out of the lift and cried out. "Help! Help us! We need a doctor. Now!"

She'd barely got the words out when Sammy appeared from around the corner. He saw them and ran over.

"What's going on?" he asked, fixing Beth firmly in the eye, trying to get a read on the situation.

She gave him the briefest of nods. "I don't know," she replied, with her voice still raised. "He was clutching at his chest and then he collapsed. I think he's had a heart attack."

Sammy knelt beside Hopkins, addressing Simon as he did. "Please, sir, give him room. He leaned over and listened to Hopkins' chest before straightening up and pulling a torch from his pocket. "I mean it sir, please step back." Simon did as he was told, getting to his feet and muttering into his cuff, not taking his eyes off of Hopkins. Sammy switched on the torch and lifted Hopkin's eyelids, shining the light into his eyes.

As Beth watched on, she sensed movement to her left and, looking up, saw another doctor running toward them. Sammy saw him at the same time and shot Beth a look. This was it. The mole.

"Step aside please," he called out as he got close.

Beth recognised him as Dr Aleks Demski, a cardiothoracic surgeon who'd been with Farringdon less than a year. She hadn't had much to do with him since his induction, but working in HR that was usually deemed a good thing.

"Is he alive?" Simon asked, agitated now as Demski leaned over the body. "Are you able to help him?" He stepped back, peering over their heads. Beth followed his gaze to see Mark and some more of the Prime Minister's aides rushing over.

"What the fuck is going on?" Mark yelled.

Demski shushed him down before getting to his feet and waving down to the loading bay where two paramedics were looking on. "Get a stretcher up here. Stat."

Beth looked at Sammy. "Where are you taking him?" she asked.

Demski ignored her. Instead, he threw out his arms as he

addressed the growing crowd. "Can everyone please take three steps back so my colleagues can get up here?"

"Is he going to die?" Mark asked.

"You and you," Demski called out, pointing at the paramedics as they wheeled a stretcher towards them. "Take him to room thirty-six. A suspected myocardial infarction."

"Excuse me," Mark said, stepping around the side of the stretcher as the paramedics hauled the Prime Minister up on top. "I'm assistant to the Prime Minister's Private Secretary. I need to know. Is he going to die?"

Beth saw the sneer of derision on Desmki's face. It was a split-second thing, a slight twist of the lip and an even slighter narrowing of the eyes, but it was there. He looked Mark in the eyes. "Sir, this man's pulse is very weak. If you want me to save his life and give him any semblance of who he was, I suggest you get out of my way. Now."

Shocked gasps and audible intakes of breath rippled around the group. Beth shifted over so she was facing Sammy. He didn't look at her.

"I'll come too," he told Demski. "Just in case."

"Not necessary Dr Raul"

"I want to help. If I can."

This time, Demski could hardly hide his anger. "Fine," he said through gritted teeth. "But you follow my instructions."

"Of course."

As the paramedics wheeled the Prime Minister away and the two doctors ran along beside them, Sammy glanced back. Beth didn't react as their eyes met. She stood and watched as they disappeared around the corner. Then, as the Prime Minister's aides and bodyguards erupted in a flurry of ringing phones and frantic conversations, she quietly slipped away. The hard part was done. It was time to get her daughter back.

38

eth already had her phone out as she zigzagged through the winding corridors that led from the rear of the hospital to the front entrance. From a world of flashing lights and medical equipment, of cold chrome and bleach, to the plush surroundings of the reception area. Once there, she slowed her pace and, holding her phone up to her ear, wound her way around the sea of reporters and other media people, making sure she was seen. And also heard.

"Yes, I've just seen him," she spoke into the mouthpiece, employing her best stage-whisper. "The Prime Minister, yes! It's awful. Awful!"

She stared off into the middle distance as she spoke, hoping to give the impression she was too engrossed in the call to focus on those around her, but watching them all the same. A few had noticeably stiffened as she'd said the words 'Prime Minister', but it needed more work. Much more.

She stopped in the middle of the room and frowned as if the person on the line was asking her a troublesome question. It was strange to her how easy she was finding this, but she supposed that was how it was when you were slap bang in the heart of the action. For days it had felt like she was on a sinking ship and now she'd dared to jump into the ocean, her only option was to swim fast, or she'd drown.

"I know," she said, raising her some more. "That's what I said too, but I've got it on good authority. Yes. He's... Dead. About two minutes ago. Heart attack."

This got the press people's attention. Heads turned to look at her, then at each other. Someone stepped forward with their hands up, blocking Beth's exit as she made for the security gate.

"Excuse me," a woman with straight blonde hair asked, stepping towards her. "Is what you said true? The Prime Minister has had a heart attack?"

Beth startled. "That was a private conversation."

"I'm Andrea Masters, BBC news," the woman said. "And if that's true, it's of national interest."

Beth stepped back as more people approached. A young man ran up to Masters with a phone pressed to his ear, nodding wildly. "I'm on with Magnuson," he whispered. "He says he's heard the same."

An older man stepped forward, covering the receiver of his phone with his hand, and nodding solemnly to the crowd. "My source has confirmed it. Massive heart attack. They tried to save him, but he's gone."

Beth didn't recognise the man, but he must have held sway over the press network because as he finished speaking, the reception area erupted in a cacophony of chatter and ringing phones. Weaving through the growing hysteria, Beth headed over to the stairwell on the far side of reception and slipped through the door. As she hurried down the stairs, she called Sammy. The plan was she'd just leave a brief message, so she was surprised when he picked up.

"Where are you?" she asked, already breathless as she took the stairs down to the employees parking garage two at a time.

"Outside surgery," he whispered, speaking fast. "They've declared it. Or rather, Demski has. I've been like his shadow since it happened, and he was calling it before we even got Hopkins into the room. Did no proper tests. I told him I'd found no pulse and he just accepted it. Like he already knew the outcome. We were right, Beth. Our risk paid off. It's done."

The words buoyed her, but she couldn't let herself celebrate just yet. "That's good. But we aren't done until Freya is safe," she told him. "I'm on my way down to the basement. I'll speak to you soon."

"Good luck, Beth. Be safe."

She hung up and ran down the last few steps and into the parking garage. Despite having an aroma of petrol, the cool underground air felt good on her face as she made her way across the forecourt to where she knew Sammy's car was parked up waiting. Space forty-six.

She looked around as she got close, but there was no one else down here. But why would there be? A circus of excitement and rumour was booming upstairs, growing more fervent and manic by the second.

Reaching under the front wheel arch on the driver's side, Beth found the keys straight away and beeped the silver Audi unlocked. Moving around to the rear, she opened the boot hatch, where she found a small metal box tucked into the side of the chassis as arranged. She lifted it out and opened it up before taking the syringe and vial from her pocket and placing them inside. She shut the box and spun the combination lock before concealing it back in the car's chassis and slamming the boot lid shut. Taking her phone from her other pocket, she side-stepped down the side of the car and opened the driver's door. As she slipped inside and settled herself behind the wheel, she glanced at her phone to see she had three missed calls, two from Louise and one from Carla. They could wait. She was about to pocket her phone and take out the burner phone when a new notification flashed up on the screen. A red box with white text:

Newsflash! Prime Minister Sir Gerald Hopkins suffers a fatal heart attack. Feared dead at age 73. More updates as they arrive.

The English student in her winced at the error. *Fatal* heart attack but only *feared* dead. But that was the nature of the rolling news services these days. They often announced things without properly checking their workings, or their grammar, so eager were they to get the exclusive on a breaking story.

Beth threw her phone onto the passenger seat and was reaching in her pocket for the burner phone when it rang. With shaking hands, she flipped it open and clicked to answer.

"Congratulations Beth," a voice said. "We have confirmation you achieved what we asked of you."

"It's done," she replied, fumbling the ignition key into its housing as she spoke. "Now let my daughter go."

"Cubic Wharf on the Isle of Dogs," the voice said. "I believe you know it well."

"Is she there?"

"She will be. Thirty minutes from now. Come alone. Tell no one."

Beth bit her lip. "And you'll let her go. Let us both go?"

"Correct. Thirty minutes. Don't be late."

They hung up and Beth chucked the burner phone onto the passenger seat alongside her personal one. Then she twisted the ignition key and switched on the engine. As the car roared into life, she clicked the seat belt into its housing and adjusted the rear-view mirror. Then she shifted the gearstick into reverse and screeched out of the space. The clock on the dashboard told her it was 11:33 a.m. It was time to finish this nightmare. Time to get her baby back.

39

News helicopters were already circling overhead as Beth pulled out of the underground parking garage and took a right towards the river. As she coasted down the street, she jammed her phone into the housing clip on the dashboard and tapped the destination into the maps feature. It told her it would take her thirty-one minutes to get there.

Don't be late, they said.

She didn't plan on being.

She indicated right and put her foot down as she pulled out onto Clerkenwell Road, swerving around cyclists and over-taking cars the way Sammy had done. It felt exhilarating and terrifying all at once, but she kept her speed up, taking a sharp right across two lanes of traffic.

Getting Freya back was the only thing on her mind, the only thing keeping her going, as Aldersgate Road became Commercial Road and then the Limehouse Link Tunnel, which would take her to the Isle of Dogs. As the orange lights on the roof of the tunnel whizzed past at fifty, sixty, seventy miles per hour she gripped the steering wheel tight, her palms were clammy and her nerves in tatters, but she couldn't slow down. She was so close. The dashboard clock said 11:47 a.m.

As she emerged from the tunnel and took a right towards the docks, her phone rang on the seat next to her. She panicked for a moment, thinking it was them calling her, telling her she was late - too late. But as she glanced over, she saw it was her own phone ringing and Sammy's name on the screen.

"Hey," she said, swiping it open and lifting it to her ear. "I'm almost there."

"Where are you meeting them?" he sounded like he was running.

"Isle of Dogs. The same place we saw Freya the other day," she replied. "Cubic Wharf. What's going on there? Is he...?"

"Don't worry, it's all gone to plan. You just focus on what you need to do. I'm on my way."

"No." Beth lurched the car to one side as she passed alongside a slow-moving delivery truck. "They said to come alone. After last time, we can't risk it."

"You sure? Because I think maybe—"

"I'll be fine," she told him. "I've got to go. As soon as I have her, I'll call you.

She hung up and threw the phone back on the seat. She was almost there. The two buildings where Freya had been held were visible down to her left. But it was almost noon.

She leaned forward on the steering wheel, gritting her teeth and pressing her foot all the way down on the pedal as she raced on towards the destination. But as she drove alongside the wasteland, she couldn't see anyone in sight and an icy panic rose inside of her.

"No! No, no, no..." she muttered to herself, slowing the car and trundling it onto the wasteland. "Don't do this."

She let the car roll to a stop, peering up through the windscreen at the two buildings. They looked as bleak and unoccupied as last time she was here but silhouetted against the dull greyness of the sky, even eerier. If that was possible.

She scanned the area but could see no sign of life. There wasn't a single bird in the sky. A dull panic filled her, sending her teeth chattering. Something had gone wrong. Then the phone rang. The burner, this time.

She scooped it up and flipped it open in one motion, holding it to her ear.

"Are you alone?" This time the voice had no digital alteration. It was a man's voice. Well-spoken, but with the hint of an accent.

"Yes. Like you told me."

"Get out of the car and walk slowly around to the rear of the nearest building. We are waiting for you."

"And Freya?" Beth asked, but the line was dead.

She pocketed both phones and got out of the car, leaving the keys in the ignition and the car idling in neutral, as Sammy had suggested. It was a miserable day, and a chill wind blew across from the river as she slammed the door shut and wrapped her jacket around her. With her head down and her hair whipping across her face, she walked across the sprawling arena, mindful of the large cracks in the concrete and piles of rubble in her path. She didn't feel scared, but she didn't feel relieved either. Not yet. They still had her little girl and things could still go wrong.

She swiftly moved around the side of the first building, glad of the shelter it provided from the wind and trying but failing to straighten herself out as she approached the rear. In front of her stood a large black four-by-four, a Suzuki, parked with the front grill pointing towards her. The windows were blacked out so she couldn't see through them, but as it was the only vehicle around; she had to assume Freya was inside. The thought of that sent a ripple of anxious energy up her spine.

She was walking towards it when the front passenger door opened and a man's voice called out, "Stop right there. Don't move."

Beth did as she was instructed, resisting the urge to raise her hands in surrender. "I just want my daughter," she said.

A man got out of the car. He was tall and slim with grey hair swept back from his face and sharp cheekbones. He wasn't exactly handsome, but clearly, he cared about his appearance. With a graceful flick of his wrist, he closed the car door as another man climbed out the other side. This man was younger than the first and a lot bigger and mean looking. He crossed his arms and stared at Beth, who shifted her attention back to the first man.

"Beth Lomax. How are you today?"

She raised her chin. "I've had better days. Had a lot better weeks. Where's Freya?

"All in good time."

"Listen," she snapped, stepping forward. "I've done my part, did what you asked of me. Now let her go." She lowered the finger she hadn't realised she was pointing at him and gulped a mouthful of air. "Please. Let her go."

The man chuckled to himself. "You have indeed fulfilled our demand and we are grateful. Believe me when I tell you this, Beth, you have made your country, and indeed the world, a better place. Hopkins was a self-serving moderate who had no desire to bring about any change unless he and his cronies benefited. It is better that he is dead."

Beth sniffed. She had no response. A second ticked by. And another.

"So?" she asked. "Where is she?"

The man chuckled again and climbed back inside the car as the back door opened. Beth froze as she saw legs emerge, followed by a grey blazer and then her darling daughter's face. It was Freya. She was alive. She looked grubby and weak and like she hadn't slept properly since she'd been taken, but she was alive. And she was coming home.

She saw Beth and burst out crying. "Mum!" She made to run but an arm snaked out from inside the car and grabbed her wrist.

"Freya, it's okay darling, don't cry," Beth told her, smiling and nodding like a mad woman. "I've come to take you home, baby. It's over. It's all over. I promise. We can..."

She trailed off as the arm's owner climbed out of the car behind Freya. A woman. Wearing a bright fuchsia pink trouser suit that didn't fit her properly.

What the hell?

Beth's eyes grew wide, her pupils burning with the cold air, but she couldn't help it. She tried to speak but her voice caught in her throat. All that came out was a weird gurgling sound.

"Hello, Beth," said the woman, taking position behind Freya and placing her hands on her shoulders. "Fancy seeing you here."

"What the...?" Beth stammered. "You? But... Why?"

Louise pursed her lips and shrugged theatrically. "Money, power, control. You know, the usual stuff."

"You fucking bitch," Beth spat, glancing instinctively at Freya as she swore. The poor girl was crying but her head was raised and her expression determined. She was tougher than Beth gave her credit. She regarded Louise. "You've put Freya and me through absolute hell. I thought we were friends. I don't understand."

"You will, darling," Louise said with a smug grin. "You see, post-Brexit, our exuberant but corrupt Prime Minister was due to sign a big deal with Braxxon Kleiner. That deal would have given them exclusive rights to sell their new heart medication in the UK."

"Yes, I know all this," Beth said, meeting Freya's gaze and shooting her a reassuring smile.

"And did you also know my husband is one of the major shareholders at Sanick and Co, Braxxon Kleiner's chief rivals?" Louise said. "They aren't at all happy with the upcoming deal and neither are their other major shareholders, who we shall simply call 'The Russians' and leave it at that. Best for everyone, we don't name any names." She wrinkled her nose at Beth, who, in turn, dug her fingernails into her palms. Seeing Louise here had shaken her, but not enough that she wasn't ready to rip the evil witch's hair out, given half a chance.

"So, it really is about money? Wow."

"Oh, come on, what isn't these days? So, with the Russians financing the whole thing, we made plans to ensure the deal didn't happen. With Hopkins dead, our kingmakers will ensure a much more affable Prime Minister takes the reins. Someone we can be sure will sign a new deal with Sanick and Co. Fifteen billion US dollars, Beth. Think of the good we can do with that money. We can pump a lot of it back into Farringdon, into the research department. Hopkins' death will mean we might find actual cures for heart and lung disease. For cancer too. This is a good thing what we've done."

Beth pulled her jacket around her, eyes flitting between her frightened child, the scary man still staring at her without blinking, and her boss. She was struggling to get her head around everything.

"You had someone murdered," she said. "That's not a good thing. You used me; you used our hospital."

Louise gripped Freya's shoulders, making her yelp. "That's right. But there was a need, I'm afraid. You see, once Sanick can trade in the UK, their goal is to roll out an experimental drug that destroys plaque and other fatty deposits in the arteries. Meaning an end to coronary heart failure. It would save millions of lives. Sanick wants to use the five hospitals under the care of the Farringdon Trust for the trial."

Beth held her nerve, eyes on Freya the whole time. If Louise hurt her, she'd... She took a deep breath. "I take it Broadhurst is in on this too."

"You couldn't be more wrong. I ran the idea by Damien some time ago, but he was adamant he wouldn't allow the trust to get into bed with one company in particular. Which is why we need to remove him, too. Put someone else in his place as head of the Trust."

"You?"

"Perhaps me. Why not?" She smiled that smug smile again. Beth hardly recognised this contemptuous harpy from the genial Louise she knew. "In fact, it was me who came up with the idea of killing two birds with one stone. You see, soon enough, questions will start being asked. Was the hospital at fault? Did we do all we could to save Hopkins? You can imagine the headlines. How the hell was he allowed to die of heart failure whilst visiting a hospital that specialised in heart problems? It's not good optics. Any way you look at it."

Beth nodded in acknowledgement. "I see. You get rid of Hopkins and make it look like the hospital was at fault. Then what? You lean on Damien Broadhurst, get him to step down."

Louise chuckled to herself as she massaged Freya's shoulders. "Exactly. We'll gently let him know that if he doesn't, then there's a very real possibility he could be prosecuted for negligence. He might be an old fool, but he's not stupid."

Beth dug her nails harder into her palms. Off in the distance, she could hear police sirens, but this was East London. It meant nothing.

"Why me?" she asked.

"Because you were there. Because out of all the staff who might have shown Hopkins around, you were the one we could get to the easiest." Freya squirmed as Louise stroked her hair, still gripping her shoulder with her other hand. "Missy here was the perfect leverage and once we knew her route to and from school, it was almost effortless. You ask why you. Why not you? It was nothing personal, Beth. And you've done your bit. We're all good."

Beth held out her hand. "Freya. Come on."

"Mum," Freya tried to walk away, but Louise held onto her. "She won't—"

"Louise, please!" Beth stared into her former friend's eyes. "It's over. I've done what you wanted. Hopkins is dead. Now let us go."

Louise sighed, then let go of Freya, shoving her forward. "Go on then, off you go."

Freya looked to be in shock. She glanced from Louise to Beth. Then, with a shriek of emotion, she ran forward.

"Oh, baby!" Beth opened her arms as her darling daughter leapt into her embrace. They hugged each other tight, hugging like they would never let go. Freya sobbed, so did Beth, both shaking with emotion. "It's okay, Frey. I'm here. You're safe." She raised her head to Louise. "What now?"

"You go home. Live your life. Forget this ever happened. And I mean, forget it. If you ever tell anyone what happened... well, we know where you live. We'll find you. Not to mention the fact you're in this up to your eyeballs. We could get you sent away for a long time, Beth. Then what would happen to Freya?"

Beth wiped her hand across her cheek. "Don't worry. I won't say a word."

"Oh, and I'll expect your resignation, of course," Louise said. "It would be awkward otherwise, don't you think? You'll be put on immediate garden leave from Monday. But you'll get a decent severance package that will more than make up for all your... troubles."

Beth stared her out before putting her arm around her daughter and turning away. It wasn't worth it. "Come on Frey. Let's go home."

But they'd only taken a few steps when Beth's phone vibrated in her pocket, and she heard the recognisable sound of a news notification. Her first impulse was to ignore it, to get away from these people as fast as possible, but as she and Freya hurried over to the car, a flurry of beeps and chimes echoed from behind her. And then someone's phone was ringing.

Beth pulled her own phone from her pocket. No. This couldn't be happening. It was too soon. Time stopped as she stared at the screen and the red notification box.

Newsflash! Prime Minister is alive, sources say. Earlier accounts stating he had suffered a fatal heart attack now discounted.

"Shit."

Freya peered over at the screen. "What is it?"

Beth shot a look over her shoulder to see Louise on the phone, yelling at whoever was on the other end. As she was looking, Louise saw her and waved her hand at the tall man on the other side of the car.

"Hey!" she screamed, pointing at Beth and Freya. "Get them!"

"Mum? What's going on?" Freya asked, as the man slammed the car door and ran towards them. "What do we do?"

Beth grabbed for her daughter's hand and yanked her forward. "We run, baby. As fast as we can."

40

Even with the car engine running, Beth realised almost immediately they wouldn't make it. Flicking a cursory glance over her shoulder, she saw the man was gaining on them with every stride, moving two metres to their one. If they carried on this trajectory toward Sammy's waiting car, he'd be on them before they reached it.

"This way."

They veered over to the riverside, down an alley that ran between an old garage and an electricity station covered in graffiti.

Beth wanted to scream. This was exactly what she'd been afraid would happen. Sammy was an experienced anaesthetist and had assured her there was enough midazolam (the same tranquilliser used for putting patients into medically-induced comas) in the new syringe to knock most men out for well over two hours. But with Hopkins' size and not knowing his exact stats, it had been guesswork. She didn't blame Sammy; she'd agreed this was the only way she could get Freya back without resorting to murder. But now they were on the run and had a scary man pursuing them.

The end of the alley opened out on the Thames Path Extension with the river in front of them. Beth glanced both ways before taking a right, yanking Freya along with her.

"This way. He's coming."

She could hear the man's footsteps echoing down the alley. Another thirty seconds and he could have them.

"Mum, I'm scared," Freya gasped as they ran alongside the river. "If he catches us, we're dead."

Beth didn't answer. She knew that already. But they'd had luck on their side even to get this far. She had to believe they could still pull it off.

Sammy's assumptions about the mole - who they now knew was Dr Demski – had been correct. He'd not checked Hopkin's vital statistics thoroughly. To try to put Beth's mind at ease, Sammy had explained how people believe whatever fits in with their already established narrative. Demski knew Hopkins was supposed to die and had already accepted that was true. With Sammy there to confirm his bias, it was a forgone conclusion. He'd made the call. Despite the whole plan being risky as hell and a total stretch, they'd got this far. They couldn't give up now. Not when they were so close.

"Stop! Now!! Come back!"

Freya yelped as the man shouted after them

"Go to hell," Beth yelled back. "Leave us alone!"

But the man kept coming. As she shot another look over her shoulder, she saw him burst out from the alley and steady himself on the metal railing in front of the river.

"Shit!" she screamed, eyeing the gun in his hand. She gripped Freya's hand like it was her only lifeline, putting the last of her energy into her legs. "He's got a gun, Frey. Run! Fast as you can!"

Not that the poor girl wasn't doing so already. But the two of them didn't stand a chance.

"Mum, this way." Freya tugged Beth to one side, and they ran down a narrow passageway that led away from the river. As they disappeared around the corner, a loud bang cracked the still, noon-day air.

He was shooting at them.

With a real gun.

With real bullets.

"Freya..." she gasped. "Where are we going?"

"Away from him." They both screamed as another gunshot rang out behind them. On they ran, Beth lamenting her lack of conditioning as her chest and sides burned with lactic acid.

"What if the others are up here waiting for us?" Beth cried. "We could be heading straight back into a trap."

"If we can get to the car, we'll be safe," Freya told her. "We have to try."

Beth had never experienced her daughter acting so brave and steadfast. A surge of pride went through her, but it was short-lived, replaced by a shudder of fear as the man shouted after them.

"Stop you fools. Or I shoot you. There's nowhere for you to go."

"Come on, Mum," Freya shouted. "We can do this."

She veered down another passageway, dragging Beth with her. With a tightness growing in Beth's chest, they ran past a row of garages and old security lockups. The man was still chasing them, but they were putting some distance between them now. He was fast but ungainly, and as they weaved their way through the zigzag network of constricting passageways, it was taking its toll on his speed.

Beth gulped down a mouthful of air and, for the first time, allowed a flicker of hope to show itself. Down the next alley they went, then another off to the right, then they seemed to cut back on themselves as the path arced all the back towards the wasteland.

At the end of the next row of garages the path split into two. Pausing for a second, Freya opted for the right-hand path but as she changed direction she skidded over on the loose gravel and went down with a scream.

"Freya!" Beth gasped, scrambling to help her up. "Come on, baby. Be strong."

"I'm all right. Let's go."

Beth scooped her up, and they set off, the two of them pawing at the air like speed swimmers desperate for traction. As they got to the end of the passage, it opened out onto a grass verge. Over to the right were the two buildings, the concrete wasteland in front of them. They'd come full circle, which meant if they ran up this sloping patch of green, Sammy's car should be a hundred metres in front of them. Beth glanced behind her, but their pursuer was nowhere in sight. She pushed Freya forward before scrambling up the grassy incline after her. But as she got to the top and stepped onto the hard concrete, her heart crashed into her stomach.

Sammy's car was gone.

Beth cast her gaze around the area. The sound of police sirens was louder now and more distinct, but still a way off. On the other side of the wasteland, she saw the black Suzuki speeding away towards the docks. But no black Audi. No getaway car. And the man with the gun was still coming.

"Mum!"

Beth spun around to see the man had emerged from the alley. He stopped running and stared up at them, the vicious snarl that had been twisting his lips softening into a sickening smile. His expression said it all.

He knew he had them.

They knew it too.

Across the far side of the concrete arena, through rows of trees, Beth could see a block of flats. Their only option now was to run as fast as they could towards them, pray they reached a more populated area before the man reached them. Once there, there'd be people. Shops they could escape into. They had a chance.

"Stop!"

They'd only travelled a few metres when a shot rang out. Freya screamed, but Beth pulled her along.

"Keep going," she told her. "It'll be okay."

But it wouldn't be okay. She knew that. There was no way. Another shot rang out, and this time a bullet pinged off the concrete in front of them. Whether it was a warning shot or poor aim, she wasn't sure. But she couldn't risk finding out.

She slowed down and gave Freya's hand a firm squeeze. "I'm sorry, baby," she told her. "I can't... We can't... He's going to..." She stopped, and holding her side, made to turn around. "Okay, we give up..."

But her words were lost in a squeal of tyres and the blare of an engine. As she turned, a black car shot across her vision. In a burst of screeching breaks and loose gravel, it drove straight into the gunman, knocking him clear off his feet and sending him tumbling over the bonnet. As the car came to a stop, she saw Sammy behind the wheel.

"Beth! Get in!" he yelled out of the open window.

Beth grabbed Freya and they ran over to the car with one last burst of effort. As they got there, Beth yanked open the back door and bundled Freya inside before clambering in after her.

"Drive," she yelled, as she slammed the door shut.

As Sammy skidded the car around in a semi-circle and opened the throttle, she turned and peered through the back windscreen. The man was lying motionless on the ground, the gun a few feet away from him.

She sat back in her seat. The sirens were close now.

"Are they for us?" she asked. "The police, I mean."

"Yes," Sammy replied, meeting her gaze in the rear-view mirror. "I was in the Peace Corps with a guy called Pat Davey, who's now Deputy Assistant Commissioner at the Met. I called him as soon as I saw the newsflash about Hopkins, and he got straight on it. They're taking this seriously. Very seriously."

"It was Louise," Beth told him, still not able to fully believe it.

"What? Our Louise? From the hospital?"

"Yes. She's part of all this. A big part." She glanced at Freya and gave her hand another squeeze. But it was less out of reassurance now and more out of relief. And love.

"Well, she won't get away with it," Sammy told her. "I've told Pat everything. Well, everything I needed to so he'd act. We'll fill them in on the complete story later. Those rotten fuckers." His eyes met Beth's once more. "Sorry, shouldn't swear."

Beside her, Freya huffed. Beth leaned over and placed her arm around her. "Don't worry, Sammy. My daughter can handle a bit of bad language. She can handle anything, can't you, darling?"

Freya sighed, but Beth couldn't tell whether it was out of embarrassment or relief, or just plain old nervous exhaustion. It was probably all three. As Sammy turned onto the road that would take them out of the Isle of Dogs and back home, Beth glanced back out of the rear windscreen. Over on the wasteland the gunman had got to his feet and was limping over to the gun. The sight twisted Beth's stomach, but he couldn't get them now. They were safe. Freya was safe. And Hopkins was alive. As three police cars hurtled past them, going the other way, she sat back against the soft leather seat. It was over. It was really over.

She closed her eyes and let out a long breath. It felt like the first time she'd exhaled fully since Freya went missing.

"Are you okay, Mum?" Freya whispered.

Beth smiled sleepily. "I am now, my darling," she said. "I am now."

41

Beth held the coffee mug to her cheek, enjoying the warmth on her face as she watched her daughter slurping up the last of her cereal. She looked so young sitting there hunched over her bowl. But then she raised her head and flicked her hair over her shoulders, and she could have been twenty-one. A grown adult. Beth smiled. She didn't envy the poor girl, straddling the two opposing worlds of childhood and adulthood. Adolescence was hard for anyone. But Beth knew her girl would cope with whatever life threw at her over the next few years. She'd more than proved that.

"Have you got a busy day?" she asked.

Freya grimaced. "Umm... English this morning, then maths and chemistry this afternoon."

"Ugh," Beth said, knowing how much Freya disliked the more science-based lessons. "But drama club after school?"

Freya grinned. "Yeah. Did I tell you we're doing Midsummer Night's Dream next? Auditions are in a few weeks; will you help me learn my lines?"

Beth returned the grin. "Of course I will. Are you going for Titania?"

"Maybe. Or maybe Hermia. Although Denise said we can audition for any part and the best person for the role will get it, regardless of gender."

Beth chuckled to herself. "I see." It was a different world from the one she'd grown up in but that was fine. It was Freya's world now. She nodded at the empty cereal bowl. "Would you like anything else?"

"No. I'm good. We'd better get going. I said I'd help Mia with her Insta post before class, you know, for her new Etsy site."

Beth hardly understood any of those words, but nodded, regardless. "Okay, you go get your coat and I'll load these things in the dishwasher."

"No worries."

Beth watched as Freya got up from the table and shuffled down the hallway. She looked like a typical fourteen-year-old girl. Self-obsessed, often surly, deeply embarrassed by most things her mother said or did. And Beth wouldn't have it any other way.

The two of them ate together every morning now. Beth made sure of that. Her therapist, Emma, had explained how it would be a good way to re-establish unity and togetherness. Breakfast was the most important meal of the day after all, and sharing this experience had indeed brought her and Freya closer. A start-the-day-as-you-mean-to-go-on kind of thing.

Both Freya and Beth had been assigned trauma counsellors for six months after their ordeal. But Beth had enjoyed her weekly sessions so much that afterwards she'd sought out Emma, and signed up for a year's programme. She'd encouraged Freya to continue too, but she'd decided against it. She didn't need to talk about it anymore, she said. Everyone always says how resilient kids are, but Beth had first-hand experience of that in the form of this clever, brave young woman she was so proud to call her daughter.

The kidnapping never really came up in conversation between the two of them now. Not because it was too harrowing a subject to deal with or because it was some dark secret, but simply because it was in the past. That part of their lives was over, and they were only looking forward.

"Ready when you are," Freya called out from the hallway.

Beth closed the dishwasher and straightened up, catching sight of herself in the mirror hanging above the table. The woman looking back at her looked older, and less carefree than she ever had been, but stronger, too. Much stronger.

It was almost eight months to the day since Freya had been taken. Since Beth had almost killed the Prime Minister. But instead, she'd foiled a sinister conspiracy that spanned the globe and had ties in both Russia and the US. Not bad going for a middle-aged divorcee who still hadn't fully revived her old exercise routine.

They'd arrested Louise and her husband, along with their cronies, as they tried to board a private jet out of the London City Airport. The last Beth had heard, there were diplomatic negotiations taking place over where they'd stand trial, but the evidence was strong and by all accounts they would get what they deserved. After everything had settled down, Beth had wondered if Sir Gerald Hopkins might have asked for a meeting to thank her for what she'd done, perhaps even invite her to Downing Street. But no one from his office had ever contacted her. Clearly, they too wanted to put this whole sorry period behind them.

"Come on, Mum! I'm going to be late."

"Sorry, darling. I'm coming." She scooped her keys up off the kitchen island and headed for the front door where Freya was waiting, eyes fixed firmly on her phone screen as usual. But as Beth nudged her out of the way so she could grab her coat off the hook, she looked up at her and smiled. The sight warmed Beth. She'd never get complacent about that smile ever again. She'd promised herself that.

"Are you seeing Sammy later?" Freya asked.

"Yeah, he's staying over. Is that okay?"

Freya shrugged. "Sure. I need to show him this TikTok video I was telling him about. He's going to love it."

"Great. I'm sure he will."

It was still early days for Beth and Sammy. She'd held him at arm's length for almost six months, swatting away his gentlemanly advances. But eventually, she'd succumbed to her own feelings. He was a good man. And he and Freya got on well. Hell, even Adam seemed less of a shit these days. Whether that would last remained to be seen, but perhaps that was how it worked when you truly moved on from someone you once loved. The hate does indeed turn to indifference. And then, one day (maybe?) a resigned friendship. Who knows? Stranger things had happened.

"Oh, by the way," Freya said. "I'm going to Lauren's after drama club for some food. I can make my own way home afterwards."

The words hung in the air between them, like they always did when Freya announced she was doing something away from her mother's protective gaze. Beth chewed her lip.

"I'll be fine, mum," Freya added. "It's a five-minute walk and I'll stick to the main roads. It won't even be fully dark then."

Beth let out a sigh. "Okay. But keep your phone charged and text me when you get to Lauren's house and when you're setting off home."

"Yes. Don't worry." She opened the door and stepped out onto the front step. "I'm not stupid!"

"I know you're not."

Beth watched as Freya walked down the garden path. Of course, she still felt protective of her young daughter, but it was important not to let that stray too far into over-protectiveness. It was something she was working on with Emma. She wanted Freya to be safe, but she had to let her breathe. She was growing up so fast, but their relationship was good again, and she trusted Freya to do the right thing. Would she ever feel fully comfortable about letting her walk home alone? Possibly. But not yet. Maybe soon. Not yet.

"Come on, mum!" Freya yelled as she got to the car, parked on the roadside. "I'm going to be late."

Beth stepped outside, smiling to herself as she closed the door. "Don't worry, darling," she called out. "I'm right behind you."

THE END

Enjoy psychological thrillers? You'll love M. I. Hattersley's next book...

THE EX

What if you found out your ex-boyfriend's former lovers were all dying in mysterious circumstances, and you were next on the list?

Get your copy by clicking here

WANT TO READ MY BOOKS FOR FREE?

To show my appreciation to you for buying this book I'd like to invite you to join my exclusive Reader's Group where you'll get the chance to read all my upcoming books for free, and before anyone else.

To join the group please click below:

www.subscribepage.com/mihattersleybooks

Can you help?

Enjoyed this book? You can make a big difference

Honest reviews of my books help bring them to the attention of other readers. If you've enjoyed this book I would be so grateful if you could spend just five minutes leaving a comment (it can be as short as you like) on the book's Amazon page.

Also by M I Hattersley

THE EX

What if you found out your ex-boyfriend's former lovers were all dying in mysterious circumstances, and you were next on the list?

Aspiring writer, Camille Fletcher is struggling to get by in the world after leaving university. But she has no idea how hard things are going to get....

First an old friend dies in tragic circumstances. Then another girl. And another. The police say they are no suspicious circumstances, they don't see a link.

But what if there was a link?

What if the rumours are true, what if your ex-boyfriend was responsible?

When do you stop dismissing the rumours as the work of internet trolls and start believing them?

Because the police don't know Camille knows...

Despite her fears, she makes a choice. She'll get to the bottom of the story herself, and expose her ex before he gets to her.

Now entangled in a twisted web of discovery, deceit and death, Camille must fight for her life and her sanity too if she's to survive.

Or will this be one story she doesn't live to tell?

From bestselling author M. I. Hattersley, The Ex is a nerve-shredding domestic thriller

Perfect for fans of Karin Slaughter, Mark Edwards, K.L. Slater, Miranda Rijks, Iain Maitland and Harlan Coben

GET YOUR COPY HERE

About the Author

M I Hattersley is a bestselling author of psychological thrillers and crime fiction.

He lives with his wife and young daughter in Derbyshire, UK

Printed in Great Britain
by Amazon

82366514R00159